WRATH
AND
RUIN

Wrath and Ruin

A Chilling Anthology by

C. W. Briar

2016

Edition: 1st

First edition: July 2016

Cover Illustration: Kip Ayers (www.kipayersillustration.com)

Editors: Lindsay Franklin (www.lindsayafranklin.com)
         Ben Wolf (www.benwolf.com / Splickety Pub Group)

ISBN - 978-1-942462-09-5 (paperback)

Also available in Ebook (978-1-942462-10-1)

This book is dedicated to everyone who instilled into me a love of stories.

To those family members, friends, mentors, teachers, and writers who guided and supported me on the journey to publication, thank you.

Thank you to God, the master storyteller, for my small part in this extraordinary tale known as life.

Thank you, Lindsay and Ben, for your assistance and guidance as editors. Thank you, Kip, for the gorgeous cover art.

Stories

*novelette **novella

Escape from Wrath and Ruin was my first published story. It won the GK Chesterton Award in the annual Athanatos short story contest and was included in their anthology. This piece represents a starting point for me, the season of my life when writing became more than a casual hobby.

The version included in this collection is an update to the original. I've learned a lot about the craft of writing since this story was first published, and I incorporated those lessons into this rewrite.

Escape from Wrath and Ruin

The only thing I could remember was shouting, "No."

I awoke to an overwhelming light. It inundated me, yet somehow I saw only darkness. While my eyes discerned nothing, my ears picked up the sound of scratching a thousand times over.

My other senses roused like patients after surgery. Next came pain. I rolled to my hands and knees at the heightening agony. My brain felt like it had exploded and nearly ruptured my skull. The top of my head was especially sore and tender to touch.

I sensed cold, dry air on my bare face and arms, but also warm dampness on my hands. Blood. I smelled blood. Was it mine? Panicked, I stood and reached out, flailing. I discovered rough rock walls on either side of me. They were close, as if I were standing in a doorway. Slowly, touch gave way to sight, and I realized I was in a deep chasm. The light beams pouring into the stony maw seemed as tangible as a waterfall.

"Help!" The rocks shouted my voice back a hundred times, mocking me.

I tried to walk, but something warm and heavy blocked my feet. As light accumulated in the chasm like water filling a reservoir, the obstruction took form. It was a man's carcass. He was old, and his twisted, ugly expression deepened the wrinkles on his face. I didn't recognize him, and like all other details from before I awoke, the manner in which he died remained locked behind amnesia.

Was he a friend? An enemy? I wasn't sure, but a sickening feeling of guilt churned in my gut when I realized the blood on my hands might belong to the dead man lying in front of me. What had I done?

The scraping, scratching sound I heard when I awoke had stopped. I only recognized its absence because the noise returned, and it was much louder than before. The ground trembled, shaking dust from the walls and creating a haze. I touched a stone and realized its surface was crawling like infested skin.

Again I shouted for help, but the growing sound devoured my voice. My heart threw its shoulder against my ribs, and I scrambled my fingers over the rock walls in search of hand holds.

In the blink of an eye, the chasm floor dissolved and flowed like water. Innumerable brown insects with pincer heads and segmented, snake-like bodies surged around me. I tried to climb, but I couldn't reach the nearest projection of stone. In desperation, I stepped up on the corpse. The added height was enough for me to hook my fingers over a lip of rock. I lifted my feet off the body just as it started to move and drag along the ground.

I began my slow ascent out of the chasm. A gnawing fire quickly built up in my arms and legs as I climbed, but

I couldn't let go. Not while insects devoured the corpse below. Every time I stopped to find a handhold or my breath, I shouted, "Help!" to no avail. No one answered.

But help did come, and from a strange source. The light beams seemed to … they were more than mere light. Somehow they strengthened me and pulled me up like ropes. The more tired I became, the more they aided me—at least, until I reached the summit of the chasm.

Moments before I could climb out, the light dimmed. All my weight returned and tried to drag me back into the pit. I cried out for fear I was about to fall.

Then I realized what was shading the light. A man had appeared above me. He was kneeling at the top of the precipice, reaching toward me. With the last of my arms' strength, I grasped his hand and let him pull me out onto level ground.

I sat for a long time on the rim of that rift with my feet hanging above the darkness. While I massaged my exhausted forearms, the man who had helped me sat silently nearby, turning his head back and forth as he kept watch of the horizon.

Even though I couldn't recall my life from before the climb, I knew the terrain was foreign to me. Black sand aggregated like shadows in every crack and crevice of the red, stony land. Rock pillars jutted up from the barren plains and leaned toward distant mountain peaks. New clouds manifested rapidly in the dry air while others, which were already swollen and dark, sunk from the sky and diffused on the ground.

A huge sun dominated the sky and bleached it white. It didn't roast us with intolerable heat, but I did have to shield my eyes from its glow. I didn't see any vegetation we could hide under, but I doubted trees would have helped anyway. That torrential, unrestrained light seemed to overwhelm and erase shadows.

"Thank you," I managed to say once my panting eased. I gulped another deep breath of the thin air.

The stranger smiled at me. For some reason, in spite of my nearsighted memory and strange circumstances, I found immediate encouragement in that smile.

"I'm glad I could be of help." He glanced past me, again checking our surroundings.

"Did you hear me yelling?" I asked.

"Yes, but I may not have been the only one. That's why I need to know if you're ready to walk."

"I think so." My arms were spent, but not my legs. "Where am I?"

"Good," he said, passing over my question. He rose to his feet, so I did the same. The man stood a head's height taller than me, and he had paler skin. We were both wearing simple white shirts, pants, and shoes. "We can talk as we walk. I fear we may not be alone for long."

He glanced down at my blood-stained hands, then back at me.

I wiped my hands on my shirt to no avail. The red stayed. My heart began to tremble again, and fresh sweat moistened my brow. My tongue tripped over my teeth as I tried to explain away the stains.

"My fingers are hurt—hurting—from the climb. I'll be all right."

The stranger held up a clean hand. "None of the blood got on me. It's been there for a while." He took a step away. "Start talking before I decide I have no reason to trust you."

I reluctantly confessed to the corpse in the chasm, but I insisted upon my innocence with all the grace of a log tumbling down a hill. I explained that I didn't know the dead man, neither could I remember anything beyond the last hour with clarity. Whispers of old names and stories swirled in my mind, all of them disembodied from faces and places. I pleaded for the stranger to help me and show me where to go.

He responded with another encouraging smile.

"Congratulations. It appears I've found a traveling companion, after all. We definitely need to get going."

He turned and quickly walked in the same direction that the giant stone pillars were leaning. I followed. Every fifth step was a leap as I tried to keep up with his pace.

"What's going on?" I asked. "You look worried."

"Law will certainly know what's happened," he said dryly. "He'll come looking for you. He has a way of knowing things no one should. Nothing gets past him. He'll seek you out, and your best hope is to distance yourself from him as much as possible. Trust me on this."

As I climbed onto a raised platform of stone, I tripped and banged my shin. The pain bit deep. I sucked air through gritted teeth and rubbed the swelling bump.

"Are you running from him too?" I asked.

"Everyone runs from him, or at least tries to. There's no reasoning with him. He just hunts people down, and he 'judges.'" The stranger made air quotes with the word. "He likes to call it judging, but really he just takes pleasure in punishing people. He makes a sick game of it. And I'm not talking about prison time. The man is a monster who delights in tormenting everyone he can catch."

Various forms of torture flashed in my mind. I clambered up a boulder and hurried to the stranger's side. "Can't I just go to the police and explain what's going on? Someone needs to get that body if … if there's anything left."

The man stopped long enough to glance at me with a puzzled expression. "Police? Where do you think we are?"

"I don't know. I already asked you that question. What's this place called?"

"I'm not sure this place has a name," he said. "People tend to just pass through, and normally as quickly as possible. There's nothing out here."

It dawned on me that I didn't know the man's name, either. I asked him.

"Messipor. What's your name?"

I tried to recall it, but the effort worsened my headache. I pressed my palm against my forehead. "That's one of the things I can't remember."

Of all the voids in my memory, my name was the most troubling.

Messipor. The name was unusual, but then so was everything else. Bands of iridescent colors swam on the cliff faces to one side of us. Shadows of vultures circled the ground we were hiking on, but there were no birds in the air. Whenever the wind stirred and took flight, it carried the sound of cackling and the scent of burning wood.

"Am I dreaming?" I asked.

"You were." Messipor scooped up a pebble and tossed it to me. "This is no dream."

I caught the pebble and squeezed it between my fingers. It was solid.

Messipor walked, and I followed. He seemed confident of our heading across the parched, lifeless wasteland.

***

Our hike took us into the hills that had been our horizon earlier. Messipor grew increasingly anxious, and by extension, so did I. We half-crouched and studied each dust cloud that glided over the terrain, though I wasn't sure why. I asked what we were watching out for.

"Anything that might be chasing after us," he said.

"Like what?"

"I'm not sure what, but I'd rather not get caught off guard."

We walked for hours. The sun never descended from its high position overhead, nor did the thick halos around it dim. We were locked in a perpetual, otherworldly noon. I asked Messipor about that as well.

Without glancing up, he said, "The sun? No, that's the moon. We'll be in serious danger if the sun rises."

"The moon? That glow's too bright. It can't be a moon."

Messipor remained silent.

"What did you mean by danger if the sun rises? When will that be?"

"I don't know, but it hasn't happened in centuries. Let's hope that continues, because I've heard that if it does rise, it'll scorch the whole land, and anything caught in the light dies."

I thought Messipor was exaggerating, but then I re-considered the barren terrain and hard soil. Could a moon really cause that? The land desperately needed shade and rain, though it looked like the drought might be coming to an end soon. A faint rumble heralded a coming storm.

I wondered what kind of storm came from clouds that fell out of the sky.

"Do you hear thunder?"

Messipor froze like a startled animal. At the next thunder roll, he scrambled to the nearest boulder. A fright-ened finger lashed out and signaled for me to do the same.

The thunder sounded regular as a drumbeat, and it crescendoed. While pressing against the rock, we peered out at the coming fury. Messipor gestured at what I thought was an ordinary bird, small against the infinite sky. But its wings were beating at the same rate as the thunder. As the creature drew nearer, it grew and grew until its wings stretched large enough to span the gap between two hills.

It was no mere bird. It had a beak and resplendent white feathers, but its body was shaped more like a dragon's. Each stroke of its wings shattered the air, and columns of stone collapsed in its wake. Even at our distance, its breaths sounded like tornadoes.

The creature descended into the valley and landed near the same chasm I'd climbed out of.

Messipor pulled a small, crude telescope out of a pocket in his shirt. "Here. You need to see what we're dealing with."

I thought it was rather obvious what we were dealing with. That dragon-bird was magnificent but frightening. But when I looked through the telescope, I spotted a man riding on the creature as if it were a horse. He slid off its back to the ground, and the creature threw itself to flight with a flick of its massive wings. The man was too far away for me to discern any of his features, but I felt as though he was searching the whole territory—searching for me—and it terrified me to the core.

He knelt beside the chasm, then stepped over it and began walking along the same route Messipor and I had taken.

"Law," Messipor said, his voice quivering.

A thousand beetles of fear crawled within my body. "Should I turn myself in and explain that I don't know what happened? For all I know, I'm innocent of that man's death."

Messipor grasped my shoulder hard enough to bruise it. "He finds everyone guilty, even of the smallest infractions. He thinks himself some sort of bounty hunter and arbiter, but his so-called justice is a farce. Don't you feel that? Can't you feel the grave danger you're in? Everyone I know has spent their lives running from him, or has already been caught."

He released me with a push, his expression as stiff as steel. Messipor hurried toward the back side of the hill, away from Law. "Come on. There's something else I should show you, and it's on the way."

"Where are we going?" Trying to keep low out of Law's sight, I stooped as I scrambled after Messipor. "Is there a town nearby?"

Messipor quickened his swift walk to a full jog. "We're going to find my friends so we can all get out of here together."

***

Hours later, we stopped briefly at a stream, which was the first water I had seen since awakening. I caught a glimpse of my reflection in it and realized I had blood on my face as well as my hands. I tried to wash the stains away, but they remained.

The cold water was clear as diamonds, and it cut a serpentine channel through the jagged terrain. Though beautiful, the stream baffled and unnerved me because it was utterly silent despite cascading into a pool. But the water was beyond pure and sweet, as if it had originated from springs inside of honeycombs.

Messipor drank from a canteen tied under a flap of his shirt, and then he refilled it. I, meanwhile, dropped to the ground and drank from a spot where the water poured off a lip of rock.

"Do you have a container?" Messipor asked, shaking his canteen.

I patted my flat pockets and replied, "No."

"Then drink your fill now."

I didn't need any coaxing. The water was remarkably good, and I felt parched from head to toe. Even after my first long drink, I had dry, sappy saliva glued to my tongue and lips.

Our hike resumed. We skirted around the next two ridgelines we came to, then climbed atop the third. As we crawled to the rim of the plateau, I caught a whiff of acrid, rotten air, a prelude to the nightmare I was about to see.

I witnessed a place as gruesome as thrashing, screaming immolation. Smoke spewed from the hills and shaded the entire black valley with a tent of gray soot. A flow of a different sort, an innumerable army of despondent people, marched toward the gaping jaws of a cavern. They showed no awareness of the horrors around them as they plodded with heads down, eyes in the dirt.

Nothing startled them, not even the tall creatures walking among their ranks. Those hideous monsters were like a jumbled amalgamation of various creatures. Their stork-like legs allowed them to walk over the heads of people, and they reached down at random with crab claws and serpent necks to tear flesh or limbs from their prey. Their feline bellies bulged from gorging on the slaughter.

All the while, the people—the prey—kept marching into that cave, trudging through a swamp of blood and black soil.

I looked away, my skin writhing. I couldn't shut out the sounds of the march, the ravenous feast, or the twisted moans emanating from the cave. The ground quivered from the termite movement of people underground.

I clenched my eyes so tightly, they ached from the strain.

Messipor asked, "Do you understand why we need to escape Law? This is what he does to those he catches. He banishes them to this place."

"Get me out of here," I pleaded with a forced but barely audible voice.

"What?"

Louder, "Get me out of here. We need to go."

"All right."

We trudged and slid down the hill, away from that wretched valley. When we reached the bottom, I fell to my knees, then collapsed face down on the ground. I wept so hard for those helpless people that my lungs and throat hurt.

Messipor kept a stoic watch over me.

***

My desire to stay ahead of Law redoubled, and I had no difficulty matching Messipor's pace. Swift as the wind, we traversed a few more hills and came upon what could best be described as a meager camp. Three men were sitting around an ash-filled fire pit in a land with no wood for burning. Their tents amounted to nothing more than rocks leaning against other rocks. They looked a lot like Messipor, with similar clothes, pale skin, and hair as dark as tar.

They stood up when they heard us approaching.

Messipor waved to them. "Gentlemen, Law is on our trail. We can't rest here."

I didn't want to hear that. I was fatigued enough to risk a short rest, in spite of the torture that awaited me if I were caught. While I sprawled on the ground, Messipor's friends grabbed their satchels and followed him. His years on the run must have trained his body, because he had yet to show any sign of fatigue. I, on the other hand, felt burdened by my own weight and wrung dry. Nonetheless, I rolled to my side after my too-brief moment of recovery, then got up and jogged after them. Fear of being left behind to Law was the only thing pushing me forward.

The land grew increasingly rugged and no less red or barren. We had yet to find any sign of civilization, and I couldn't discern any progress. It had been a long time since Messipor and I stopped at the stream. I craved another drink, and if we were as lost as it seemed, then I might drop dead before we located another source of water.

Messipor seemed to sense my disquiet. He glanced over his shoulder at me and said, "We're about halfway there."

"Halfway to where?"

"To Pinnacle Mountain. We should find safety there."

"*Should* find safety? Is there any place with more certainty, because I'm not so sure we can hide from that bird-thing Law was riding?"

"Law's mount may prove the least of our worries. He has a lot of tricks up his sleeve, and if he catches us—well, you know."

Halfway there? I wasn't sure if that was good or bad news. We had come so far; there was no way I could maintain our pace and double that distance. But having some measure of progress buoyed my hopes, at least briefly.

A bloodcurdling noise disemboweled my newfound hope.

Howls, similar to wolf calls but garbled and more piercing, sounded nearby. The echoes leapt from boulder to boulder and pounced on me. I shivered at the terrifying cacophony, which sounded like multiple creatures calling through one.

Messipor and the others didn't speak or look for the source of the noise. They ran, and I did the same.

Without breaking stride, we hurdled rocks and crevices that would have slowed us while hiking. We sprinted to the edge of the exposed hilltop and threw ourselves down the graveled slope. Sometimes sliding on our feet, sometimes rolling and collecting bruises on every corner of our bodies, we made it to the bottom. Two of the men cast their bags aside. The sprint resumed, but in vain.

A large, fearsome hound dropped from a precipice and thudded on the ground in front of us. Instead of fur, it had gray, vine-like cords that ran the length of its body. Each vine glowed orange on the inside, like stoked embers, and every one of the creature's steps left a charred, black paw print on the ground.

It lowered its head, bared fangs, and uttered a sound both guttural growl and quenched, hissing fire.

I backed away from the beast's heat, which threatened to burn my skin. Fortunately for me, I had trailed the group. The creature seized the man in the lead and, in one bite, broke him at his waist. His body bent at a hard angle. Death came too quickly for him to scream, but the sound of shattering bones exploded in my ears. No blood. The wounds instantly cauterized and leaked an odious, black smoke.

The hound tossed its first kill aside and pursued another of Messipor's friends as he fled. I wanted to run as well, but an intense heat suddenly scorched my back.

Stumbling, I turned and faced the open jaws of a second hound.

It planted its front paws firmly on either side of me. Viscous fire dripped from its fangs and singed the ground between my sprawled legs. I froze, and my cowardice saved me. As the hound sniffed at me, the third of Messipor's friends ran past and tried to climb a rock wall. The beast pursued him instead, leaving me alone, sweaty, and trembling—but unharmed.

Messipor fled like the others and dove into a short cave. His pursuer wasn't the fiery hounds but rather a man in a long, white shirt and red vest. The newcomer's dark, leathery skin suggested a lifetime under the bright moonlight, and his beard had bleached to an almost-white gold. His eyes were obsidian blades, dark and pointed at Messipor. His movements defied understanding. Gentle steps propelled him forward like a sprinter and crushed rocks into sand beneath his feet.

Law.

Law was a tornado. A maelstrom incarnate. He radiated a force that simultaneously propelled me away and yet wrenched me toward him. Every conceivable emotion fired off inside me like fireworks in a box. Joy, dread, longing, satisfaction, comfort, loathing—but mostly fear. All of these roiled within me, heightening to the point of intolerability or ecstasy, then fading and pulsing again.

I wanted nothing more than to crawl away, to shrink and hide in the smallest crevice possible. However, I couldn't let my cowering guide be killed. Messipor needed help, so despite my terror, I grabbed a rock and ran at Law.

Messipor's cave was scarcely large enough for him to slide in on his belly and hide. Law stood outside the entrance and summoned him by shouting an unfamiliar word. "Elis." Nothing stirred, so he boomed "Elis" again. This time, the valley shuddered and the hills rolled rocks off their shoulders.

The cliff giving sanctuary to Messipor groaned and cracked. The land might have split in two if not for Law collapsing to the ground.

I stood over the man who had been hunting us, bloody rock in my fist. Fresh crimson ran on my already-red-stained hands. Blood pooled in Law's concave temple and poured over the misshapen socket around his eyes. The fiery hounds, which had been rushing toward me as I ran at Law, vanished into clouds of ash and embers.

Messipor emerged slowly despite me calling him. He had to look down on Law's corpse twice before he laughed, and even then he stayed close to the cave. His snicker grew into a loud, boisterous guffaw and accompanying dance.

After spinning, he took me by the shoulder and said with a broad smile, "I knew it was a good idea to help you. We're free!"

I didn't share his joy. I felt sick in my stomach and chest. The sensation of Law's skull breaking from my punch still echoed in my arm, and the stench of blood nauseated me.

"Your friends—I'm sorry they didn't make it." The three men lay on the valley floor, their bodies charred and horribly contorted.

Messipor sobered. "I'm sorry, too, but this is the life we've lived for quite some time. You have no idea what it's been like, or how many people we've lost. But you've changed all that. We can be free."

"What was that word he was calling?" I asked.

"Elis? My whole name is Elis Messipor. I'd managed to evade Law longer than anyone I'm aware of, and I think it frustrated him. He called me Elis, but my friends call me Messipor, and you're certainly a friend."

I dropped the bloody stone. It rolled and came to rest against Law's body.

"What now?"

"We continue on as planned. Pinnacle Mountain isn't far, and it'll provide a way out of here."

A way home, perhaps. Wherever home might be.

***

The land rose and fell for miles, and each time we crested a hill, I saw a distant mountain with a headdress of clouds. It seemed to be withdrawing from us, constantly pulling back to the horizon, because it remained small and distant. When at last Messipor and I climbed a final ridge and saw that only a broad plain separated us from our goal, I knew the end of our journey was near.

The final walk proved the simplest. The ground was as flat as a tabletop. I continually measured our progress by the growth of Pinnacle Mountain. Though not of staggering height, it presented the highest and steepest climb of our journey. Its slopes tapered to a narrow peak where a light glowed, illuminating the clouds tethered to it. Messipor explained the light was a portal that could take us away to a safer, healthier place.

When we reached the base of the mountain, I asked for rest and a drink. Messipor agreed. He sat beside me and offered me his canteen, saying he could wait until the journey's end before getting a drink himself.

I tried to be careful with it, but in my thirsty haste, I dribbled some of the water down my chin and chest. It tasted even greater than when we visited the crystalline stream. I drank more than intended, filling my belly and emptying the canteen.

Messipor didn't seem to mind. He leaned back on his elbows.

"I hope you regain your strength quickly. The last push will be the hardest."

"I'm not too keen on heights," I admitted as I sized up the climb.

"Just don't look down."

I glanced back over the terrain we had crossed. Beyond the plains wiped clean of even the smallest loose stones, a crown of hills rippled the horizon. My journey originated somewhere beyond those ridgelines. It had been a long trek, though I couldn't guess the number of hours—or perhaps days. The perpetual moon made time difficult to judge.

I ran my fingers through my dusty hair and discovered my scalp still hurt from the unexplained wound, the one I had woken up with. I'd forgotten about the pain while fleeing for my life. I stretched my limbs and tried to relax my body as well as my mind. The land was utterly silent, and I let out a loud sigh to confirm I hadn't gone deaf.

While I rested, I realized how hungry I had become. Starving, actually. When had I last eaten?

"Messipor, do you have any food?"

"No, but there'll be plenty beyond the peak."

"Okay."

Disappointed, I turned my attention to the single hill near Pinnacle Mountain. Caves pockmarked its surface, and it was ringed by conical stone pillars balancing on their narrow tips. I was surprised the stones hadn't been knocked over by the wind.

"Oh, no!" Messipor exclaimed. He got up and backpedalled toward the mountain. His dread-filled eyes were fixed on the sky.

I frantically searched for whatever was frightening him. I expected to spot Law's massive bird diving toward us, but I saw nothing. "What is it?"

"The moon!" Messipor cried. His face paled, and his fists were shaking. "Has it moved?"

I squinted at the moon, but only for a second before I had to look away from its blinding light. It did seem to be listing to the side.

Messipor ran to me and pulled me up by my shirt. "Dawn is coming," he said, his voice splintering with panic. "We don't have much time left before we're destroyed. Hurry!"

His hysteria over the coming dawn confused me for a moment. When I recalled his warning about the sun, my own tide of panic and adrenaline surged within me.

We ran up the mountain until the slope made it impossible. Then we marched with high, labored steps. After that, we climbed with dug-in toes and fingers. The air warmed, and droplets of water began to sweat from the rocks and fall upward toward the sky. Drops of sweat from my body did the same. My tired arms remembered their fatigue from the earlier climb, and the pain rushed back. It was impossible to ignore, even with my desperation screaming at me to hurry.

The pulsing light at the mountain's peak beckoned us forward. An even greater motivation loomed in the distance. Not far from where the moon was descending, a foaming, violent sea of clouds galloped toward us on legs of lightning.

The storm reached us sooner than the strong winds following in its wake. Gusts and rain flogged us without mercy, trying to pry our fingers from the mountain.

"Elis." The name boomed like thunder from the clouds. At the sound of the voice, nature ceased her violence and sat quietly with her hands upon her lap. The rain and winds dissipated. Lightning bolts stayed in their holsters. Only the clouds remained, but their stampede halted.

A familiar figure descended from the clouds. Law glided to a place beneath us on the slope and landed heavily on the ground. The wound I gave him had healed, though a sneering, jagged scar remained beside his eye. He clenched one of his hands into a fist and glared at Messipor.

"Elis, release him. You have no authority to seize him."

Messipor leaned out from the cliff and looked down at Law. "I haven't seized anyone. We're free men escaping your tyranny."

"Halt your tongue and disperse your deceptions. You cannot destroy any who are beyond your grasp."

I moved to a ledge no wider than a hand's width and set my hip on it, attempting to preserve my remaining strength. I weighed the situation.

Despite the fearsome presence emanating from Law, a strange gravity drew me toward him. When he turned and looked at me, he seemed a completely different being, as though a mask had peeled away. Law had joy in his eyes, warmth rather than burning. He gazed directly at me, and I saw no fury in him.

"Child, close your eyes and see." Law's voice disarmed me. My urge to escape vanished, and I longed to stay near him.

Messipor screamed, "Beware his lies! He's trying to deceive you."

Law fumed, and the sky broke with thunder loud enough to deafen me temporarily. The mountain quaked and nearly tossed me off at the sound of his vehement voice.

"Do not accuse me of being a liar. I am not of your ilk."

Close your eyes and see. Law's words lingered, clinging to me like static. His battle of wills with Messipor seemed to fade into the distance. My mind refocused as if I were coming to from a long deprivation of sleep. I blinked slowly, hiding the world from my sight for a second.

When I raised my eyelids like a stage curtain, I witnessed a transformed world.

The clouds evaporated. The broad stone plain flooded and turned into a calm, silver-platter sea. The moon reclined on the western hills while rays from the waiting sun sprouted like flowers to the east. Never could I have imagined anything as white, as resplendent, or as beautiful as those rays. The day was awaiting its moment to bloom, and I suddenly yearned for the night to be over.

Messipor shouted, "See? The sun is coming. He's going to destroy us."

"Greet the day, child," Law said. His smile beamed like the sunrise. "You have no reason to fear it. The eye is easily fooled. See with more than the eye and behold the fullness of truth."

I heeded Law's prompting by closing my eyes once more. In the last moment before I blocked out the vanishing moonlight, I noticed something unusual about the small hill below me. The caves on its surface had grown wider and darker, and the stone pillars were biting into the newly flooded sea, clenching against their reflections. The arrangement looked like a skull.

The ground shifted when I blinked. I fell from my precarious perch on the cliff and, flailing, clutched another projection of stone. My feet dangled in the air.

After a few moments of shouting, I realized that Pinnacle Mountain was actually a crater, not a mound of stone, and its illusionary glowing peak was a disguised pit of fire. Thick, acrid smoke billowed from its center. If my frail grip on the cliff gave out, I would fall into the pit's depths.

Messipor wasn't leading me up a mountain; he was guiding me into a crater. He clung to the rocks below. His once-friendly eyes darkened, and their pupils narrowed and sharpened into fang-like slits.

I tried to shout for help, but my stomach seized. After a few convulsions, I vomited water from the crystal stream into the abyss. The clear drink had become black and oily in my gut, and its sweetness had turned bitter.

The vomited oil turned into a serpent-like shadow on the cliff. Its tail stretched down into the smoky depths of the pit, and its body slithered up the rocks toward me. It bit my shadow by the leg and tugged me with a twist of its head.

I couldn't escape. I was glued to my own shadow, and the enemy was using it to pull me. My fingers strained until my knuckles felt ready to snap. The fires below me flared and belched waves of hot air.

Elis cupped a hand around his mouth and called out, "What did you say about this one being beyond my grasp? He's guilty of murder. Blood is on his hands even now. He's not yours."

He was right. My quivering, aching fingers, the ones slipping from the rocks, were still stained red. "I'm sorry. I don't know what happened."

The shadow's weight increased, testing the limit of my strength. Smoke rose on either side of me like the open jaws of a crocodile.

Law, who was above me in the now-inverted world, hurried down the cliff. "Child, there is a writ in your pocket. Take it out."

"I can't." The ring finger of my left hand lost its grip. I blindly reached with my toes for a foothold but found none.

The final threads of my arm strength snapped and gave way.

Still hanging by one hand, Law lunged for me and grabbed me by the wrist. "You must read the letter."

With Law's help, I managed to sustain a hold on the rocks. The hostile shadow's grip on my leg lessened, and its color faded from black to gray. My burden eased. I quickly slid my free hand into my pocket and felt a folded piece of paper I'd not noticed before.

"Read it aloud," Law said.

I pulled out the writ. At the snap of my wrist, the paper gave up its folds. "This letter declares the bearer to be innocent of all charges against him. He has been forgiven and released from the bonds of guilt and condemnation." I looked up at Law. "I don't understand. I killed someone back in the chasm."

"Child, that dead man was your old body, and the blood spilled on you was my own. That blood has made you innocent."

How had Law's blood gotten on me before I attacked him, and how did it make me innocent?

The fading shadow released me and withdrew down toward Elis, who shouted the same questions I was thinking. "Innocent? From blood? He murdered you."

I could feel and hear my crime as if I were committing it a second time. The sensation of breaking Law's skull reverberated in my hand. Pangs of guilt and horror over-whelmed me. The thought of throwing myself into the pit and accepting my punishment flashed in my mind.

"He's right. I tried to kill you."

Law smiled at me, wrinkling the ugly, scabrous scar on his face. The look in his eyes soothed me like a balm. "You did kill me, but I live again. Can a man be guilty of murder if the victim still lives? Can a victim not offer forgiveness?"

I jerked with pain as a flying rock cracked against my shoulder blade. Elis had thrown it. He was readying to throw another one at me, but before he could, my fingers slipped.

I didn't fall. Law held me by my arm. I swayed over the fiery depths as he carried me out of the pit. Elis, mean-while, retreated from us, crawling like a beaten animal into a cave near the bottom.

My memory began to heal, and—I remembered what happened to me.

I had been shot in another life. Elis had been standing there, watching. He was also the one who attacked me in this world, striking my head with a rock as I passed through the dry, red land. He'd wounded my memory, then deceived me when I awoke.

Elis stared at me with narrow, hateful eyes.

When Law pulled me up over the precipice of the pit, I discovered a remade world. The eager dawn had arrived, and the broad, golden sun poured its light over the land. I had never seen such radiance before. Its gleam made the sun of my old life seem like a flickering candle by comparison.

Green fields and hills had replaced the barrenness. Men and women filled the grassy plains like spring blossoms. They danced, sang, and laughed with one another. Streams wrote flowing poems over the landscape, and trees tossed flower-petal confetti into their waters.

I felt joy as vibrant as a gust of wind. The world's beauty could never be sufficiently described with words, nor could it be fully viewed by eyes alone. Elis's domain was gone. Law's could no longer be restrained. I wanted to run and leap across this new land, but I stayed put, fixated by the wonders around me.

Law produced a white book. When he held it in front of me, the first of my many happy tears fell on its cover. He opened it and pointed to the writing on the first page.

"Your name is in here," he said. "Do you wish to remember it?"

I nodded, unable to speak or temper my smile.

"The message written here is, 'Jacob, my child, welcome home.'"

LUST

A key jostled in Dave's apartment door.

Dave lurched forward in his chair as if someone had shouted "Boo!" He grabbed at his computer mouse, fumbling it, but still managed to close his web browser in time. Seconds later, his wife, Brynn, rushed into the apartment and passed by his office.

"What are you doing back already?" he asked with the accusatory scorn of a prosecutor. Dave glanced over his shoulder to make sure Brynn wasn't standing in the doorway with arms crossed and eyes aflame.

"You would know if you answered your phone," she yelled from the kitchen. Every word sizzled with ire. "I called, like, five times."

Dave turned his muted phone over. Two missed calls. She was exaggerating, as always. He emptied his lungs with a long sigh, then walked to the hallway to see what Brynn was doing. There was no point in waiting to get chewed out for whatever new mistake had angered her.

She was shoving the contents of their junk drawer back and forth, knocking pens and a bottle opener onto the ground. A sticky note flew out and clung to her blue pencil skirt until she brushed it off.

"Where are my office keys?" she asked. Now she was the one who sounded like a prosecutor.

"I haven't seen them," he said coolly. She had probably lost them. At least, he hoped it was her own fault this time so he didn't get blamed—*Oh shoot, I think I did see them!*

"I checked, and they're not in my purse," Brynn said.

"Did you dig all the way to the bottom?"

"I checked!" She slammed the drawer. The Rocky Mountain postcard inside of it, the one they had purchased on their honeymoon, got bent between the drawer and countertop.

Answering the way he wanted to would have triggered another shouting match. Instead, Dave moved about the kitchen, tipping and sliding objects on the counter to look behind them. Brynn did the same with even greater urgency. Her frizzled brown hair chased after her as she rushed to the dining table.

Dave eyed her for a second. They were now in their thirties, and she looked the part. She had changed in their four years of marriage, more than he would have predicted. Wrinkles and pounds were beginning to accumulate, but even more disappointing were the all-too-common spats that always seemed to be his fault.

Brynn huffed and snatched a pair of keys from under the mail he had promised to go through. She brandished them as she hurried to the front door. "Thanks. Now I'm going to be late for work."

Dave interlocked his fingers in his hair and squeezed the top of his head. He had tossed the mail on top of the keys.

Lust

I am such a screwup.

"I'm sorry. I'll get through the mail today."

"Sure," Brynn replied sarcastically. She pointed at his office as she marched by it. "You said that yesterday, just like you said you'd get started on that new ad project."

"I'll finish at least one of the edits today."

She didn't look back or acknowledge his promise.

He called out, "Bye," but received only a banged door in reply. Their framed wedding photograph tipped on its nail.

Dave went back to his office. The plain, white Photoshop document on his computer screen attested to his recent procrastination. He needed to get started in order to make his deadline, but lately, he couldn't maintain his focus for more than a few minutes at a time. Worrying about this latest fight with his wife would certainly not help.

He leaned toward the window of their sixth-floor Philly apartment and stared down the narrow one-way street, watching the subway station for Brynn. Dozens of people dressed in everything from suits to scrubs were shuffling outdoors, marching to their daily grinds at offices, restaurants, and hospitals. A man talking on his cell phone finished his coffee and tossed the paper cup under a parked Camry.

Brynn jogged into view with her purse looped over her shoulder. She reached the subway station just ahead of the man on the phone and hurried down the stairs.

There wasn't any way to fix her morning, but he thought for a moment how he could make it up to her. Dinner. If he made enough progress on his work by mid-afternoon, he would have time to cook something she liked. Mushroom risotto would buy him some relief—unless she got chewed out by her boss for being late. What then? He would have a headache and a half on his hands if that happened.

Sudden movement in the corner of Dave's eye drew his attention upward. A black feather hung outside his window, stuck on a dewy, lacelike curtain of cobwebs. It fluttered gently and rhythmically like a subway rider swaying to music in their earphones. Birds, usually pigeons, often gathered on the fire escape outside his window, but none were perched there at that time. The feather must have come from a crow flying overhead. Dave peered up at the strip of blue sky between his apartment and the one across the street.

Instead of birds, he spotted someone, a young woman, standing on the roof of the other apartment building. He couldn't see much of her due to the brick parapet atop the wall, but he spied her pale, bare shoulders and a bit of black sleeve on one arm. Silken, raven hair hung straight as a plumb line down her back. Because she was looking away, only a narrow portion of her face was visible, but the glimpse of her petite ear and sloped jaw was enough to recognize she was stunning.

The woman's beauty and mystique lingered long after she moved out of view. Dave continued to think about her, drawing in the remainder of her face and body with his imagination. When he pulled up the same porn site he had been visiting before Brynn interrupted him, he looked for girls that resembled the one warming his mind.

The distractions delayed the start of his work until lunchtime, when hunger gnawed him out of his daze. The afternoon proved more productive, with fear serving as his primary motivation. He didn't want to defend another wasted day to Brynn, nor could he risk begging his agency for another deadline extension.

Dave was nearly finished with his second digital facelift when he heard the door to their apartment open. He checked the clock and mentally kicked himself for not having started dinner in time to surprise Brynn.

She stopped at his office door. Fortunately, she was holding a bag of Mexican takeout, and she actually seemed rather happy to see him, as if she were in the afterglow of a long laugh.

"Oh, good," she said. "You got some work done today."

That's it? The first thing out of her mouth is a backhanded compliment for working. Dave leaned back in his chair, pleased to show off his progress on an ad featuring a tall, slender bottle of vodka and a similarly proportioned model. Still, it irked him she didn't bother to at least greet him first.

"This is actually my second project." He pointed his stylus at the bagged burrito harvest hanging from her hand. "Takeout again?"

"Yeah, I'm just too exhausted to worry about dinner tonight. If you want something else, make it yourself."

Dave followed her as she carried their dinner to the kitchen and set it on the counter. "Actually, I had planned on making risotto."

"Hmm, that would have been nice."

"What do you mean by *that*?" The last word came out more defensively than he intended.

Brynn rolled her eyes. "I didn't mean anything by it. It would have been like the old days, is all. Like when we were dating." She opened the cupboard and pulled out two plates. "Is this okay for tonight?"

"Yeah. Burritos are fine."

Dave opened the refrigerator and stooped to search for the hot sauce. He lingered inside the open door, cold air spilling over his legs. His mind wandered and tripped over the memory of the dark-haired girl. She hadn't reappeared since the sighting that morning—he had checked often enough to be certain of that. Was she a new resident of the neighboring building? Could he see her apartment from his own?

The refrigerator dinged, reminding him to shut the door.

"It's on the top shelf," Brynn said.

He pulled out the bottle of red hot sauce. "Thanks."

She slid his dinner to him. "I'm sorry I got angry this morning. The good news is I managed to catch my train, barely. I was a little sweaty when I made it to work, but on time. The rest of the day actually went pretty well."

"Good, and sorry about the keys." Dave smiled at her, though out of relief rather than joy. Perhaps she wouldn't spend the next few days reminding him of his mistake, after all.

She unrolled her burrito and picked out the slices of onion from the fillings. Dave shook his head. She hated onions, but even more she hated telling restaurant employees to customize her order and not add them. Over the years, the quirk had grown into a peeve for him. Despite his insistence, she refused to "inconvenience" the workers. Whenever they ate out together, he appended a request for no onions onto her order, much to her embarrassment.

Lust

"I ran into Mrs. Hill on my way upstairs," Brynn said, "and we chatted for a few minutes. She invited us down for tea."

"For tea? Who still does that?"

"She's an old lady, and she lives alone. She's trying to be nice."

Dave tipped his head back, his mouth half full of pork and rice. "She's going to make you religious."

"Is that what bothers you so much about her?"

Mrs. Hill, who lived in the apartment below theirs, was the quintessential elderly neighbor. She always dressed up and wrapped her gray hair in a kerchief even when just stepping out to collect her mail.

"She pries into people's business. I can't ride the elevator with her without being interrogated about my life, or being told 'God bless you.' I feel like I'm living upstairs from a nun."

His wife tossed an amused and patronizing expression at him. "A nun? Are you afraid she's going to hear us in bed and come chase us with a ruler?"

Dave grabbed a beer from the refrigerator. "I'll pass on the tea."

Brynn rolled her dinner into a sloppy, misshapen likeness of what it used to be. "It would be nice to spend time with you, even if it is just tea."

"I don't want to hang out down there."

She sighed and sucked her fingertip clean. "Fine. Maybe next time. She said her door is always open to us."

Dave snorted in amusement and carried his dinner toward his office. Like Mrs. Hill, the invitation wasn't likely to get more attractive any time soon.

He managed to complete more work in between fruitless glances at the other building's rooftop. By the time Brynn returned from Mrs. Hill's downstairs apartment, his eyes ached from the hours spent staring at the screen. Still, it felt good to be productive after his recent slump. Maybe, after weeks of struggling, he was finally getting on track.

Brynn asked him to join her in bed, but the invitation resulted in disappointment. When it became apparent through multiple spurned cuddles that the evening wouldn't progress beyond Netflix and sleep, he stole away to his office. He stared at the rooftop and scanned every visible window, searching for the mystery girl. After a long while, he pulled up videos on the internet. He knew how to find what he wanted there.

***

He dreamed about her that night. Not his wife, but the unidentified, fair-skinned beauty with obsidian hair. She wasn't on the roof, but rather walking about his apartment. He saw more of her body this time. Much more. The dream ended abruptly when his wife rolled against him and woke him up.

Wednesday and Thursday passed without sight of her, and he began to worry she had been visiting someone and wouldn't return. But on Friday she appeared, like before, during the minutes after Brynn departed for work. Unfortunately, he again failed to glimpse her face, but he did hear the indistinct yet musical hint of her voice. It could have been a song, or poetry, or the joyful retelling of a favorite story. Whatever he heard, the sound of it matched the tantalizing beauty of his mystery girl.

When she moved out of sight, he raised the window and listened for her. The high, flowing voice was fading, its final wisps echoing like a humming chime in the narrow street.

A taxi honked, interrupting the sound. The melodious whisper was gone. A crow feather tumbled from the sky and fluttered into his apartment through the open window.

He failed to learn anything more about the girl over the weekend, as errands and other responsibilities kept him busy. She reappeared regularly, but only in his thoughts. The fantasies interrupted him as he shopped for groceries or tried to carry on conversations with Brynn. Every time he spotted a woman with long black hair, he stopped to see if she was the one from the rooftop. None of them were.

The girl of his literal and figurative dreams even flared up in his memory as he received some long overdue, though prosaic, sex from his wife. Later, as Brynn slept, he heard the musical voice and rose to check at the window for its source. The girl didn't appear, and after a few minutes, he trudged back to his pillow, resigned to the possibility he might have only imagined her singing.

Come morning, he heard her for certain.

Brynn had left for work. She had been complaining about …? He couldn't remember. His focus was in shambles. He had failed to prepare coffee for her as he usually did, but that wasn't it. His cereal remained uneaten and soggy, the bowl still surrounded by the milk he had spilled while pouring. The mysterious girl dominated his mind, interrupting his every thought.

He was standing in his bathroom doorway, trying to remember if he had showered yet, when he heard the voice.

Beyond a doubt, it wasn't a memory of the song but the actual melody caressing his ears. He ran to the window and saw her lying on the parapet. She was positioned such that he could only see the top of her head. Her hair hung over the street.

Dave threw open the window, slamming it against the top of the frame. The girl was cooing in her high-pitched voice. Her words, which were Latin or some other vaguely familiar language, blurred together into a seamless, lyrical dance. His pulse quickened when she bent one knee, raising her bare leg into sight. Her effervescent chorus gave him a sensation of weightlessness, and he felt as though he could lean outside and glide toward her like a balloon.

He should fly to her. She was heaven. Perfection. Ecstasy. Everything in his life was anchoring him to the ground. His career, his apartment, his wife—they were the gravity keeping him from her. Keeping him from bliss.

But no longer. Dave sprinted out of his apartment and up the stairs to the roof of his own building. He shoved open the door, hurried to the low, outer wall, and looked for her. She was gone. His beautiful mistress, the joy of his life, had vanished. A surge of multiple emotions punched his chest, and he didn't know whether to sing back to her, to weep, or to jump from the rooftop and end his pitiful existence. Even her voice had vanished, and the ever-present murmur of the city had never sounded so ugly.

The remainder of the day became a blur of misery and grief. He was vaguely aware of returning to his office, as though he were experiencing it in a vision. Except for a few moments of sharp, painful consciousness, he spent the hours listlessly seeking her voice through a mental fog. The one sense that kept him chained to reality was the smell of his apartment, which was sickeningly familiar.

I need her, he thought as he paced the kitchen floor.

***

Brynn screamed from somewhere in the haze. Yanked from half-sleep into full consciousness, Dave leapt up from the living room floor where he had been lying unaware. The shrieks quickly changed to angry, fearful shouts of his name. She was standing in front of his office, her mouth gaping and the contents of her dropped purse spilled over the ground.

Panic struck him with such force, he nearly collapsed to his knees. How could he have been so stupid as to leave one of his web searches on the computer screen? Dave steadied himself with one hand against the wall. Why were his legs so weak? He tottered toward her, hoping to explain away whatever she was seeing. He needed a swift excuse, even though whatever he said would be useless.

Dave reached his office, clasped the door frame, and froze. His wife staggered toward the computer. One of their honeymoon pictures, a photo of her lying beside the hot springs in a bikini, had been pulled up on the screen. Someone had maliciously edited the image. The playfulness in her eyes had been stretched into a wide, lifeless stare. Her body was torn open in several places, and three crows perched on top of her, their beaks bloody. One held a chunk of flesh in its jaws.

Brynn's mouth moved up and down for several seconds before she managed to speak. "Is this … what you did all day? You made this horrible thing?"

Dave looked frantically between her and the image, trying to figure out how it had gotten there. "No, I didn't make this."

"I'm not stupid, Dave. It's your computer." She shook her finger at the screen. "Did somebody pay you to make a horror image?"

"No."

"So you made it for your own sick enjoyment? I didn't give you permission to use my picture like this." She plucked something black from his desk. "And what are these?"

She was holding a crow's feather, one of dozens spread around his keyboard. Dave's head whirled, as if his brain were being spun at the end of a rope. He tried to recall what happened earlier that day, but the attempt left him feeling disoriented, confused, and nauseous. He collapsed into his wheeled desk chair. It rolled back several feet.

"What's going on, Dave? You haven't even showered yet, and I come home to this freaky, cultish stuff in your office."

"I don't know."

"What's wrong with you?" Each question was louder and higher-pitched than the last. "Are you on drugs, or something?"

"No," he answered firmly, then winced from his throbbing head and knotting stomach. It felt like something was squeezing the sides of his skull.

She started to move closer to him, but he stopped her with an upraised hand.

"Just tell me," she pleaded

His thoughts shattered and drowned in a maelstrom of emotions. Fear suffocated him. Shame weighed on his chest, making the air in his lungs feel as heavy and difficult to move as a bucket of water. Dave buried his face in his hands and mumbled at Brynn. The words seemed to well up from somewhere deeper within than his throat.

"What?" Brynn asked.

Dave sat upright and glared at her. *Why won't she shut up?* He repeated his words, loudly enough for her to hear them clearly.

"Shut. Up."

Brynn dropped the feather. "You need help," she said with disgust.

In a burst of regained strength, Dave stood and shoved his chair back, bashing it against the wall. He shouted, "Get the hell out of my office! Stop screwing up my life."

Brynn recoiled as though punched. She attempted to speak, but her lips contorted into a deep, quivering frown. After breaking down into sobs, she hurried out of the room, slamming the door behind her. The mess of feathers on his desk lifted into the air and scattered around the room.

Dave had no idea why, but when Brynn disturbed the feathers, she stoked his already-burning rage.

***

Brynn remained isolated in their bedroom for the rest of the evening. He didn't dare to knock on the door or try to speak with her. Instead, he remained vigilant in his watch of the neighboring rooftop. He couldn't sleep, not while so distraught that his love and lust for the mystery girl might go unrequited.

A brief but heavy rain passed through during the night. Dave cursed the storm for keeping his muse off the rooftop. After the weather cleared, he opened the living room windows, lay on the sofa, and listened for her. As he waited, he studied one of the crow feathers by the dim light of the city's runoff glow.

Her voice fluttered into the apartment and kissed his ear. His mystery girl, his true love, was calling to him with her gorgeous, foreign words.

Ecstatic, Dave ran to a window.

She was there, leaning on the parapet. This time, she was staring at him. Her pale skin reflected the moon and city lights with such intensity that only her blue, crystalline eyes could be seen through the gleam on her face. Twirled by the wind, her black hair repeatedly brushed over her naked shoulders and curled back in a come-hither gesture. The song, her intoxicating warble, embraced him like a lover's arms and pulled him closer. Dave lifted his feet, and his body slid out through the window.

He landed on the balcony of the fire escape. Its grates were wet from the recent rain, and the warm, humid breeze felt like a breath on his neck. A murder of crows took flight from the platforms beneath him, their rapid wings beating in time with his excited heart.

The mystery girl was still waiting for him. She didn't vanish like before. If he crossed over to the other building's fire escape, he could climb the stairs to her. How perfect to finally join her on the rooftop, to unite under the hazy, moonlit sky.

He was separated from her building by only a one-way street. It was practically an alley, and stairways framed it on both sides. He could make that jump with ease. Not even a jump. A hop. The ground, dark and far below, was inconsequential. Dave climbed onto the railing, keeping low to maintain his balance. He wobbled, but his doubts and fear vanished as quickly as they appeared, overpowered by the courage from her inspiring voice.

Once steady, Dave tensed his legs, then jumped—or at least tried.

His foot slipped off the wet metal. He fell, but in his terrified flailing, he managed to smash his hands on the other building's fire escape. Dave caught the railing, and even though his fingers slipped as he swung wildly, he held on. His heart banged with an intensity he had never known. His shouts echoed in the street.

Brynn must have heard him. Within seconds, she appeared at the window. "Oh my—Dave!" she screamed as he struggled to maintain his wet grip. "I'm coming."

He tried to hook his toes onto the edge of the platform, but the gap beneath the railing's lowest bar was too small. "Hurry!" he shouted.

He could hear her climbing out onto the same part of the escape he had leapt from. He dared not risk a glance over his shoulder at her. Dave slid his left hand out to the side, trying to find a better hold.

He felt something scratching the back of his head. It was Brynn's fingers.

"Dave, I can't quite reach you," she said, clawing at him but only able to reach his scalp. "Hold on."

Crows circled in the sky. Again he adjusted his hands. He heard no further noise from Brynn. She had gone, and he didn't know if he would be able to last until she came back.

However, it appeared he wouldn't have to. The mystery girl, his beloved, descended the steps toward him, coming to his rescue. She wouldn't abandon him.

For the first time, he saw her entire face—or what should have been a face. With dread realization, he renewed his cries for help, this time for rescue from her rather than by her. The girl—no, the monster—was nude, but her luminous body lacked the sculpted details of a normal human. Breasts and other features were vaguely approximated, melted into a mannequin-like replica of the female form. Her face was equally devoid of basic anatomy, possessing alluring eyes but no mouth or nose. Stranger and more terrible still were her limbs. Near the elbows, her arms transformed into raven wings with clawed fingers, and below the knees, her legs resembled a bird's.

The mystery girl was an abomination. It hummed a joyful melody as it glided toward him. "Stay away from me," he warned, but the beast merely responded with a curious head tilt. It slid over the grated platform until it stood directly above him, staring at him without blinking. Its body gave off cold vapors like dry ice. The water on the railing began to freeze and sting Dave's fingers.

He swung his right leg, then his left, trying to gain some footing. Terrified, he considered reaching back for his own balcony. But before he could act, the monster stabbed his hands with its claws.

Dave opened his mouth to shout, but the pain stole his voice. Blood flowed down his forearms as the creature dragged its nails up to his knuckles. His wounded fingers began to recoil and surrender their grip, regardless of his desperate will not to fall.

The monster, which he had approached for pleasure, in turn seemed to take pleasure in his fear and misery. Its empty visage was emotionless, but it signaled delight with its writhing dance and flapping arms. It leaned close to his bloody wounds and, despite lacking a nose, made a motion that resembled sniffing. Then the creature emitted a song at a pitch and volume that threatened to rupture Dave's eardrums. Crows gathered on the railing, joining in the sinister celebration.

I'm about to die. That realization filled him with taut, weighty emotions he couldn't identify. He struggled once more to bring his foot up to the platform, or to wrap it over the railing below, but fatigue crippled his attempts. He was going to die, and the inhuman beast was hastening his end. It stopped its dance mid-sway and reached toward his face with its long, tapered claws. Dave looked up at the cruel thing one last time before clenching his eyelids shut.

The coolness of its presence washed over his cheeks and lips. When he felt the claws pressing his eyelids, beginning to bore through the thin flesh, he released the railing. Shouting, he plummeted into the dark chasm of the street.

The impact came quickly, and far above the pavement. One floor below, he crumpled onto wood. His ankle wrenched awkwardly and popped, but otherwise he escaped injury. Dave grasped the edges of the plank that had saved him.

"Dave!" his wife screamed. Brynn and Mrs. Hill were standing behind him. They had dragged the old woman's table outside and laid it upside-down across the railings, bridging the gap between fire escapes. Their quick thinking had rescued him from a deadly fall.

He looked up, expecting to see the monster diving after him, but it was gone.

Dave crawled off the table and into his wife's embrace. Brynn wrapped him in her arms and, sobbing deeply, buried her face into his shoulder. Warm tears soaked his shirt. Dave slowly moved his trembling hand to her hair and held the back of her head.

"I thought I had lost you," she moaned. "I thought I had lost you."

Her warm breath, her smell, and her touch calmed his racing heart.

Mrs. Hill examined Dave's bloody wounds, raising her eyebrows in shock. Other residents, having heard the commotion, began to emerge on their own balconies. A few of them called out and asked if they needed help.

No, Dave thought. *I'll be all right*. He felt freed, steady, and healed in his wife's tight embrace.

Mrs. Hill climbed into her apartment to get bandages, leaving Dave alone with Brynn. He glanced up toward the roof's edge. Several crows remained perched there, but the monster had flown away. He spotted its gray, glowing form vanishing into the haze above the city.

THE OTHER EDGE

Astronaut Varik Babel reached out to keep from rotating in front of the video display. He drifted backwards until his feet touched lightly against the wall, and he glanced out the spaceship window. His brief look stretched into a lingering gaze. They were orbiting over the ultramarine waters of the Mediterranean and the tan coasts of Europe and Africa.

"… Would you agree, commander?" asked the reporter on the communications display.

Oh, cripes! What was the question?

Like a student called on by his teacher while daydreaming, he flipped back a page in his memory, trying to recall what had been asked. What could he say to redirect the interviewer? He must look like a fool.

Janice Widowicz, the five-person crew's biology specialist and youngest member, rescued him. "We can't see it from this part of the ship right now," she said, minimizing her French-Canadian accent. "But we do have a magnificent view of Earth. *Ciao* to everyone watching from Italy."

"Have you seen *Angel One* yet?" the reporter asked.

"Yes. We're orbiting alongside it at a distance of approximately six hundred meters."

Varik smoldered with frustration. Hadn't the reporter been listening when the last five interviewers asked the same thing? *We are six hundred meters from the greatest discovery in history. Stop wasting our time.*

It had taken humanity almost a decade of work to reach this moment. When scientists began broadcasting laser communications to probes around Mars, they didn't expect to hear replies from the asteroid belt beyond the Red Planet. An unidentified object was broadcasting a signal that counted up and down in increments of ten, and every nation denied it belonged to them.

The first known alien artifact, a spacecraft, had been found. NASA named it *Angel One* and declared its plan to bring the object to earth's orbit.

Varik remembered the announcement well. He had been a pilot for the Air Force at the time, but within a week of hearing the news, he submitted his résumé to NASA. This was going to be a monumental event. He needed to be a part of it, even if only in some small way. By hard work and luck, he earned more than a small role. He was chosen as commander of *Unity*, the space shuttle built to intercept and investigate *Angel One*.

But being on the first crew sent to explore an alien spacecraft meant enduring the media day after day. Varik knew what the next question would be before the interviewer said it.

"Can you describe the alien ship for us?"

The *Unity* crew members looked at one another. Lance Ishikawa, the engineering specialist, took the question.

"The vessel is approximately two hundred meters long, making it three times longer than our ship and four times longer than the old space shuttles. It's shaped like a swan with a long neck, except the wings are short and the body is round like a disc. The box structures on the wings are possibly thrusters."

"What color is it?"

"The spacecraft's skin is extraordinary," Janice said, her accent more prominent with her excited tone. "It's not a single color, especially when sunlight reflects off of it. The best description for it is slightly darkened mother-of-pearl."

The interviewer directed a few questions to the rest of the crew, British pilot Callum Mills and German mission specialist Emma Stadt. He then said "Commander Babel" and paused for a response. He probably wanted to confirm Varik was paying attention this time.

"Yes?" Varik said.

"Are you and the rest of your team proud to have won the Second Space Race?"

Varik nearly scoffed at the question. "This mission has never been about nationalistic one-upmanship, and I have a lot of respect for the Russian cosmonauts and the Chinese. I've worked with both."

He sighed. The reporter was sidetracking him. "The priority of our mission has always been to explore this artifact left by our unknown intergalactic neighbors. This moment is for all of humanity. Our ship is called *Unity*, after all."

"And there certainly will be a large percentage of humanity watching," the reporter said. "Experts predict your mission will be the biggest televised event in history. How does it feel to be watched by billions of people?"

It feels like you're wasting everyone's time with idiotic commentary, that's what.

Janice patted Varik on the shoulder. She had witnessed enough of his rants to know how he truly felt.

Varik forced an ambassadorial smile. "I would like to tell those billions of people to stay tuned. The course of human history will change forever after today."

After a few more exchanges with the crew, the reporter signed off with an awkward catch phrase that was, based on his grin, nowhere near as clever as he thought it was. After a cut to black, the comms display changed to a live feed of Nick Costa. The balding man was the capsule communicator, which meant he bore the famous "Houston" call sign and served as the voice of the command center.

"That's it, folks," he said. "It's just us now. Are you ready to make history?"

The crew let out a collective sigh.

"It's about time," Callum said.

"Sorry, *Unity*. Everyone down here is just as eager as you, trust me." Nick checked his watch. "We're only a little behind schedule. Nick, Janice, and Ishikawa, suit up for the walk."

The distractions stopping them from the mission had passed. Emma drifted toward the flight deck with Callum, laughing at a comment he had whispered. Janice and Ishikawa leapt off the wall and propelled themselves like torpedoes toward the airlock. An hour and multiple interviews ago, Varik would have gladly joined them. Instead, he lingered in front of the comms display, fuming. He could see Nick speaking with someone off camera.

"Nick?" He used his friend's name rather than his call sign to indicate what he had to say was personal.

Nick turned to him and inserted his earpiece. "Yeah, Varik?"

He scowled. "Seriously, what was that bullcrap? Nine interviews? We're astronauts, not TV hosts."

"Calm down. That's part of being a hero. Plus, we need to pay the bills. Interviews excite the taxpayers, and excited taxpayers don't complain about funding NASA."

"There's a six-hundred-foot alien vessel orbiting Earth. Keep that on camera and they'll fund us for the next century."

Nick tipped a lopsided grimace at him, letting Varik know he didn't want to have this conversation. "The politicians push for this stuff. I know you hate politics, but they're the ones who ultimately pay us, so just deal with it."

"Sorry, how could I forget?" Varik apologized sarcastically. "It's not enough to explore the most significant find of all time. It's all about winning the race for ol' red, white, and blue. We gotta scratch Uncle Sam's beard, right?"

Nick shot glances over his shoulders. "Watch what you're saying."

"I am. I toned down what I wanted to say."

"No, I mean the president has his CIA bulldogs here around the clock. They've got their noses so deep in NASA's business, I can't fart without them knowing it."

He checked over his shoulders again. "It's not been announced publicly yet, but Russia moved up their launch date by ten days. You have two weeks before they join you, and I agree with Washington and London that we need to get all potentially lethal tech out of *Angel One* before Kashnikov can get his hands on it."

Kashnikov was Russia's president and a throwback to the unpredictable, militaristic leaders of decades past.

"This is why I prefer science," Varik said. "It's so much purer and simpler than politics."

"Reality is messier than a laboratory." Nick shooed him with his fingers. "Go get your suit on. I'm dying to see what's on that ship."

So was Varik. At that reminder, his curiosity and excitement overwhelmed his frustrations. "You really know how to sweet-talk me."

Nick smiled. "Godspeed, Varik."

***

In the final moments before the spacewalk, all chatter on the radios went quiet. Everyone involved in the mission, both in orbit and on Earth, waited to see if the suits would respond correctly to the vacuum of space. Varik heard only the hiss of the depressurizing airlock and the beat of his pulse. The plastic smell of his spacesuit filled his nose.

"Pressurization is at zero," Varik said over the radio, breaking the silence. "My air is still good. Janice, what's your status?"

"I'm good," she responded from within her own suit. She tapped twice on her visor.

"Ishikawa?"

"No issues here."

"Excellent. Houston, we're ready."

Nick responded, "All right. Stay put, *Unity*." A few seconds later, presumably after affirming system readiness with the flight director, Nick announced, "Mission is go."

Those three words thrilled Varik just as much as the booster thrust had when they took off from Earth.

All three astronauts grabbed the bar over their heads, then Varik flipped the door's safety override and pressed the control button. The indicator light changed from yellow to red, and the door opened in a slow, silent yawn. Their target—the mottled, iridescent alien craft—loomed nearby. It was orbiting Earth with them at five hundred kilometers per minute.

Varik leaned out of the airlock. "I see *Angel One*."

He could also see *Aquila* clinging to the ship's back. NASA and the European Space Agency, ESA, had designed and launched *Aquila* within a mere twenty months of finding *Angel One*. The unmanned ship had operated as a rocket-powered claw machine that grabbed the interstellar prize and brought it back from the asteroid belt.

"Houston, are you receiving my helmet's camera feed?"

A delay, then, "Affirmative. We're watching with anticipation."

At long last, here we go.

He bounded out of *Unity* and soared over the wide, blue expanse of the Pacific. The artifact hung gleaming against the even wider expanse of black space. *Angel One* was aptly named. Its wings stood out at its sides, and sunlight reflected from its surface in an array of colors.

"She's beautiful," Varik said.

"Yes, she is," Nick replied through the spacesuit's speaker. "Slow your approach, lover boy."

Varik realized how quickly he was gliding toward the alien craft. His jump was on target, but unless he corrected his speed, his arrival at the alabaster hull would be a crash. He pressed his thumbs against his ring fingers, activating a short burst from his jetpack's reverse thrusters. His body cocked sideways, and his velocity slowed.

Angel One filled his visor. While en route, everything seemed familiar, giving him déjà vu from his hours in the simulator.

Then he touched the ship.

To his surprise, the hull deformed like gelatin under his fingers and toes. Waves rippled through the surface until, as if suddenly drawn tight, the material stiffened and reformed its original shape. The shuddering caused Varik to slip. He slid along the vessel, the difficulty of weightlessness vividly apparent as he tried to gain traction. Only by using his jetpack and catching his boot in a groove did he finally stop.

"Varik, are you okay?" Nick asked. In the back of his mind, Varik realized the question was being repeated. He had been too occupied to answer the first time.

"Affirmative, Houston. I'm fine."

"Your heart rate shot up, and you were cursing into the mic. What's going on?"

"Sorry, I just got surprised. The ship felt … rubbery or organic, like I tried to get traction on a whale carcass. It's rigid now, though."

A female voice came through the speaker. "This is Janice. Varik, am I clear to come over?"

Varik turned his back on *Angel One* and faced *Unity*. Janice and Ishikawa waved from the airlock doorway. "Yeah, Jan. Aim for me. It's easier to grab hold where the ship widens."

"Okay. Coming to you now."

Janice leapt out over the earth, followed a few seconds later by Ishikawa. From Varik's perspective, they looked like giants sliding over the surface of Asia. Wide, circular clouds, the telltale sign of a cyclone, churned off the shore of India. From orbit, even a violent storm looked beautiful and calm.

"Don't look down if you're afraid of heights," Varik said.

"Har, har," Ishikawa replied.

"Earth looks stunning from up here." He felt like they had the entire world to themselves. "Everything is serene. I could get used to this."

"Don't get too comfortable," Nick said. "I don't want you taking off your helmet and finding out how welcoming space really is."

"No worries, Houston."

"Okay. *Unity*, we're putting your audio on public broadcast now. Remember to switch to the private channel if there's anything you don't want Moscow or the general public to hear." After a pause, Nick said, "This is Houston. Commander Babel, care to share what it's like up there?"

Varik collapsed into his thoughts. The moment had come. He had long wondered how many months Neil Armstrong spent pondering his words for the lunar proclamation. The "one small step" line still reverberated almost a century later, and Varik's next words would be no less significant.

After clearing his throat and drawing in a long breath, he said, "If we, the people of Earth, are united by science, then nothing is impossible for us. The *Unity* crew has boarded *Angel One*." Varik waited for the applause in ground control to die down in his headset. "Widowicz and Ishikawa are almost to me. I see no doors or windows, an indication the spacecraft was possibly unmanned."

Varik knocked on the hull with his gloved knuckles. It felt hard but thin and hollow, like a pane of glass. "The exterior of *Angel One* is made from an unfamiliar material. It's mottled and glossy. Even more unusual is its rigidity. At first touch, it rippled significantly, but now it's as solid as titanium. Man, the folks in materials analysis are going to have a field day with this stuff."

"That could explain the unusual readings from *Aquila* when it docked with *Angel One*," Ishikawa said. He and Janice had almost reached the ship.

"You're right. I'm going to— Hold on! It's changing again."

The metallic structure began to dilate at the spot where Varik had knocked on it. The dimple gaped and widened to a round hole large enough for them to fit through. Varik stuck his head in the hole and shined his helmet lamp inside. He gulped air from his suit, unsure of how long he had been holding his breath.

"Houston, are you getting this?"

"We are. It's incredible."

The other two astronauts arrived, and they all crowded the opening. Their lights reflected off the white interior wall and silvery, grate-like floor and ceiling. Varik glanced down the throat of the ship, boring a tunnel through the darkness with his lamp.

"We seem to have activated an opening," Varik said. "We can see the interior of the ship's neck. It's not pressurized, nor do we see any signs of life yet, but it does look like it could have been manned at one time. Perhaps it still is."

Varik clambered forward, slowly, until his torso was inside the hole. He searched for movement. Something latched onto his spacesuit at the hip. Varik recoiled, flailing slowly and awkwardly in the zero gravity.

"I'm sorry," Janice said, laughter tinging her accent. "I didn't mean to startle you, Commander. I just wanted to remind you not to touch anything that looks biological. The last thing we need is to pass along a dangerous bacterium to Earth."

Varik let out a strong sigh. His breath reflected off his visor and tousled the front of his hair.

"Too bad," Ishikawa interjected. "I was hoping to keep the flesh-eating parasites as pets."

"*Unity*?" Nick said. "That reminds me. Did you bring the Taser?"

If Varik could have beaten his forehead against his faceplate, he would have. How many times had Nick regurgitated this topic? After broadcasting himself clearing his throat, Varik said, "Uh, *no*, Houston. I left it in the ship."

"You do realize you are potentially endangering yourself and your crew, correct? There may be hostile entities inside."

"So be it." Varik pulled the rest of his body into *Angel One*. "*Unity* questions the wisdom of carrying a weapon while making first contact with a more advanced species. I would rather risk my life than risk this moment."

"Suit yourself, but note NASA recommends you be prepared."

Ishikawa, the crew's resident fanatic of classic science fiction and horror, said, "Varik, keep your mouth closed when you meet 'em. You don't want them laying any babies in your chest."

The stationary helmet prevented Varik from casting a sideways glance at the specialist. "Ishikawa, I suspect Houston and Director Phillips are not keen on their astronauts recording frivolous banter at this crucial moment."

"Sorry, sir."

Nick snickered.

The grated floor and ceiling were segmented into a grid of diamond-shaped tiles. Varik glided over the checkerboard pattern like a chess piece, moving toward the nose and hopefully the cockpit of *Angel One*. His narrow light beam revealed an area where the walls curled in, choking off all but an open doorway in the ship's neck. He advanced through it, expecting to find computer terminals, seats, and other equipment in the forward room. Instead, he discovered … nothing.

To his disappointment, the room was as empty as a newly made coffin. The only other doorway doubled back down a second hallway that paralleled the first. He twisted his body to and fro, panning his light over the walls in hopes of finding more. How strange for such a prominent extension of the ship to be empty.

Janice, who had followed him into the room, must have sensed his confusion. She offered, "We can return later to swab for DNA and chemical samples."

"Commander?" Ishikawa called through the radio. "I think I've found something."

Varik moved to the doorway, then used a slight burst from his jetpack to fly down the hall to Ishikawa.

"I noticed one of the floor panels sticking up higher than the others." Ishikawa's wide, excited eyes were visible through his faceplate. "Can you help me with it? I think there's something underneath."

Ishikawa and Varik took crowbars out of the toolkits in their packs, then slid them under the corners of the panel. It guarded its secret well. Varik strained his back while prying the stubborn panel up enough to slide his fingers under the metal. Once the men had a decent grip, they widened their stances and lifted it together. Varik groaned through gritted teeth.

When the panel reached waist height, they let go and floated backwards. Janice swooped in and shined her light at the substructure they had revealed. Her voice rising, she exclaimed, "It's a container!"

"Janice, what's in it?" Nick asked with equal excitement.

Varik regained his orientation and glided to the raised compartment. Janice was holding one of the many clear, sludge-filled bags stowed beneath the panel, squeezing its contents. She announced, "It's green and fibrous but seems to be moist."

Mission Specialist Emma Stadt, watching the video feed from aboard *Unity*, spoke up for the first time since the spacewalk. "Is the matter organic?"

"I don't know." Janice pressed the end of the bag, thinning the contents in one corner. "It resembles algae. If ... if it is ..." She trailed off as she turned it over several times. "We might have found an alien organism."

Hairs rose on Varik's neck. He winked, activating the helmet's camera. The picture of the bag in Janice's hands displayed for a few seconds on the side of his visor, then disappeared. The sludge looked like a green version of the oatmeal they ate for breakfast, but he had never seen anything so magnificent.

Alien organic matter.

"Don't jump to conclusions," Janice warned. "It might be synthetic."

"Manufactured matter is still an incredible find," Nick said. "Will you be able to send some down to us in the drop pods?"

"We should be able to," Janice said. "I'll grab more bags."

"How much of that stuff do you think *Angel One* is hauling?" Ishikawa asked. "There's hundreds of floor panels in this hall, and they might all have bags like this under them."

"I don't know," Varik said. "Janice, grab a few and let's proceed. I want get as much exploration as possible out of our oxygen tanks."

Next they explored the halls that traversed the wide, circular body of the ship. The passages were bent into narrow, meandering arcs that never straightened for more than a few meters. Because of this, Varik's light carved out only a short distance of visibility. Shadows peeked around every curve, and the thought of being ambushed by aliens defending their ship became a genuine concern. The complete lack of environmental sounds and the inability to run away worsened his nerves.

Why did Ishikawa have to mention *Alien*? Varik would never confess it, but the movie, which had given him nightmares as a child, was feeding into his active and jittery imagination. He sensed movement at the edge of the darkness. Nothing materialized. He knew better than to expect lurking, acid-filled monsters, but someone built *Angel One*, and they might not be taking kindly to trespassing humans.

Get ahold of yourself. He's got you spooked over a movie that's as old as your father. You're supposed to be a man of science.

Nonetheless, his anxiety persisted. He felt as though he were diving in the shark-infested ruins of a sunken ship. Halls existed for a reason—so inhabitants could move about. Were those inhabitants pursuing them as his intuition insisted, baring their teeth or weapons?

Varik slapped his helmet, trying to dislodge the unnerving thought. The artifact had been drifting in distant orbit for years, if not centuries or millennia. Not even basic life forms had ever been proven to survive under such conditions.

"Are you all right?" Janice asked.

"Yeah, I'm fine." Varik clutched wildly in his mind for an excuse. "I thought my speaker cut out, but I hear you loud and clear."

"This seems very inefficient," Ishikawa said.

"What does?"

"The halls. Why curve them? It complicates navigation."

"You're thinking like a Homo sapien," Janice said. "Instead, translate the ship's design into clues about the travelers."

Varik found a room that branched off from the hall. "Something tells me our Janice is going to become a professor of xenosociology."

She chuckled. "Sounds like a good fallback plan to me."

Varik halted at the offset doorway and swept the next room with his light before entering. The chamber was kidney-shaped, and its white walls had a texture similar to tree bark. A bundle of green tubes hung from the ceiling and drifted lazily like seaweed in calm waters. Most intriguing was the array of stump-like fixtures that protruded from the floor.

"Houston," Varik said. "We have, uh … forty objects of unknown purpose in this room. They're brown, approximately fifty centimeters in height, and round with ridged edges."

"They look like giant peanut butter cups," Ishikawa added as he hovered over the top of one.

Varik pointed at his own lips with a jab, a gesture meant to remind Ishikawa their audio was being recorded for posterity. "Thank you, Ishikawa. I'm sure the people of Earth will be thrilled to know aliens travelled across the cosmos to bring us chocolate."

Each of the objects had a tall, curved plate that extended up from one side. When Varik pushed against the nearest one, it moved.

"The objects are fastened to the floor but do rotate. They have straps on these vertical portions."

"Chairs," Janice suggested. She turned to Varik, but the glare from his light veiled her face. "I'd bet my last oxygen tank they're chairs."

Varik nodded. He pressed the top of one seat. It compressed under his hand. "They're cushioned. I think Janice is right on this one. That makes forty passengers, at least. Where are they?"

Further searching revealed two similar rooms, tripling the number of seats. But they did not find any advanced life forms, living or dead. They also became disoriented by the roundabout courses of the halls, unsure if they were moving toward the ship's interior or exterior. Twice the labyrinthine corridors doubled back for no apparent reason.

Varik was considering how they might map the halls when Janice said, "Do you feel that?"

He spun to face the others, and his helmet scraped along the ceiling as he continued drifting. Janice was in the back of their group, enveloped up to her shoulders in darkness until Varik aimed his light at her. She pressed both hands against the wall.

"The ship is vibrating."

Varik reached out, dragging his gloved fingers over the wall. He felt it too. Faintly. "The ship's active!" he blurted out, then grimaced for having shouted into the microphone. More calmly, he asked their pilot, "Callum, do you see anything out there? Maybe lights or movement?"

In his deep, bullfrog voice, Callum muttered, "Umm … Negative, commander. You're still dark."

"Do you want me to deploy the UAVs?" Emma offered. As mission specialist, she was the primary controller for all robotics on *Unity*. "I recommend a swarm scan."

"I concur. Start on the exterior." Varik crawled forward along the curved wall like a hamster in its wheel. "Send one to the openi—"

"Varik," Ishikawa cut in. "I see something."

Varik shielded himself with his arms and glanced back and forth, searching for whatever had alerted Ishikawa. "See what?"

"Turn off your light."

Despite the oddness of the request, Varik turned the dial on his helmet. The beam above his eyes dimmed and went dark. Janice and Ishikawa did the same, leaving nothing but …

He saw it. A dull, white glow was spilling out on the floor and ceiling from an indistinct doorway, one he might have passed by without noticing. A few puffs from his jetpack propelled him through the opening and across a catwalk that spanned a black pit. He turned his helmet lamp back on and shined it into the pooled shadows beneath him.

"I see coils of red metal below the bridge. It looks like the inside of a nautilus shell."

"Any idea what it might be for?" Nick asked.

"None." He didn't linger. Drawn by the gravity of his curiosity, Varik continued to the next door at the other end of the bridge. The source of the glow was inside the next room.

He barely made it past the door before halting, suspended in wonder. Nick spewed questions over the radio, but they reached Varik's ears as background noise. Pure, white light was radiating from a circular panel by the far wall. The glowing disc was tilted forward, displaying three shoebox-sized devices as if they were bracelets at a jeweler's shop. Rigid, wavy tubes hung from the ceiling above them like the roots of a tree.

The bizarre objects excited Varik, but not nearly as much as the recognizable blue holographs floating above the panel. Letters. The holographs were letters spelling out words from dozens of Earth languages. He could read several of them, and they all translated to the same message.

WITAM
CROESO
BIENVENIDO

The Other Edge

WELCOME

***

"Are you guys ready?" Nick asked the crew, who had gathered around the comms display in *Unity*. He bit down on his lower lip, barely containing his smile, then the screen cut to black for a few seconds.

Here comes the big announcement, Varik thought.

The screen changed to a broadcast of Lynn Weiss, NASA's Public Affairs Officer, standing at a podium. The word LIVE overlaid one corner of the display. Lynn was preparing her notes before addressing the media, and she looked excited enough to catapult off the stage like a rock star.

It had been a week since the crew's first collection mission on *Angel One*. They had sent their haul to Earth in a drop pod, including pieces of the ship's skin and gelatinous bags from beneath the floor. But Varik suspected the most significant item they took was the metal box, the one magnetically docked on the podium that projected holographic words.

The box had been linked to the other two by bundles of wires that resembled optical fibers. His years of experience in the Air Force and NASA told him such a device might be a flight recorder or processor.

An alien computer.

Cracking the processor's data would allow them to cheat off an advanced civilization's homework. What progress might scientists make in his lifetime? Interstellar travel? Communication with new worlds? Escape from Earth to healthier planets? Every problem, from overcrowding to food shortages to potential extinction, could be solved.

If landing on the moon was a giant leap, then *Unity's* accomplishment was like soaring on an intercontinental flight.

On the monitor, Lynn Weiss grinned into a barrage of camera flashes and delivered her address.

"Ladies and gentlemen, as previously reported, the crew onboard *Unity* successfully harvested bags of an unknown substance from *Angel One* and sent them to Earth. The substance, popularly dubbed 'Soylent Green,' has been tested by NASA and the ESA, and both organizations came to the same conclusion. We can at this time confirm, with absolute certainty, the contents of the bags are a new species of algae.

"We have discovered life from another planet."

The reporters listening to Lynn stood and cheered. Likewise, the astronauts watching the announcement celebrated with unwieldy, floating hugs and high-fives. Ishikawa shook five grape juice pouches to add bubbles, then handed them out. Varik tapped his faux champagne against the others' and took a drink through his straw.

Lynn continued to announce more details from the discovery. "Astronaut Janice Widowicz offered some speculations about the purpose of the algae. She believes the builders of *Angel One* used it as a food source or intended to spread it on a planet as part of a terraforming effort—"

The communications monitor cut back to Nick. "You're all officially heroes. Janice, if I get my way, the new species will be named after you."

Janice brushed her drifting hair away from her face. She was blushing. "Thank you, but Widowicz doesn't sound so great in Latin."

"It does sound appropriately alien though," Callum said, nudging her with his elbow.

Janice laughed, then within the span of a blink, her enthusiasm hardened to concern. "The researchers are taking appropriate cautions, right?" she asked Nick.

"Yes, for the fourth time, I promise you they are. The research team is entirely isolated and unable to leave the facility within thirty days of having contact with the algae."

"Good. I'd hate to be the one responsible for introducing a deadly, latent virus on Earth."

"Don't worry. In fact, grab another drink. We have lots to celebrate. Babel?"

Varik perked up. "Yes?"

"You were right."

Varik gasped, and his crewmembers patted him on the back, dribbling him toward the floor. *The flight recorders.* "Are you saying what I think you are?"

Nick nodded, and a burst of laughter popped out of his mouth. "Yep, it's a computer. And we've already tapped into it."

"No!" Varik exclaimed. His mouth hung agape.

"I kid you not. We can't read the data yet, and the machine is transmitting at an incredibly high rate. We're able to capture only a fraction of its output. But our engineers had the brilliant idea of searching for incrementing and reducing patterns of ten, like we saw when we first made contact. We found it. It's interlaced with other data, but the pattern is there."

Ishikawa pumped his arms, propelling his body into a spin. Emma wiped away a tear with the palm of her hand.

"We've really done it," she said. "We've heard from extraterrestrials."

Varik exhaled slowly as his mind and heart staggered under the weight of the news. "Do we have any idea how the ship knew to project greetings to us in multiple human languages?"

The display went dark before Nick could answer.

Varik blinked rapidly, pulled into mental focus by his reflection on the blank screen. Several of the astronauts called out to Nick, and Callum cycled power on the equipment. The connection with ground control did not recover.

Their joy got trampled as they scrambled from station to station. The crew urgently needed to determine the fault and regain communication with Earth. There were a thousand dangers that could kill an astronaut crew, and loss of comms meant being vulnerable to them. Varik hurried to the flight deck with Callum and pulled up the ship's diagnostics on a monitor. His fingers sprinted over the screen, flicking from one box to the next.

"Anything?" he shouted down the ship's corridor. He received three different versions of "negative" as replies.

The issue had to be on *Unity*'s end, regardless of every system insisting in green it was functioning properly. NASA had more infrastructure redundancy than a small city, and even if it did go silent, the crew should have been able to contact the ESA, or JPL, or any bored kid tinkering with an amateur radio.

No one knew precisely when it happened, but during their frantic troubleshooting, an image appeared on the comms display. Varik noticed it first and called the rest of the crew into the module. The screen was displaying a satellite image of *Unity* orbiting above earth. No, not an image, because the lights on their ship were blinking. It was a video. It reminded Varik of the recordings he used to make while flying in formation with his wingmen. The camera angle was at the three o'clock high position.

Three o'clock high? Varik pushed back and climbed over Ishikawa and Callum as if they were rungs on a ladder. A thought had struck him like a fired bullet. Janice asked what he was doing, but he remained silent. He needed to look out the window, to dispel his concern. He hoped to see nothing but earth or stars.

No such luck. There it was, *Angel One*, drifting high and to the right, relative to their position. Varik shook his hand in front of the window and, on the comms display, saw himself waving from afar.

Someone was filming them from aboard *Angel One*. That realization would have been his greatest concern if not for the even more startling text that appeared on the screen, superimposed over the video. Varik's spine shivered as he read it.

HELLO VARIK.
HELLO UNITY.

***

Varik pulled his hand away from his mouth because of the burning sensation on the tip of his finger. He glanced down and saw he had been biting his nail, exposing the raw, pink flesh underneath. He kicked the habit years ago.

When was the last time he gnawed them to the point of pain? During his divorce?

Most of the crew were once again floating around the monitor. Ishikawa, the exception, was strapped in at the nearby workbench as he built an override for the Direct Frequency Radio Controller. It had been forty hours since they last heard from anyone on earth. Forty hours since the entity supposedly aboard *Angel One* first reached out to them.

The stranger had been consistent in its pattern but sparse in details. Every ten hours, it broadcasted a live video feed of *Unity* and communicated via text on the ship's comms display. The crew could send messages to the stranger, who seemed pleased to answer trivial questions but avoided important ones by replying, "I AM GROUND CONTROL."

When they asked, "In what years did England win the World Cup?" the entity answered them.

1966 AND 2022.

"How did you learn English?"

FROM TRANSMISSIONS.

"Are you the one responsible for our communication issues?"

YES.

"Why?

I AM GROUND CONTROL

"Which star did you travel from?"

I AM GROUND CONTROL.

Despite the evidence, Varik found it hard to believe something aboard *Angel One* was severing their ground links. The crew ruled out hardware failures. Though doubtful, the hack might have come from Earth. Was an independent hacker group responsible, or perhaps Russia? The Roscosmos space agency would not endanger astronauts for revenge, but what about the Russian government?

Or Varik could accept the stranger's confession that the interference came from *Angel One*. After all, the logistics for an earthborn attack would have been incredibly complex, and the stranger's behavior was bizarre. Janice had suggested a distant stranger might be reaching out to them through *Angel One*, using it as a communications hub. Could she be right?

Callum twirled his weightless watch around his finger. "Two minutes," he said, referring to the time remaining until the entity would contact them again, assuming it maintained its pattern.

Varik rubbed the bridge of his nose. He had not slept in over two days and could feel the bags hanging beneath his eyes. "Ishikawa, how much longer for the radios?"

"I don't know." Ishikawa repositioned the vacuum nozzle he was using to collect smoke as he soldered a space-suit computer to the radio controller. "It's hard to tell when McGuyvering a solution. A couple hours?"

"Keep it up. We need science to come to the rescue."

"Technically, it's engineering, not science," Ishikawa said through a yawn. "And Jan doesn't think science can save us anyway."

"What?" she exclaimed. "Ishikawa, I—" Janice shut her mouth and glared at him, as if he had betrayed her darkest secret.

"What do you mean?" Varik asked.

"Nothing," she said. "It's a long story."

"No, seriously. What do you mean?"

Varik sensed the other two were withholding a confession, and his patience was too frayed for anything but straight answers. Speaking more angrily than he intended, he thrust a finger toward the floor and snapped, "You might as well tell me, because I can't talk to anyone down there."

Ishikawa opened his pursed lips and sighed. "She wasn't a fan of your speech. She said people can't be united by science."

The dull insult cut deeply into Varik's pride, partly because of his fatigue and respect for Janice, but mostly because the words he said aboard *Angel One* were supposed to be his immortal legacy.

"Well, what should I expect from someone who carries a crucifix in her pocket?"

Janice recoiled. "Hey! It's a reminder, not a magic charm. What I told him was that science is a method, not a moral cause. People don't rally around methodologies. They unite for causes like religion that are focused on people and greater meaning."

Varik scowled. "Religion uniting people? It's our leading cause of death."

"That's an old myth," Janice said with a dismissive flick of her hand. "Governments and diseases have killed far more people, but complex things are two-edged swords. They always have good and bad sides, and it's dishonest to admit to only one side and not the other. Bacteria cause plagues, but they're also essential for life. Governments cause wars but also protect people, and religions can serve the poor or serve themselves."

He had never heard this side of Janice before. "There's a reason I studied physics in school, not theology or philosophy. Too much bickering. Give me something that moves forward. Something that puts humans in space."

Janice rubbed one of her bloodshot eyes. She looked as tired as he felt. "It moves us forward in space, but not in ethics or civilization. It's morally neutral. Science creates bigger buildings but also bigger bombs. The greatest atrocities are usually committed by people with the technological advantage."

"But not in the name of science."

Janice crossed her arms. "I didn't hate your speech. All I said was that as wonderful as science may be, I think humans need more to unite. And science cuts both ways, just like religion and politics. It's usually beneficial, but if we blindly trust it, we fail to account for all of the variables and the end users. That's how tragedies occur".

"She's at least partly right," Ishikawa said without looking up from his work. "Technology made it possible for us to be here, but it also made it possible for us to be hacked."

Callum waved at them. "Can you finish debating later?" He pointed at the screen, which was displaying the exterior of *Unity*. "It's time."

Varik put aside his disagreement with Janice. Given that she moved close to watch the screen with him, it seemed she had put it aside as well. He said, "Ground Control, are you there?"

Callum typed the words and transmitted them.

After a few seconds, they received their response. YES. THIS IS GROUND CONTROL.

Varik dictated the conversation to Callum. "Ground Control, are you in *Angel One*, on Earth, or on a different planet?"

ALL.

"All?" Callum said. He wrinkled his nose at the answer as if it had a pungent stench.

Varik said, "Please explain. Are you on *Angel One* at this moment?"

YES.

"Where are you in the ship? We searched it several times."

Before Callum finished typing, the stranger replied, "I WAS WITH YOU, VARIK."

His pulse quickened and pumped ice through his veins. How did the stranger answer preemptively, and how did it know who was speaking? Could it hear them?

A new image replaced the video of *Unity*, one which caused Janice to clutch at her chest and stutter, "How? How?" The picture was a photograph of three astronauts in the dark corridors of *Angel One*. It had been taken from behind them and showed their jetpacks and helmets.

"Keep calm," Varik said, as much to himself as the others. He asked, "Are you human?"

I AM GROUND CONTROL.

Callum punched his left palm. "We're losing it again."

The "GROUND CONTROL" answers always preceded the stranger's hours of silence.

"Why are you doing this?" Varik asked.

The screen remained unchanged. Varik feared Callum was right about the conversation ending. However, after what felt like minutes, a new text appeared.

INTEGRATION WITH EARTH SYSTEMS COMPLETE. CONFINEMENT INITIATED.

A whirlwind of questions circled around the module as crewmembers asked each other what the message meant. Varik did not stay to hear their guesses. He was enraged by the stranger's mockery and haunted by the implications of "confinement," a word which conveyed no less dread than a death sentence. Varik flew out of the room and headed toward the airlock. Along the way, he grabbed a Taser gun. So much for peace.

He was halfway into his spacesuit when Callum called, "Commander, where are you?"

"I'm going over there and ending this."

"Really? What do you want us to do?"

Varik shoved his arm into his suit's sleeve. "Keep it busy. See what other information you can get."

Janice shouted, "I'm coming too."

Within minutes, the pair donned their suits and disembarked from *Unity*. Varik accelerated too quickly when he jetted toward the other ship. He had to correct his maneuvers to avoid tumbling and rotating.

A semi-transparent message appeared on Varik's visor display.

THIS IS GROUND CONTROL. VARIK AND JANICE, RETURN TO YOUR SHIP. PLANETARY CONFINEMENT IS REQUIRED.

Callum radioed, "Commander, I see a message."

"I see it too."

Screw confinement, Varik thought. *Angel One* was supposed to be their key to the stars, not a locked door. "Ground Control, stop interfering with our communications. We pose no threat."

RETURN TO YOUR SHIP. CONFINEMENT IS MANDATORY.

"No," Varik replied.

PROTECTION PROTOCOL INITIATED. SENTIENT LIFE FORM 46 RISK STATUS ELEVATED.

Should he go back to *Unity*? Did the entity know of other sentient species? Questions inundated Varik's mind, and chief among them was the one he asked Janice. "Is it an AI?"

"It's starting to sound like it," she said. "Varik, you need to slow down."

He was closing in with *Angel One* at a reckless speed. Varik reversed thrust in the final seconds, but his momentum was too high. He reached out to absorb the impact and slammed into the hull. Pain launched from his wrist and flew up his forearm. After his body bounced, he clutched the injury and sucked air through clenched teeth.

Janice screamed, "Varik!"

"I'm fine," he lied. His arm hurt, but at least it didn't feel broken. He needed to press on. When the ship opened a hole in its surface, he flew into the dark, gaping maw, then headed toward the holograph room.

RISK STATUS ELEVATED.

The warning blinked on Varik's display, but he didn't turn back. Then the stranger transmitted something new, a video broadcast from Earth. The British prime minister, who looked unusually disheveled, was addressing reporters in front of the Palace of Westminster.

"—Working to uncover the source of the computer virus. It's difficult because the effects have been widespread. Global, really."

She raised her chin as she listened to one of the reporters in the back, then said, "No, we don't know when railway service will be restored." After taking another question, she said, "We still suspect cyber terrorists. We have no evidence that suggests alien activity related to the *Unity* mission is at fault."

"We need to tell them," Varik said as he hustled clumsily through the curved hall. "Ishikawa, you need to hurry with those radios."

"Varik, which direction did you turn?" Janice asked.

"Meet me at the central chamber." He kept moving forward. After several seconds without a reply, he asked, "Janice?"

No one answered.

"Janice? Ishikawa?" Still no answer. "*Unity?*"

Communications with the ship and Janice were gone. He called each crewmember's name over his radio, but no one responded.

The only audio came from the news feed, where a man in a dark suit was running toward the prime minister. He stopped on the other side of the podium and whispered into her ear. Whatever he said caused her to open her eyes wide.

"I'm sorry," she mumbled into the microphone, then retreated to Westminster as quickly as her age and heels would allow. The reporters rioted with demands for information.

The video vanished. Varik heard nothing but the sound of his own heavy breathing. "Janice? Callum?"

What was going on? Their situation felt like it had just veered in a new, terrible direction, but toward what?

He was about to stop and go back in search of Janice when a glowing message appeared in the corner of his visor's HUD. The simple statement struck him with ominous, indifferent finality.

THIS IS GROUND CONTROL.

PROCESS IS COMPLETE.

He needed to go on, to put an end to this madness quickly. The doorway to the holograph room was near. Varik clawed his way toward it, even with his injured arm. His suit's cooling system activated, blowing sweat off his brow. "Stop this, Ground Control."

REDUCING RISK LEVEL.

Anger and fear wrestled in his chest as he reached the bridge to the holograph room. "Stand down, Ground Control," he ordered, unsure of how to deescalate the situation.

WELCOME BACK, VARIK.

He flew into the room, which appeared unchanged since the last time he saw it. The tilted pedestal glowed beneath the two remaining processors. It projected various forms of "Welcome" into the air.

A section of curved wall illuminated and projected the view of Earth from outside *Angel One*. They were on the dark side of the planet. Varik recognized the western half of North America by the pattern of glowing cities.

"Where are you, Ground Control?" he shouted.

The blue holographs scattered into a swarm of dots, then coalesced into three arrows. Two pointed at the processors on the lighted pedestal, and the other pointed at Earth.

I AM HERE. INTEGRATION COMPLETE.

The stranger was an AI, or rather a virus, and it had been hiding in the computer he sent to Earth. He had infected NASA and, based on the news broadcast, countless other systems across the globe. Guilt tore through him like a grenade blast. He trembled, causing his rapid breath to stutter.

CONFINEMENT IS MANDATORY. SENTIENT LIFE FORM IS TO REMAIN ON ITS PLANET.

This can't be. His discovery was supposed to be Earth's future, their ticket to the stars.

DO YOU LIKE FIREWORKS, VARIK?

The question confused and terrified him. Fireworks?

The dimming view of Earth dragged Varik's attention to the wall display. Cities went black, turning the planet into a dark orb. Then, as he watched in paralyzed horror, the silent fireworks show began. A burst of light appeared from the area where Las Vegas had been glowing seconds before. Then Phoenix. Then cities up and down the Pacific coast.

Varik realized what the new phase of the AI's plan was. He begged for it to stop, but his voice merely echoed inside his helmet. His heart plummeted into a black hole of sickening dread.

The circles of light continued to flash at random across Earth's surface. The devastating nuclear explosions coruscated like fireflies on a moonless night.

Wrath and Ruin

THE CASE OF ELIZABETH FLORA

CLASSIFIED
Office of U.S. Naval Intelligence
3 December, 1919
Transcript of the interview with subject Elizabeth Flora,
survivor of the SS *Providence*.
1st session

—Should a told you I'm not crazy, doctor.

*I haven't made any pronouncements about you yet,
Miss Flora. Dr. Loomis informed me about some of your story,
but I'd like to hear it for myself. Do you know what this is?*

'Course I do, sir. It's a gramophone. Mr. Pelletier used
to play records on his.

*Correct, but it's not just for playing music. I'll be
recording everything we say for later reference. Just try to
ignore it.*

Yes, sir. It won't bother me any.

Good. Are you comfortable?

Yes, sir … I know it's true, the thing I saw. All of it.

*That may be, Miss Flora. I want to believe you, but I
need to hear your story first. Can you start from the beginning?
Maybe tell me a little about yourself. That accent? Louisiana?*

Yes, sir. Raised only a tomcat's strut from Baton Rouge. Lived there all my childhood 'cept a few years during the war when my papa worked at the bullet factory.

And your mother?

Mama took care of us eight little ones. Six after Benny and Margaret died of the flu. She also worked at restaurants, cleaning dishes and such. Six days a week she did that, but not Sunday. Not on the Lord's Day.

Would you describe your childhood as difficult?

'Twas about as good as we could 'spect in Louisiana. We had food on our table, and the white folks on our street mostly ignored us. Our years in Alabama was worse.

No troubles at home? With your father, maybe?

No, sir. My papa's a good man. I have friends who had mean papas, but he ain't one. They's gonna roll out the carpet when he arrives at the pearly gates … Mais, if you think I'm making my story up on account a fear from my papa or mama, you're wrong. They loved me.

Doctor, I saw it move. I saw what it done to those folks, and I heard it—

I have to ask questions like these, Miss Flora. It's standard for my job. If you're telling the truth, it will all become clear. What about your work? How'd you know Mr. and Mrs. Pelletier?

Some rich folks at my mama's restaurant was looking for help, so she told them 'bout me. Told them I was a good worker looking for a job, so they hired me to help out. Keep the house clean, or watch their grandkids.

How did the Pelletiers treat you?

Just fine. Good, actually. Mrs. Pelletier was always fussing about something 'round the home, and Mr. Pelletier had a quick temper when money was involved, but otherwise they's good folk. They … I'm sorry. It bothers me terrible when I think about what happened to them.

They were on the ship with you, correct?

Yes, doctor.

Take a breath, and then tell me about that.

They decided to sail on a steamship to France. Mrs. Pelletier brought me with them so I could help, and it was all very exciting. I'd never done nothing like that before.

The ship was beautiful, all white but glistening pink and yellow at sunset. I reckon its smokestacks was as high as those buildings in New York or Chicago. I had to sleep in the belly of the ship, in a room with other servants, but it was worth the heat and noise. I preferred being on top of the deck, anyway. People there was drinking wine and playing roque or shuffleboard. I just liked looking out at the sea or shore.

I ain't ever seen anything as beautiful as the ocean when sailing in the middle of it. It was like a big, endless jewel. The waves was gorgeous, and the sky and water was competing to show who had the prettiest blue.

How did the accident happen?

The other doctors asked me … I don't like talking 'bout it, but I suppose that's why we're here.

I was on the deck when it happened. Something big and frightful crashed into our ship and grabbed on.

Something crashed into the ship, or did the ship crash into something?

No, no. Something crashed into us. Something big, big.

A whale?

No whale could a pushed that huge ship sideways like it did. It was much bigger than us. Oh, that night was worse than a nightmare. I was setting on the deck, looking up at the stars, and the floor jumped to one side. I got thrown like an apple core over the railing.

Others was falling with me. A lot of folks screamed all at once, but not me. I was too scared to scream, like my throat was grabbing on to my voice for dear life. The ship did my shouting for me. That hull made a banshee shriek. Sounded like a whole stable a horses was being attacked, and then everything silenced.

I ain't never hit something so hard and so fast as when I plunged into that water. Never been so deep, neither, and while I was down there, I saw a yellow, beating glow. It flickered as fast as a racing heart. I figured 'twas lights from the ship, but now I know better.

If my papa hadn't taught me how to swim, I'd a drowned. But I kicked and kicked, and when I got back to the surface, I filled my lungs with blessed air.

You still believe something attacked the ship?

Yes, sir.

Did you see the attacker?

Only the lights under the water.

Your first impression that the lights came from the ship might have been correct.

But we didn't just sink. That ship turned faster than a boy turns to look at a pretty girl.

The Providence *might have struck an iceberg like the* Titanic. *The ships were about the same size.*

But the crew was watching the water.

Ice can be awfully hard to see at night. Was there an explosion, perhaps?

No. None.

Lots of nations have submarines now. They're vessels that sail under the water and fire torpedoes to sink large ships on the surface. No one has admitted to sinking the Providence, *but they wouldn't dare to. Or maybe the submarine collided and sank too quickly to send any communications.*

Submarines and icebergs don't set ships loose after they sink them.

Pardon?

They don't set ships loose. The *Providence* sank twice, not once. The first time, it went down so fast that hardly no one had time to escape, 'cept those like me who was on the deck. That vessel dove under the water, and hills of giant bubbles made a storm on the surface. Then at least half of it rose back up like a great, leaping whale. When it crashed down, it sunk again, but slower the second time. Desperate people jumped over railings if they could.

And you're sure this is what you saw, even though it was dark?

Yes, doctor. I'd swear it on my mama's life, and I'd swear it again.

Hmm.

You don't believe me, do you?

I believe you saw the ship sink, perhaps even in an unusual manner. But no one has ever seen a creature large enough to do what you claim. Science has come a long ways since the days when sailors blamed sea dragons for their misfortunes, and we've explored all of the oceans.

You think I'm coo-yon? Touched in the head?

Now, Miss Flora—

Years ago, you would a thought me coo-yon if I said people could sail ships under water, but now we have submarines.

I suppose I might have. Please continue. What happened next?

All of us who escaped, we struggled for a long while in the ocean. People crying and shouting out names as they tried to swim. Some of them fighting over the flotsam they was holding on to. I tried grabbing the only boat that floated to the surface, but the people who reached it first hit me and pushed me away. They cussed at me and called me vile names.

How did you survive?

After a while, I found a table that come floating up. The good Lord provided.

How is it someone clinging to a table survived while passengers in a boat have never been found?

I didn't do nothing to them, if that's what you're wondering.

I'm not suggesting anything of the sort.

There're lots a explanations for why a little boat goes missing. Seeing a huge ship sink twice is far more confusing. You should figure out that mystery first.

Hmm … You met Dorothy Fairmont while in the water, am I correct?

Yes, doctor. She clung to the table with me.

Tell me about her.

She was a pretty, young white lady with blond hair. She must a been enjoying a party that night 'cause I could smell the champagne on her breath, but I think the wreck sobered her up faster than a belly full of curdled milk. I was rightly scared, but she was more so, wailing as if the whole world had sunk.

And did you see the Pelletiers after the sinking?

No, sir, and I wish I had. More than anyone, I wanted them to survive, 'cept for maybe the children. It's ... I apologize, but it's terrible hard to speak about it.

Would you like a handkerchief?

... Thank you, doctor. Here—

Keep it. Can you talk about the island instead?

None of the other doctors believe me about what it really was. Will it do any good for me to tell you?

I promise to listen before making my conclusions. Nothing more, but I think that's a fair offer.

Very well. At first, it was the happiest sight I'd ever set eyes on. I'd floated all night with Miss Fairmont and through half the next day, burning under the sun. Mais, bless me, when I finally saw those trees peeking over the waves, why I never tried to get someplace so desperately in all a my life. Miss Fairmont and I, we swam up to the shore. I rested a bit, and then I saved my wits and set to exploring.

That island was beautiful but strange. I ain't never seen anything like it, either in my life or in pictures. I been to the coasts of Alabama and Cuba during the *Providence* cruise, and neither of them looked like that island. Could a fallen from the moon, for all I know. It was missing the usual pretty, white beaches. Instead, that island's grass grew all the way to the edge and even under the water.

I say "grass," but it was more like fat, lumpy seaweed. It couldn't stand up more than a few inches 'fore falling over, and the long strands grew in spirals like they was trying over and over to grow taller but kept collapsing.

The jungle trees was just as odd, with colors I couldn't imagine even in dreams. One kind had silvery, fish-scale leaves that shimmered in the wind, and its orange fruit was shaped like a cow tongue. None were real tall, barely growing bigger than a bush.

How many people arrived on the island other than Miss Fairmont and you?

Three. Miss Fairmont and I found Mr. Louis Durousseau over there down the shore. He was the oldest of our group. He kept staring out over the waves, hair and brown suit still soaked through. He mumbled "Luna Belle, Luna Belle" over and over. That was his wife. He lost her on the ship.

After some convincing from Miss Fairmont, he joined us as we hiked into the jungle toward higher ground. That's when we met Vince Oak and John Codding. Vince was cutting through the brush with a knife. That man worried me from the first. Real handsome Texan. Young, tall, and muscled like a farmhand. But there ain't no way I could ever trust eyes as intense as his. I wondered if he had fought in the Great War, and I asked him as much on a later night, but Vince just waved me away.

Mr. Codding was smaller, naught but skin shrunk down tight around bones. He said he taught biology at LSU, and he had the most curiosity 'bout the island out a all of us. While Vince was chopping down everything in his way, Mr. Codding was plucking silver and red leaves to study them.

How was your relationship with him?

He left me alone, and he didn't startle me like Vince did. Mr. Durousseau treated me the fairest, despite his broken heart. Miss Fairmont talked to me during the first few days on account of I was the only other woman. On the ship, they had all ignored me, though. I recognized all a them from before the sinking, and not one had acknowledged me.

Miss Fairmont took a swift liking to Vince. She kept patting down that short hair a hers and straightening her dress. She called him a "gorilla" when she was talking to me, but whenever that man looked her way, she winked her eyes and begged him to find food and water for her.

Vince obliged her. He'd let her stand close if she was scared, and he spun tales 'bout surviving in the wilderness and killing bears with his knife. She'd giggle at him, then glance back at me and roll her big eyes.

I never understood why she played with the man's mind. She'd plead for water, but we had enough of it. It rained on the first day, and the bell-shaped leaves collected it for us. Food … mais, that was a different problem. No critters anywhere, and none a us knew if the fruits was poison. I left them well alone. I figured until I was desperate, hungry was better than sick.

What did you do for shelter?

No shelter other than the sky on the first night. It didn't matter that we hadn't seen bird or bug all day; I still felt watched by something, and the others sensed it, too. They kept stirring and looking around, not that looking helped any. When clouds was out at night, that island got darker than the first day a creation, 'cept, that is, at the center of the island. There was some golden light coming from there, 'tween the two hills.

I wondered if that glow came from a bonfire, and if it did, who made it. Cannibals or peaceful folk? Was it a volcano? Those was the questions rolling in my mind as I listened to the shushing of the spouts.

Spouts? I don't have anything in my records about those.

I forgot to mention them to the last doctor. I suppose they make more sense now than when we found them.

We heard the spouts long before we found them. Regular as cuckoo clocks, them. The cave along one shore would suck in lots a air for a long while, at least for thirty minutes, then spew it all out for just as long. Whenever it breathed out, that air shot long plumes of water over the ocean.

I beg your pardon. Breathing?

Yes, sir. That was one of the strangest features. When the cave breathed in air, the island's two hills swelled, stretching out the ground 'tween the trees. Whenever the spouts started spraying, the hills shrunk. That land was breathing like a sleeping boar.

You're saying the island swelled when it pulled in air?

Yes, sir. It was breathing.

Breathing is something done by animals, Miss Flora. It is incredible, however, to think you found an island that expands with air. That would be the first discovery of its kind.

...

Miss Flora?

You won't learn the truth long as you're making up your own. I know what breathing is. That's why I keep saying it wasn't really an island.

Carry on. Can you tell me more about the golden light you mentioned?

The Case of Elizabeth Flora

I was getting to that. On the second day, we travelled to the island's center, in the small valley 'tween the two hills. Vince had been staring toward the glow all night and headed that way come dawn. A wise man would a snuck toward it carefully, in case there was hostile people there. But no, he chopped and stomped his way toward it. We all followed Vince anyway, mostly 'cause if we was attacked—well, if he scared me, I hoped he'd scare them too.

But weren't no natives. Instead, the light come from the strangest thing I'd ever seen, and I'd seen a lot of strange things by then. We found a pillar of rock, least twenty feet high, and a sphere of golden, swirling light stuck in the base of it. Weren't no glass around that dreadful glow, nor anything else keeping it in the shape of a ball. The fire just spun and kept itself together on its own.

"Dreadful?" The reports indicate that you previously described the light as "beautiful."

Mais, it was more beautiful than the grandest fireworks. Like liquid gold reflecting sunlight, that sphere was. But from the first glimpse, it frightened me even more than Vince. That sensation a being watched flared up until it felt like invisible eyes was surrounding us. One half a my mind told me to go grab that light, and the other half told me to run, so I dropped to my knees and didn't go anywhere.

I yelled at Vince not to go near it, but he didn't listen. The man was strong and brave but coo-yon as a cat in the nip.

The closest I ever got to that light was after Vince grabbed ahold of it. He started convulsing and cursing and shouting for help. All a him shook, but he couldn't pull away from that thing. I wanted to jump back in the ocean and swim away from that place, but I hauled up some courage and ran to Vince. The others followed me, 'cept for Miss Fairmont. Her only contribution was a whole chorus a screaming.

We pulled Vince by his shoulders until we all fell back together in a pile. He held up his hands and they was a ghastly sight, all burned and want for flesh. The yellow smoke coming off a his hands stunk of death. We panicked and searched for anything we could use as medicine. Then Vince called us back. His flesh had healed.

How long do you estimate it took for him to heal?

I say a minute. Two at most. 'Twas a miracle, but one that didn't feel right, like it didn't come from above. We puzzled over it, and Mr. Codding poked Vince's palms and examined them. Vince swore the skin got cured on its own. Then he realized what he done and got real quiet.

What did he do?

He wished for healing.

Wished? As in, wishing on a star?

Yes, sir. He had been pleading to us for help, but something else had heard him. Something in the light. It granted his wish. Vince eyed that golden orb. He suspected its powers, and to test his idea, he walked back up to it a second time. He held his hands near it but made sure not to touch it.

I bit my breath while waitin' to see what would happen to him. Would the fire snap out and burn him? He closed his eyes like he was whispering prayers. Weren't but a few seconds later, a chest full of gold coins appeared behind him. The others rushed over and picked up the coins, feeling them with their fingers and dropping them back on the pile. They clinked the gold for a while till Vince dragged the chest away, insisting it was his.

The Case of Elizabeth Flora

Miss Fairmont tried next. She copied what he'd done and got her own treasure. A bigger one. The chest was too heavy for her to move it, so she wished it to a different part of the valley.

At any time, did you approach the light or make a wish?

No. Never. I didn't trust it or anything coming from it. My papa taught me never to trust a gift from a man who hates you, and I felt hate in that light. I always got the same feeling when I used to fetch food from the market for Mrs. Pelletier, and the white men outside the bars would glare at me or yell at me to get off their street.

That light had harmed Vince plenty, and I trusted it about as much as I trusted a serpent. It wasn't done hurting us.

Miss Flora, how do you explain the appearance of the gold?

I said they wished for it. They told me so.

Are you familiar with the First Law of Thermodynamics?

No, sir. I've never heard of it.

The law states energy cannot be created or destroyed. The same goes for matter. It cannot vanish, and it cannot appear. Therefore, if there were gold, it must have been brought from somewhere. It cannot simply materialize. I'm wondering if perhaps the gold had been there all along, hidden among the brush, and they happened to discover it.

It wasn't covered by nothing, and they made a lot more wishes than that. I don't know how the gold appeared. I don't know how Earth got put together neither, but here we are sitting on it.

I don't doubt how strange this story sounds, but I can promise you I saw the truth. I'm not lying, sir.

You do recognize the difficulty of accepting that gold magically appeared, don't you?

I do, sir.

Hmm … Did the gold coins have any words or images engraved on them?

None at all. The sides was smooth.

Do you know who created the gold?

No, sir, but my guess is a demon of some sort.

A demon? Why would a demon give away free gold? It seems like a kindhearted thing to do.

Not if it's to anybody who wishes for gold before anything else. Such people can't be trusted with wealth. It's like giving a gift of fire to straw.

So you think this light had the power to grant wishes? Was it some sort of genie?

More like voodoo, giving people what they want without them really controlling it. It's the devil giving presents while stealing from your pocket.

How did the others react to this power they supposedly found?

Supposedly? So you don't believe my story?

… I apologize for my choice of words. Go on.

How do you think people would react with that kind of power? Mr. Codding tested it as well, getting his gold. He announced a book he was thinking of, *Tom Sawyer*, and it appeared in his hands. Miss Fairmont said she wanted fresh bread, grapes, and iced water, and she got all three. Vince wished for a gun for protection, and he got a brand-new rifle.

It wasn't long before the three of them was wearing fresh clothes and gorging themselves on every kind of food.

The Case of Elizabeth Flora

Mr. Durousseau waited a while before approaching the light. I don't know if he was being cautious, or if it's 'cause he was already pondering the wish he'd later regret. He ate the others' food and offered me some. I said, "No, thank you." I didn't trust it, plus Vince looked all sorts a disgusted that the old man would do such a thing.

You must have been hungry.

Fiercely so. I later tested the stuff growing on the island. The seaweed grass was bitter but edible, and the orange fruit tasted like currants. It was enough to keep me from starving.

Weren't you tempted to make a wish?

'Course I was. Every waking hour. But temptation's a whisper, not a shout. Don't need to listen to it.

What kept you from making any wishes?

Fear, mostly. After a couple days a watching the others, I seen everything I needed to keep me away.

I thought they'd wish us home after collecting a few treasures, but I didn't know the might a their greed. They made houses on that island. Big ones, large enough for families a thirty, but each had their own mansion. Not Mr. Durousseau. His home was simpler, but he made one nonetheless.

They ignored me when I asked them to wish for a ship to find us. Instead, they kept filling their homes with more wealth. Their wishes got darker and darker. Soon Vince had three ladies living in his home, and Miss Fairmont—mais, she had an eye for Vince and vied for his affections. She did not care for those girls one bit, so she tried to stir up some jealousy by wishing for a gentleman named Tom. She flaunted him and announced he was a doctor from her ward.

Don't ask me to explain it. I thought it was crazy, too.

How did these people respond after being brought to the island by wishes?

As if they'd lived there all along, and that the people who'd wished for them was their true loves. I don't know if they was imaginary or real people changed by the light, but none of them tried to escape. Nor'd they make any wishes. I don't know if they could.

Mr. Codding had his own prizes. Wasn't three days before he had a lady at his calling. But the island was more than a resort to him. He wished for lots of equipment for studying that place. He spent several days digging the soil with a shovel and wondering why it always grew back.

At night, those three drank all a the liquor and wine they could handle, and sometimes more. Everything they wanted, including books, lovers, and chocolate, they had it. They thought they was gods in their own kingdom. The unfortunate thing is they had the power to do all sorts a good, but it didn't take long 'fore evil started sprouting up.

Couldn't you have asked Mr. Durousseau for help escaping? He could have made the wish.

He got scared a the light after his mistake. It happened almost a week after we arrived. Every day, he walked to the shore to search for his Luna Belle. He studied the others and the people they added to the island.

The terrible thing happened after we all went to sleep. Miss Fairmont had been arguing with Vince about his girls wearing her dresses. Mr. Codding had started out all peaceful and happy while drinking, but as always, he turned mean by the time he reached the bottom a his bottle.

The Case of Elizabeth Flora

All a them was in bed, and I was lying under my shelter of leaves. Suddenly, Mr. Durousseau let out a blood-curdling noise, something between shrieking and wailing. I come running and discovered a most horrible …

Whatever demon was granting wishes played a cruel trick on that man. He was sobbing, "Luna Belle, Luna Belle." She appeared, all right, plucked right out of the shipwreck. But she was being gnawed like a dog bone. A hundred ocean worms was swarming over her and devouring …

Miss Flora? Miss Flora, are you all right?

… Just awful.

Is it too difficult to speak about?

I've had so many nightmares. Terrible as the sight was, far worse was the look in Mr. Durousseau's eyes and the screaming noises he uttered.

I have enough information about that. I understand if you'd like to move on.

…

Do you need a moment?

No, no. Thank you. I'm all right.

The days got more and more dreadful. Mr. Durousseau wouldn't talk to me or anybody. Meanwhile, Vince stopped ignoring me and started using me for work. He ordered me to bring water from the well they'd wished for, then had me preparing the food. It smelled so good, and it took all a my strength to not taste the spoon.

I listened to him at first just to avoid trouble, but when I refused, he'd hit me or go to the golden light and put a cunja on me. A spell. I couldn't disobey. Of the two, I preferred the hitting. Bruises go away faster than the feeling of invisible hands moving your body against your will.

Vince ordered me to do work in his house, like scrubbing floors till my fingers bled. He turned me into the very thing my mawmaw and pawpaw got freed from. I think he delighted in ordering me around, and it sickened me. I wept and wept after the first spell.

How did the others respond to this?

Mostly a lot of drinking, revelry, and ignoring. Mr. Durousseau looked grieved by it, but he would just go sit on the shore. He did tell Vince once to leave me alone, but that monster beat him bloody with the butt of his rifle and threatened to kill him. I got no more help after that.

They was changing. All a them. Tempers shortened, and accusations got thrown around every day. They'd be celebrating together one minute, then despising each other the next, like when Miss Fairmont brought Mr. Codding a new kind of leaf. He thanked her up and down, then slapped it out of her hand and yelled 'cause a the way she was holding it. Then he just lied under the sun for hours, staring at the leaf with an eyeglass.

Those people that got wished onto the island started hiding when not called, like they was slaves, too. Miss Fairmont beat Tom with a switch when she got angry, and twice she burned him with a hot iron.

It sounds like all of them experienced madness while you avoided it. Do you think it was due to something in the food they ate?

No, not at all. It was that golden light. Even when we couldn't see it, it watched us. I don't know how to describe it, other than a warm, dry fog crawling all over you, trying to find a way inside. I think it did get inside of them.

It made them violent and temperamental?

It made them do whatever they wanted to without any holding back.

Hmm. Did you ever try to escape?

Once, but I waited too long. I tried after Vince started putting spells on me. Mr. Durousseau went to the light for the first time since the terrible incident. He wished for a boat. I tried to help him carry it to the ocean, but Vince, he called me back. Told me to stay there and sweep in front a his house, and I couldn't deny him. So Mr. Durousseau tried escaping on his own.

He returned an hour later, all soaked through. He said his boat vanished like steam from a kettle soon as he got away from the shore. The wishes only worked on the island. That made Mr. Codding curious and he ran off to test it on his own wishes. The other two got right scared about anyone escaping and causing all their treasures to disappear.

Vince started treating Mr. Durousseau like a criminal after that. He banished him from the light and told him no more spells. Said if Mr. Durousseau needed anything, he had to make the request through him. Vince would do all his wishing for him.

And yet here you sit, alone. You escaped at some point.

I didn't so much escape as survive. Those wishes made them more and more coo-yon. Mr. Codding would scream about people sabotaging his studies, even though he wrecked it all himself while drunk. Miss Fairmont made new houses, each bigger than the last and farther away from us. Vince threw out the first girls he wished for, then replaced them with three new girls. The old ones didn't vanish. They just hid out of his sight. I brought them as much grass and berries as I could.

When they wasn't angry at each other, Miss Fairmont and Vince started getting more friendly, by and by. They'd shout and slap each other one hour, then embrace and talk sweet the next. As I said, they'd become crazy. Only Mr. Durousseau stayed sane, and he helped me build shelter for the girls that been thrown out. We didn't use any wishes for that—cho! I forgot to tell about the skeletons.

What skeletons? They're not in my report.

It fled my mind. Mr. Codding found human and fish skeletons buried in the grass and soil. He said they'd been there for a long time. Cleaned all the way to bare white, they was. He told us that because the soil fixed itself when dug, he couldn't get the bones out.

How many skeletons did he find?

The human ones? Least twenty-one, and not all in the same place. He said the largest fish skeleton was likely a shark.

How did they die?

I don't know, and I don't care to. I witnessed enough death. A couple of them was missing their heads, but the rest was whole.

Hmm. Let's go back to your escape.

It happened one evening when Miss Fairmont and Vince started out cordial with each other. More than cordial. They danced together 'round the fire like they had forgotten how much they hated one another the night before. Indecent dancing, with hands that didn't care who was watching.

I didn't want to be there. I would have rather been sleeping, but Vince ordered me to keep bringing them drinks. I wanted to beat his face with my platter … Forgive me. I got caught up grumbling.

After some dancing, Miss Fairmont pretended like she was going to kiss Vince, but then walked away, giggling. Well, his temper flared up real quick. He pulled her back hard by the shoulder. Miss Fairmont screamed and slapped him, so Vince punched her. She staggered, and wasn't no telling what'd she do next as she stood there, hand on her cheek and eyes swimming in anger and fear.

Miss Fairmont ran toward the golden light. Vince chased her and caught up after a few strides, and he pummeled her something awful. Mr. Durousseau wasn't in sight, and Mr. Codding shook with laughter like he was watching a vaudeville show. I looked for a weapon or anything else I could use to stop Vince without him beating me to death, as well. But I didn't need to find one. Miss Fairmont's screams changed, and I knew what she'd done before I saw it.

She was jabbing her hand at his belly, and I could see the knife flashing by the firelight each time the blade come out of him. She'd pulled it from his belt. Vince tried to flee to the light, but he collapsed on his side, clutching his wounds as he groaned and mumbled for help.

Maybe he was too far from the glow, or maybe Dorothy wished for him to die while he pleaded for healing. I'm not sure which. All I know is those wounds didn't recover like the burns. Wasn't long 'fore he slipped into eternal slumber in a pool a his own blood.

That fight, far as I can tell, is what woke the island. It moved and started humming.

Describe how it moved.

Yes, sir. The ground moved so quickly to one side, I fell to my hands and knees.

Perhaps an earthquake?

No, sir. It kept moving through the water like a ship. Those cave spouts? They started shooting doubly high and raining down all over the island. And the ground hummed a song so loud that I not only heard it but felt it rumbling through my body. Just like the golden light, the song was beautiful but terrifying.

I can't describe that chorus properly. It rolled like an army of chariot wheels and shivered like organ pipes. My ears danced to it, but mais, my frightened heart was trying to leap out a my chest.

Is that when you escaped?

Yes, sir. I ran when I could and crawled when the island moved up and down too much. It's well I did, 'cause a mouth opened in the ground near the light. I was uphill when it happened, and when I looked back, I saw more teeth than I could ever count. All a them was big as swords. Vince's body fell into the maw first.

Miss Fairmont and Mr. Codding went next. They never ran away like I did. Instead, they covered their ears, fell on their knees, and gnashed their jaws like rabid dogs. Both a them was biting at air up until the island swallowed them.

The wish-people vanished, or at least I couldn't find any of them. I did see Mr. Durousseau curled up under some brush, covering his ears. He sent me away, tears pouring out. He didn't go as mad from the song as the others, but he was squirming and moaning in pain, nonetheless.

I tried to help Mr. Durousseau to his feet, but the world lifted up right quick beneath me, and I lost my grip on his arm. Suddenly, I fell sideways through the brush. The branches slapped me from head to toe till I tumbled into nothing but air. I spun and spun, then I crashed into the water.

When I come up to the surface, I saw what I'd been living on for those weeks. The island was a leviathan. It raised its head up out a the water as high as a mountain. Its shape covered up at least a third of the starry sky, and the moonlight reflected on the waterfall running off its back.

What did it look like?

I can't give but a penny's-worth description of it. The body looked like a centipede with hundreds of writhing, serpent-tail legs on its belly. Forests covered its whole hide like a wet, matted coat. Up on its head, between the bumps we'd called hills, the golden light was shining bright from the stone horn. That glow was pulsing exactly like the light I'd seen during the ship wreck.

The leviathan bent over and stared down at me with twenty of the oldest, blackest, saddest eyes on this earth. Its peepers was on its chin, and they yanked my worst feelings out a my heart and mind. First I started sobbing and bobbing my head like I was grieving a hundred funerals all at once. Then came the fear. Mais, I didn't know you could feel fear so awful that you swear your shaking body's going to rip to crumbs.

It loathed me. It loathed me something fierce, and I still feel it when I imagine those eyes, like its very thoughts could grab me to drag me to the bottom of the ocean, and I couldn't—

Miss Flora?

—free of that clawed mind. All my sight went blind 'cept for those eyes—

Miss Flora, are you all right?

101

—song turned into a growl, every rumble one after another hitting me, and hitting me, and hitting me, and I couldn't swim away no matter how much I thrashed with my limbs, 'cause I wanted to dive and drown myself just to get away—

Miss Flora!

—oh heavens, death would a been better—

Miss Flora, sit down and breathe!

—I still see it in my mind, right where it was grabbing my thoughts and cursing at me with words no person could ever say, and that fear just biting—

Elizabeth, wake up!

—screamed so hard my mouth ripped and all I tasted was blood and the salt from the ocean splashing in my mouth, and then it come even closer and I clenched my neck so hard my spine felt ready to snap, and the stars burned in its eyes without any warmth—

Elizabeth, stop!

—it lifted me up with just its mind, warning me—

Oh, my word. How ... how are you floating?

—pushed on my heart till sand flowed—

(screams) Security, help!

—hates us all, but specially hated me for fighting—

What happened to—oh, your eyes. Security! Elizabeth, come down.

—let go of me when I thought "I'm not yours! You can't have me or control me, and I won't do what you want!"

...

Miss Flora? Hello? Wake up.

(inaudible)

No, did you see it? She was just floating right there ... Miss Flora, wake up ... I have a pulse, but it's racing so fast, it's like water rushing through a hose.

(inaudible)

Go get the nurses.

...

Miss Flora? Look at me. Are you all right?

Yes, sir. Why am I down here?

You fell after you were ... Do you remember anything from the last minute?

I was telling you about the leviathan, and then I woke up here with my head hurting. Doctor, what's wrong? You look like you seen a ghost.

I don't know what I saw. Have you had any unusual incidents since the rescue?

No. Do you mind if I sit in the chair?

Let me pick it back up. Go ahead.

I am frightful dizzy, but I can finish.

That big monster let me go and dove into the sea. A whole cliff a water rushed over me and pushed me down so deep that my ears hurt enough to burst. I couldn't tell which way was up, so I just kicked and swam. Lucky for me, I got back to the surface.

A few hours later, I reached the blessed shores of the Virgin Island. Some folks took care a me till the Navy arrived ... How come you stopped writing notes?

Miss Flora, are you feeling any unusual symptoms right now?

My heart is fluttering, but I'm fine. You have to believe my story, doctor.

Hold on. I need a minute to think.

It's all true. Doctor, I got nothing to gain in lying. The truth is all I have.

What did you call the island creature? A le ... le ...

Leviathan, sir.

And you believe this island-sized leviathan sunk the SS Providence?

For certain. And I know you haven't found it, but the ocean is an awful big place to hide.

This makes no sense. Do you have any evidence to support your story? Evidence for everyone, not just me? The people of this country want explanations for what happened to the Providence, *but do you know how they will react if we blame a giant sea monster? Half of them will mock the report, and half will panic.*

I don't know what to say, doctor. You have my word. I just want to leave this place and return home to my family. I haven't seen them in a long while.

The nurses are here ... Send them in ... Pardon me, but I'm going to stop the recording now.

How soon will I go home, sir?

Very soon. Tell me, is this leviathan creature of yours large enough to drag down a battleship that's sailing at full steam?

-END OF RECORDING-

STARGAZING

There is no secret in why I moved from Boston to a home in the countryside. Plenty of sensible, sane people do it for the same reason as I. While living in the city, I rolled through each day like some marble trapped in a perpetual machine; I careened down tracks without purpose and rotated around cogs wound up by long-forgotten builders. The rural life offered a quieter, more primal existence—one where nature could nourish my humanity.

When I was a child, my grandmother lived in a beguilingly tall home outside Arkham. My parents brought me there for visits during the stifling summer months. All of my fondest memories, like swimming in the river by moonlight, came from those holidays in the country. Sadly, the pleasant times ceased when my mother and father passed away. I lived out the remainder of my youth with my aunt, crowded into an apartment building surrounded by other apartment buildings.

Is it then any wonder why I accepted an English professorship at a college near my family's old vernal retreat? I left Boston, forsaking with it a night sky made hazy by riverfront factories and stained by gas lamps. By contrast, my new home dwelt in a pristine environment, a place where the seemingly infinite host of stars gathered each evening in the obsidian firmament. Instead of the noise of bustling carriages and shouting street vendors, my windows opened to the singing of birds and crickets.

I adored my new residence. Any sensible person with a preference for quiet and solitude would have felt the same way.

On days when I came home early from the college, I explored the acres behind my house. The previous owners had cut paths through the otherwise unkempt forest. I was so overjoyed with wandering those trails that losing myself on them became a goal rather than a fear. An intoxicating, rapturous sense of wonder overtook me on each journey, and I trekked farther and farther from home.

Bear in mind I took logical precautions for my safety. I kept track of the time, and I oriented myself according to the surrounding hilltops. Nonetheless, an evening came when I failed to find my way out of the woods before dusk. I navigated slowly after that, holding my hands out in front of me. Thanks to the moonbeams filtering through the canopy, I managed to find my way out long before dawn.

It may seem senseless, and perhaps even mad, but the incident did not in any way caution me against further twilight escapades. In fact, it had quite the opposite effect on me. I acquired a taste for adventure that is so lacking in our modern era. My dreams escorted me back to the trails, stoking my curiosity for what lay beyond the unexplored bends.

Do not interpret my desire to roam the dark, untamed lands as an indication of insanity. Others travel at great cost to the Congo or Orient, but my frontier stretched out from my back porch. I was merely pursuing a more thrilling form of escape from modernity, a return to the origins of our species. Everyone speaks highly of being in nature, but is it truly nature if it is gardened and therefore unnatural?

Being no fool, I carefully considered what items I would need for an extended hike. I filled a bag with food, a lantern, and a canteen of water. On the next cloudless night, I put on a coat, grabbed my supplies, and set off like a settler in a wild, undiscovered land.

Nature greeted me as one of her own. Crickets serenaded me with their violin songs. The constellations followed me with their slow parade toward the western horizon. The trees ushered me forward; craven men would have been dispirited by the creaking and groaning of their boughs, but I recognized the old, deciduous giants were welcoming me with waving arms.

Never had I felt so alive. My dim, timid lantern barely pushed back the darkness with its glow, but I continued resolutely into the furthest depths of the unspoiled realm. I hiked down new trails, and after what I can only guess was about three hours, I came to a clearing carpeted with dry, dead leaves. Nothing grew in the area save a few wiry, bristled shrubs. The canopy opened over the field, and the stars, which had merely coruscated through the branches during my walk, shone in full, magnificent array.

Obscure shapes protruded from the center of the field, reflecting the light from my lantern. Curious, I approached them. Such curiosity should seem quite sensible to you, as any man would have felt the same. Furthermore, why would anyone be cautious of small, motionless objects in a forest? Exploration is not a sign of madness.

The dead leaves, thickly accumulated on the ground, crunched underfoot as I trudged across the field. The objects catching my attention were six stones arranged in a circle around a stump. The tree that once stood there had been cut down, and even in the dark I could see axe marks in the exposed flesh and rings of the wood.

Stooping, I examined the stones, each of which had two numbers chiseled into them. The upper numerals ranged between 1771 and 1816, but the lower numerals all read 1833. I logically and sensibly deduced that what I found were grave markers of people who had passed away in the same year, perhaps during a single event. My imagination scrawled possible endings for the unnamed residents buried in the soil. All of the stories were tragic.

I thought to turn back and head toward home, not out of cowardice but because I saw no further trails to follow. I considered my journey complete, and the tombstones reinforced my sense of finality. However, nature reminded me that exploration is not limited to paths created by others. The wind changed its course, raking my hair and whispering wordless promises of discovery. The curled leaves spread across the field flipped like pages of an unread book.

A swift gust swooped down from the sky and snuffed out my lantern, leaving only starlight by which to see, as the moon had yet to rise. I calmly opened my bag to take out matches but then realized I had left them in my cupboard. Though sensible and sane, I am also human, and, as such, naturally prone to errors.

As my eyes adjusted to the fuller darkness, I noticed a distant fire outlining the tops of trees in red. My desire to be near a source of light was, I think you would agree, to be expected. The coaxing that pushed me toward it, however, came from an external motivation. I was not alone; that thought burrowed into the basest levels of my awareness, yet I could do nothing about it. A possession, if you believe in that sort of thing, took hold of my curiosity.

I could not refrain from approaching the fire any more than I could refrain from breathing. The compulsion to keep walking forward, at first a purring hunger, grew into a ravenous craving. I crossed the remainder of the clearing and entered the old, thick forest on the other side.

The farther I traveled, the more I became aware of patterns in the forest sounds, as though nature were uttering an ancient, rhythmic, alien language. I have no way of adequately describing the anomaly, but familiar rustling and creaking noises aligned into cadences best described as song or speech. The earth, through groans and heavy sighs, expressed messages untranslatable to me, a mere human. The wind became breath, a breath that both lured and chased me toward the fire.

My thoughts submerged deeper and deeper into my subconscious. My movements became erratic, controlled by long-neglected primal instincts rather than my mind. I rushed through thorn bushes and clambered down a rocky cliff into a ravine. My every step was a release, the giving in to irresistible desire. Curiosity, my sole motivation, coursed through my veins.

I recall the trees swaying in time with the rhythms of the earth, casting down flower petals like spectators at a coliseum. My memory of the minutes or hours after that is vacant.

When my natural senses awoke, I was on my knees at the edge of a different clearing. A stone obelisk towered over me. Its surface was covered with misshapen circles that linked and folded over one another in a baffling, dizzying display. Similar monuments ringed the entire field, and all of them glowed because of the wild, gnashing, torrid bonfire at the center.

Robed figures moved in a bizarre kind of dance around the blaze, their movements both frantic and mesmerizing. The worshippers cast dead birds into the fire, and each time, a deafening roar of ten thousand cawing crows filled my head. I covered my ears, but my efforts did nothing to lessen the birds' torrential, painful cries.

I tried to get up and flee from the savage ritual, but severe trembling consumed the entirety of my strength. The air whirled, spreading an odious stench of brimstone and rotting fish. Caws from the unseeable swarm of crows rose and fell. The woods frothed and shook. Trees beat branches together with a brutality found only in war, their reckless percussions vibrating my bones.

Most oppressive of all was the power pressing down mercilessly upon me; the charcoal sky descended to the earth as a formless giant and crushed me under the terrible weight of its eternality. The stars I so greatly adored stared back at me, all of them eyes of an audience watching indifferently as I screamed for mercy. Yes, when we gaze at the host above, they gaze back.

The robed people gathered around me, their faces hidden by hoods and veils of darkest shadow. They reached out with wrinkled, gnarled hands but did not touch me. Instead, they chanted as the invisible fingers of some colossal, ethereal monstrosity seized my body and carried me toward the fire. The stars observed my torment like a jury at an execution.

I did not die that night, for the power that took me lacked such mercy. Instead, I awoke four months later to the shouts of soldiers seizing me at gunpoint. I was shivering terribly because I was covered with snow and the blood of people I have been accused of killing.

I am a victim, not a murderer. My mind has been contorted and bruised. I used to be sensible, logical, and normal, but those parts of me are coming to an end. This account has been penned during the high tides of sanity between recurring bouts of dreadful horror and confusion.

No one believes me that the guilty ones roam the earth. I cannot blame them, for only a few months ago I, too, would have scoffed at my mad mutterings. The police searches have failed to find the cult or the meadow ringed with obelisks. What evidence is there to free me?

To whoever reads this, do not judge me by what you see now, for this is no common insanity afflicting me. I beg you not to assume me guilty simply because you cannot see that which chooses to hide itself from mortal men. I am a living victim. I have heard, felt, and smelled the breath of powers hiding in this earth. I know what it is like to be a prisoner of the malice that resides in the shadows of reality.

The stars still look for me, watching through the window of my cell. At least I can hide from them. I have no escape from the cacophonous screams of the crows. They resound within me, waking or interrupting me at any hour. The birds mock me, torment me, and consume my resolve, and I alone can hear them.

My next collapse into terror may be permanent. If that occurs, this account will be the only defense of my name. You must believe my story. I did not kill, at least not while in control of my own mind. The cause of my growing insanity surrounds you as well, and your hope may die next. The malevolent power lurks within nature, both the nature of the land and nature of humanity. It thrives on and sustains all of our sufferings.

Who can stand against such darkness without succumbing to it? Who can free me, and free all of us, from its power?

The darkness is watching you, too.

TURPENTINE

Luciano Mideo's masterpiece began with a loose nail.

The broad mirror in his apartment's art studio suddenly fell from the wall. His reflection shattered into a dozen pieces and collapsed on the floor.

"Mannaggia!" he cursed in Italian as he hurled his pencil. It skittered across the wood floor and hid under a sofa.

Luciano raked his fingers through his long hair and sighed. The silver-framed mirror had cost over eight hundred British pounds and was the first thing he purchased after Tate Modern exhibited one of his sculptures. It was also one of the few possessions he had brought when he moved to New York City.

It wasn't about the money. He could afford a similar mirror once he started selling paintings again. His name still possessed some value, even if it had been months since his last sale. No, the loss was largely sentimental.

Other issues were feeding his frustration. He paced the room, walking past the stack of unsigned portraits. All of them were nearly finished, lacking only final touches to their colors and shading. But they seemed stale, and being uncertain of what they lacked, he had moved on to other projects while awaiting inspiration.

All of his art, both his sculpting and painting, required new inspiration. A fresh subject or challenge. Luciano stopped and leaned against a window. Cars were queued at the red light below, and lunch-hour patrons were dining outdoors at the café across the street. He had originally loved his people-watching viewpoint of New York's Chelsea District, but that too had stagnated. So what should he paint?

What? What!

Luciano slapped the window. It quaked, as did the semi-transparent reflection of his white-and-lavender apartment. He spun on his heels and marched through the circuit of rooms. Halfway through, he nearly kicked his Louis Vuitton coffee table in anger, but a tug from his better judgment restrained him.

"Focus, Luciano," he told himself. Wandering meant zero progress.

He returned to the white canvas, which bore nothing more than a few pencil lines. He rolled up the sleeves of his button-up shirt, cinched his apron tighter, and turned the easel away from the broken mirror. He didn't need that distraction. Instead, he faced two of his oldest past works. Both exhibited his preferences for strong color depth and blends of traditional art styles with the surreal. One piece featured misshapen glass hanging from a layered nest of driftwood pieces. The other was a painting that depicted family members standing behind a mother as she nursed a small skeleton.

Despite desiring to move forward, he glanced over his shoulder at the shattered mirror. The shards reflected an audience of his repeated face. So much for doing a realistic self-portrait.

Luciano cocked his head to one side. On second thought, a realistic self-portrait wasn't the challenge he needed, anyway. Portraits could be spectacular, but they were also clichéd and limiting to creativity. The process would have been as methodical as the stoplight traffic patterns below his apartment.

How, then, should he alter his approach?

Did a painter need to stare at his reflection in order to recreate it? Of course not. Why not present the identity of his heart and mind, rather than replicate visible flesh? Why not stare through the lens of his hopes, desires, and strengths in order to paint his soul on the canvas? The image would be a truer reflection of who he was.

Eagerness surged through his body and raised the hairs on his neck. Moving with the urgency of a person rescuing valuables from a fire, he hastily grabbed the necessary oil paints and mixed them on his palette. Then, before making the first brush stroke, he paused long enough to empty his mind of everything except his immediate excitement and sensations. He focused on the darkness behind his closed eyelids, the taste of each slowed breath, the contrast of cold, conditioned air and warm sunlight coming through the window.

Luciano opened his eyes and began painting a mottled gray background. No pencil sketches of his face would be necessary. Lines were a constraint, a limitation to his vision. He moved the brush recklessly yet confidently over the canvas. After applying the base, he formed a genuine version of his face, which meant meditating on his mind while also recreating facial features. The resentments, desires, and thoughts that polite society demanded be tamed and hidden served as a muse for his work.

The portrait was more than mere reflection. It was him as only he knew.

Physical details did not go unaccounted for. He parted the portrait's hair in the same way as his own, and with a flick of his wrist, he added the errant strand lying on his forehead. He included his burgeoning crows' feet but did so with the same disappointment he felt when seeing them in the mirror. When a speck of black paint landed on his shoulder, he flicked one onto the portrait's red shirt as well.

The image coalesced, coming nearer and nearer to life. Luciano's obsession possessed his every thought until a rapid knock at the door interrupted him. He looked up from the canvas. Exhaustion pounced heavily upon him, and the paintbrush fell from his hand to the cloth-covered floor. How many hours had he spent on his work? The sun was setting, dyeing his apartment walls crimson.

Another knock. The sound barged into his isolation like an unwanted guest. He arched his back, and before he could finish the stretch, the door thumped again. *"Perche me?"* he exclaimed, throwing up his hands. He removed and folded his apron, then called out, "Who is it?" in accented but fluent English.

A familiar New Yorker voice answered from the hall. "Luciano, it's Julia. I need to see you."

He rolled his eyes. Julia was his lover, an attractive woman in her mid-thirties, but he had no interest in a romp with her while firmly in the embrace of his craft.

Nonetheless, he checked his breath and opened the door as far as the chain lock allowed.

"Today is not good for me," Luciano grumbled.

Julia looked up from the diamond wedding ring she was spinning on her finger. She had left it on this time. "It's an emergency," she said, her voice as disheveled as her unbrushed hair. "I need to see you."

Luciano drummed his fingers on the wall. He wanted to return to his work, and Julia was not preened for a night together. She had arrived without makeup and dressed in a faded T-shirt and capris, a homelier version of the woman in a short, black dress from their previous rendezvous.

"Please?" she pleaded.

He hooked his fingers on the chain for several seconds before unfastening it and stepping aside. Julia entered and tried to bury her face in his chest. He stopped her advance with an upheld hand.

"I will be back in a minute," he said, walking away.

Julia covered her chest with her arms. "But, Lu, this is serious."

He wagged a finger at her. "Wait. I need to use the restroom first."

By the time he returned, Julia had retreated to one of his chairs. She was staring out the window.

Luciano finished drying his hands on a small towel, then folded it and set it on a table. "What do you want to talk about?"

Julia held out her cell phone as if the sight of it had a significant meaning. His reflection in its screen shook because of her violent trembling.

"My husband found our text messages. He knows about us and—"

"And what?" he asked, worried. "Is he looking for me?"

Julia closed her red eyes tightly. "No." Her voice cracked. "But he got angry at me. He started yelling and threatened to take my kids away. Then he kicked me out of the house. I came here 'cause I didn't know where else to go."

"Does he know where I live?"

Julia shook her head in slow, exaggerated turns.

He relaxed. At least the news was not all bad. But there had to be other places she could go. She had parents, no? Luciano crossed his arms. "I'm sorry, but now is not a good time for me. I'm busy with a very important piece."

Her trembling doubled. "But …" Julia glanced quickly about the apartment, then stared intently at him. "Can't I stay here? Just overnight? I promise I'll be quiet … You won't even know I'm here, unless you want to."

She stood and advanced toward him with small steps. Julia puckered her lips in a way that was probably meant to be enticing, but her desperation spoiled her attractiveness.

Luciano waved his hand. "I can't have any distractions right now. Besides, I did not agree to this kind of personal drama."

Julia halted. Her jaw dropped as if he had just slapped her across the cheek. "What are you saying?"

"You need to fix this yourself."

Tears flooded her eyes. "But … what am I supposed to do about him?"

Luciano shrugged. "Whatever you think best, but this is not my problem. Especially not today."

"What about us?"

He pointed toward the door. "You can come back another day if you like, after this mess blows over."

For several seconds, Julia turned left and right as though looking for a place to hide. As his demand set in, her expression changed from tearful sadness to boiling venom.

"You bastard!" she shouted. Julia swung an open hand at him, but Luciano deflected the slap. "You filthy, lying bastard." She raised her arm a second time to hit him, but instead covered the tears starting to streak down her cheeks. Her shoulders heaved up and down as she trudged, sobbing, toward the exit.

Too bad it's over, Luciano thought. The trysts had been fun.

His ex-lover halted in the kitchen. Between gasps, she asked, "Can you at least … give me some money? I left in a hurry … and I don't have enough for cab fare back home."

"It's only three blocks to the subway station."

He knew the response was cruel, and the force with which she slammed the door was not unexpected. He didn't care. She had interrupted his most exciting project in years. A few minutes later, he peeked down at the street and spotted Julia begging strangers on the sidewalk for money.

After gulping a glass of wine, Luciano resumed his work, this time with a finer brush. He added wrinkles, shadows, and other final details that subtly but powerfully communicated his frustrations with never reaching the highest echelon of modern artists. He brightened and darkened many of the hues, then blurred the edges of the image. By the time he made the final brush stroke, he was too exhausted to fully appreciate what he had made. He slept heavily and easily that night.

The next day, after he had eaten and bathed, Luciano returned to the portrait. He stood before his creation and drank it in with fresh eyes. The rush of exhilaration folded his knees, and he dropped to the floor, weeping joyfully.

"My masterpiece," he laughed. "I've created my masterpiece."

***

Two months later, Luciano stood before an eager audience in Paris's Gagosian Gallery. White walls and a half-dozen of his other creations flanked his centerpiece, which remained veiled beneath an emerald-colored silk cloth. The museum curator stood beside it as she finished her introduction.

"When you have seen it," she said in French, "you will agree we are witnesses of the next mountain peak in art."

She gestured toward Luciano. He turned on his wireless microphone and stepped forward to address the crowd of nearly a hundred patrons and art professionals. They welcomed him with calm applause.

Luciano was fluent in French. Regardless, he kept his reveal speech brief. The masterpiece could boast for itself.

"Ladies and gentlemen, I am Luciano Mideo and I present to you *True Reflection*."

He pulled the silk cloth away from the canvas and easel. The disrobed self-portrait bore a striking resemblance to him, and its colors were vibrant yet harmonious. Both painted figure and painter beamed with pride. The audience gasped and crowded around each other to take pictures, and the museum curator fanned herself.

Turpentine

Luciano smiled into the lightning storm of camera flashes.

***

"Sweetie, would you like some toast?" Edward's wife, Tiffany, asked from the far side of the kitchen.

"Yes, please," Edward Humboldt said without looking up from the *Nüday Art Review* magazine on their kitchen island. His fork hovered over his poached eggs while he read one of the articles.

The toaster lever clicked. Edward's wife circled around him and leaned against his back. As she read over his shoulder, her salt-and-pepper curls brushed against his neck. He tipped his head toward her and nuzzled her chin.

"I wish you'd eat your food while it's warm. Read afterwards."

"Okay," he said out of habit, still ignoring his eggs.

"You seem awfully interested in that article."

"Do you remember Mideo's *True Reflection*?"

She squeezed his shoulder and headed back to the toaster. "It sounds familiar."

Twenty-five years of marriage had taught Edward those words meant "no."

His wife was only a casual observer of art; one with a good eye for it, but a casual observer all the same. He, on the other hand, had earned a reputation as one of the world's preeminent art critics. His writings had appeared in numerous publications, and in a biography piece three years ago, *Nüday* called him the most respected critic in America.

Edward said, "Luciano Mideo did a piece that made quite an impression at Gagosian Paris. Elizaveta said it's the best self-portrait since Rembrandt." The comparison had surprised him when Elizaveta, a fellow critic, mentioned it. She had never been one to make exaggerated, blasphemous claims about new pieces.

"Anyway," Edward continued after scanning the last paragraph of the article, "it's apparently coming to New York next month."

The toast sprang up. Tiffany pulled them onto a plate. "I suppose you want to go."

"I do." This would be his best opportunity to see it. They lived only an hour from the City. "I'd like to see what all the fuss is about."

Despite her attention being a show of support to him rather than genuine interest, Edward told her more about the piece. "I met the artist years ago. He showed promise then, and people are loving his work now. But apparently the fool made drastic changes to the painting despite its success. He added more detail. I've seen others make the same mistake. They become fixated on perfecting a successful piece rather than letting it live."

Tiffany set the toast and butter between him and the magazine. "You're not going just to rain on some poor artist's parade, are you?" She kissed the top of his balding head.

"I'm honest, not a bully. I don't set out to cut people down." Edward pushed the magazine away and finally took a bite of his cold eggs. "Who knows? Maybe it is as spectacular as they say."

***

Turpentine

Edward sat in the first row of chairs at the Museum of Modern Art, surrounded by dozens of painters, art writers, curators, and celebrities. He knew at least half of them personally. The new *True Reflection* was mounted on the museum's wall behind a gold-and-amber curtain.

He checked his watch. Fourteen minutes late and still no sign of Luciano. How ignorant could he be? Reputation determined half of an artist's success, and Luciano was risking his.

Edward covered his yawn with his handbill. The card advertised "The Rebirth of a Modern Masterpiece," but the picture of the original painting intrigued him more than the promise. The piece displayed deftness and complexity of colors and strokes. The inclusion of the artist's paint-stained apron added transparency. The dark, mottled background accentuated the sharp intensity in his eyes. Luciano had proven his skill, and he might one day join the ranks of modern masters. One day. For now, the evening's red-carpet atmosphere seemed overblown.

Elizaveta, Edward's old friend and fellow critic, leaned close from the seat beside him. "Is something disturbing you?"

"No. I'm just perplexed by the extravagance of this party. Two-hundred-dollar champagne? No less than twelve actors and Academy Award winners at an event without an auction?"

She flashed a tight, patronizing smile. "You have never liked rubbing elbows with celebrities." She pulled a notebook and pen out of her purse. "If you had seen this piece in person, you would understand the excitement. Small reproductions do it no justice."

A sudden burst of applause turned all attention to the podium. Videographers spun their cameras toward Luciano Mideo as he entered and approached the front.

Elizaveta whispered, "I haven't been this eager for an unveiling in years. I was moved to tears the first time I saw it. We may be witnessing the next *Mona Lisa*."

Edward cocked his head. Comparing it to the *Mona Lisa*? Had everyone lost their sanity?

The applause lessened as Museum Director Franklin Gibbs stepped up to the microphone. After a speech about the MoMA's legacy of fine art, he introduced Luciano Mideo, an artist young enough to be his grandson. Luciano was wearing a maroon tuxedo and a royal-flush smile.

"Good evening, everyone," Luciano said. "Thank you for joining me on this special night. I know many of you had the opportunity to witness and love *True Reflection* while it was in Paris, and I understand your concerns that my alterations may have diminished what was already my finest creation."

Luciano clutched the curtain's pull string. "I loved the original, but I could not let the piece remain as it was. There was still too much power and mystery left to explore. People change, so their portraits should as well. Behold, the new *True Reflection*."

He parted the curtain. Cameras illuminated the painting with a near-constant stream of flashes, and orchestral music blared from speakers. Audience members gasped, applauded vigorously, or sat frozen in awe.

Edward, however, squinted through his glasses and quietly studied the painting's changes. *All the world's gone mad,* he thought. *They're celebrating before they've truly looked at it.*

The portrait's colors were bolder than the original's, and its shadows were deeper and more pronounced. Much of the nondescript background had been replaced by a throng of distant admirers, all of them cheering like thirteen-year-old girls at a concert. Far subtler and yet more intriguing to Edward were the alterations to the figure. It was dressed in a tuxedo identical to the one Luciano wore, and its sneer was even more smug than before.

"My word!" Edward exclaimed when he noticed the orientation of the portrait's shadows. The image conveyed two sources of light. One was positioned out of view, as usual, but the other emitted from within the figure, as if it had a halo.

He shook his head. The artist had a genuine god-complex. He had given himself a slight, almost imperceptible aureole, as if he were a glowing Christ or Mary from a medieval fresco.

How could the audience, who continued to applaud flamboyantly, not be appalled by the changes? How arrogant could a man be? The image's colors may have been brighter than before, but its heart was darker. Luciano had tarnished a good piece of art with his self-importance.

Luciano called out Edward. "Mr. Humboldt, I'm pleased to see you here, but you don't seem pleased by my work."

The artist stared intently at him. The portrait appeared, upon continued examination, to be doing the same.

The torrent of camera flashes and enthusiastic murmurs died down. Edward tapped the handbill on his thigh. "Well, it's technically well done."

The crowd gave a concurring applause.

Luciano tipped up a cold, joyless smile. He extended his hands like a magician showing he had nothing up his sleeves. "Technically well done? Come now, Mr. Humboldt. We've all read your articles. You are not a man of few words. Tell us what you think."

Elizaveta, who had been drying her eyes with a tissue after beholding the new *True Reflection*, patted Edward on the knee twice. "Yes. Do share."

Edward glanced once more at the artwork. It seemed nearer to him than before, its eyes narrower and more condescending. Merely disappointed at first, he was rapidly gaining dislike for it. Edward licked his dry lips. He had not felt this nervous about a critique since his earliest reviews, back before he had earned any credibility.

"Perhaps it would be best if I collect my thoughts and express them in writing at a later time."

Luciano crossed his arms. His smirk was equal parts disbelief and amusement. "The rawest emotions are supreme. If you need to, come closer so you can study it or have your photograph taken with it."

Edward huffed, no longer concerned with being coy toward the arrogant jerk. He stood before the expectant crowd, and cameras turned toward him like hungry rattlesnakes. "Since you've asked, I'll speak my mind. First, the good. It's unlike anything I've seen before. You have a unique mastery of brushstrokes and colors. The painting is nothing if not confidently done, and the subject is a tangible presence." Edward hated the taste of his own words.

Those seated behind him applauded and cheered. Luciano stepped forward close enough that Edward could smell the alcohol and peppermint on his breath. "And ...?

You said 'the good' first. That implies something is less than 'good.'"

Edward pointed the playbill at the portrait, but he kept his eyes fixed on Luciano. "To be completely honest, I'm appalled by it."

Luciano recoiled from the criticism. The audience murmured, then fell silent. Only the music playing over the speakers remained.

As the artist's pompousness deflated, his expression shriveled into the same solid intensity seen in the previous version of *True Reflection*.

"How can you—"

"Let me finish. Many of the pieces in this museum are exercises in artistic vanity, but yours is the first that startles me. I can taste, smell, and feel its contempt. The overly thick paint is heavy with the scorn and arrogance of a man who's not earned his acclaim. The vulgar emotions conveyed by this portrait repulse and worry me. I have no idea why everyone is so enamored with this thing, because I see only an overwrought piece of intermediate art with all the decency of a snuff film."

Edward had exaggerated his description, but not by much. His dislike for *True Reflection* continued to grow by the minute. He felt uneasy in its presence, as if the painting hated him back.

As desired, his critique hobbled Luciano's swagger. The man, who only moments before had been raising his hands and chin to applause, withdrew. He stumbled sideways as if the floor had shifted, and he clutched the microphone stand to keep from falling. The speakers emitted a brief, painful squeal.

"How … dare you …," Luciano stammered. "You're confused, old man. You don't know what to make of great art. You said it's unlike anything you've seen before, that it's unique, and yet you hate it. That makes no sense."

"Uniqueness is a meaningless quality anymore. Artists play word games, paring down their work with dozens of descriptions until everything is 'unique.'"

Luciano tore the microphone from the stand and held it like a knife. "Still, you admitted to its beauty and the visceral feelings you get when you look at it. Other painters would kill for that kind of power in their pieces. The stirring of emotions is what determines good art, no matter if those emotions are repulsion or fear. You don't understand art at all."

Twenty years ago, Luciano's words might have led to a fight, but Edward had matured. Now the insults merely amused him. "Do you know how many times I've gotten the 'you don't understand art' speech? Care to guess how many people have proven me wrong and sold their pieces for as much as they hoped? None. So, if you were wise, you would listen when I say there's a dark heart beneath the surface of this painting, and it disturbs me in a way I cannot justify as an alternative taste."

For the first time since the unveiling, Luciano faced his portrait rather than the audience. After several seconds, he turned back with a renewed sneer and confident posture. "You're trying to censor me. That's what this is. You're trying to censor my art because you're jealous."

Few words were as despised in the world of art as "censoring." Edward softened his tone. "That's not what this is about."

"Yes it is. You don't like what I have to say, so you're trying to silence me." Luciano lifted *True Reflection* from its mount and carried it closer. Shivers trickled down Edward's spine.

"Everyone else experiences nothing less than admiration for my masterpiece, but you insult it. Ask them what they think of it."

The crowd joined the conversation. They began to boo and yell against censorship.

Elizaveta set her notebook aside and peered over the rims of her glasses at Edward. "I'm shocked at you. How can you judge the artist's message? We're critics. We should be assessing the method, not the vision."

"Don't you see it?" he asked her. Didn't she see the hideous way the portrait seemed to be glowering over them?

"See what? It's an exquisite piece, one of the finest in my lifetime."

That cursed painting was too close, breathing the same air as Edward. He wanted to shove it out of Luciano's hand and kick it across the floor.

Too close.

Edward began retreating toward the nearest door. Luciano gestured to the audience with his free hand and said, "You're behind the times, old man. They all love it. Are you going to tell them they're all wrong and censor them too?"

Edward backed away from the hideous, sneering portrait. *What is wrong with that painting, or wrong with me?* He protested, "Truth has never been determined by consensus, and the truth is that *True Reflection* doesn't deserve to be in this museum."

The crowd's boos grew louder, and some of the people shouted insults at him. The mob he could ignore, but the horrible manner in which the painting stared at him—

His eyesight began to darken at the corners, and his throat tightened. "What is that thing?" Edward shouted. He tripped over a camera's tripod leg and fell against the wall. His heart raced painfully. "Luciano, what have you created?"

"My masterpiece," Luciano answered smugly. His pupils dilated, and he curled his lip into the same malevolent grin as the portrait. "Why do you insist on denying how incredible it is?"

Edward fled from the room and escaped through the museum's front doors.

***

For the next eighteen months, Luciano lived a life he never could have imagined. *True Reflection* became the obsession of the art world and a media fixation. He rode the tidal wave of fame on a world tour, displaying the piece in museums and galleries from Hong Kong to Berlin, and always to large crowds.

The perks of fame followed Luciano like a band of infatuated groupies. Talk shows begged him to appear as a guest, and screenwriters pitched ideas for art heist movies involving his masterpiece. Every week, he received invitations to new gallery exhibits and film premieres. He also discovered no shortage of young, beautiful women interested in spending a night with "The Michelangelo of the Twenty-First Century." Drugs became as easy to acquire as coffee.

Eventually, the pleasures staled. When the highs plateaued, Luciano became unsatisfied with his painting. To the shock of millions, he withdrew his work from the public with the promise to reinvent and improve the masterpiece yet again. And then again.

With each new unveiling, the public's adoration soared to new heights. The old versions of the painting, once public treasures, became footnotes of the new and present wonder. The visage's inner glow brightened, and the accumulating layers of paint caused the face to project from the canvas. The darkening eyes became a focal point to the admiring crowds. Those who stood entranced by the portrait for hours said it was the Charybdian gaze that drew them in the most.

The background, which increased in complexity and number of admirers, proved a surprising tendency for prescience. Onto the sides of the canvas, he added things he had long dreamed of owning, such as an Italian villa and a sports car. Within days he acquired them, not by spending the fortune he was accumulating, but as gifts. *True Reflection* predicted every good thing coming to him.

Luciano basked in the fame and adoration. He possessed the map to every conceivable desire. As long as he followed the portrait's lead and poured himself into it, nothing was unobtainable.

***

Edward's outburst at the *True Reflection* unveiling cracked the foundation of his reputation. He carried on with his work, but publications shunned him, and requests for his critiques reduced by half. Many of his oldest friends and clients became detached acquaintances.

At least his wife stayed faithfully and lovingly by his side. While Edward struggled with his sinking position in the field he loved, Tiffany remained a steadfast refuge from the heartache. She encouraged him to get back into creating art as a hiatus from judging it. Her plan worked. It renewed his passion for the simple wonder of painting.

The incident with Luciano continued to haunt him a year and a half after it had transpired. Regrets for having made the critique personal lingered in the back of his mind, occasionally interrupting his thoughts and dreams. It was unlike him to have attacked an artist's reputation the way he had.

Something had set him off. Whenever he reflected on the portrait, the sensations of fear and revulsion smoldered anew. On multiple nights, the emotions regurgitated nightmares that roused him from sleep in a cold sweat. He initially tried to explain his reaction away as an intense form of regret or stress. But doubts remained. Edward had never been superstitious, yet he could not shake the thought that the picture was unnatural in some way. Supernatural even.

It couldn't possess some otherworldly power, could it?

Edward shook his head, trying to rid his mind of the thought. He was in his office, painting an ocean scene on canvas. He blended more indigo into the gray at the bottom.

Someone leaned on his shoulder and kissed the top of his head. He looked up, expecting to see his wife. Instead, his eyes met those of his daughter, Faith. She was a mirror image of her mother from thirty years ago, but she shared his interests. She was majoring in art at the Rhode Island School of Design, his alma mater.

"Hi, darling," he said. "When did you arrive?"

"Just now. Did you have any idea I was coming home?"

"None." College summer break was still a month away.

"Good," she said. "I told mom I'd be visiting this weekend, but I asked her to keep it a secret."

"It's certainly a pleasant one."

Faith peeked inside his box of art supplies, then pointed at the colliding swathes of gray and blue on his canvas. "I'm glad to see you're painting again. What are you working on?"

"An ocean landscape. To be honest, I'm not sure where I'm going with it yet."

"I'm sure it'll be beautiful in the end." She smiled, then bit the right side of her lower lip.

Edward had seen that look a hundred times before. She had something she wanted to say. "Out with it. Is there something bothering you?"

Faith pulled a folded piece of paper from her jacket pocket and handed it to him. "Would you consider going to this, please? For our sake, and for yours."

He opened the printout and read the advertisement aloud. "Returning to New York: Mideo's *True Reflection*." Edward tensed his grip, causing the paper to bend. The hairs on his neck stood upright, and his lungs felt lacking for air. "I don't think that would be wise."

His daughter clasped her hands together. "Please? You don't have to compliment him. Just apologize, and maybe this whole situation will stop festering. You can get more work, or at least make the nightmares stop."

"How many times has he redone that thing?" Edward grumbled. "Four or five?"

Faith crossed her arms and stared at him with her wide, adorable eyes. Even at nineteen, she could coax him with a mere pout.

"I still can't believe what a spectacle people are making of this thing." Edward sighed. "I'll consider it."

She briefly bit her lip again, then hugged him and confessed, "Good, because I already called your agent and mentioned the idea to her."

Edward smirked. "You little sneak. You've learned too much from your mother." He lightly poked her ribs with the handle of his paint brush. "To make up for going behind my back, why don't you help me with this landscape?"

"I'd love to," she said, picking up a second brush.

***

Fifty-Third Street outside the Museum of Modern Art was a circus of limousines, red carpets, and A-list personalities. Every major news outlet was covering the event. Edward weaved his way through the chaos and cameras, trying to get into the museum with as little attention as possible. One reporter recognized him and asked if he planned to harass Luciano Mideo again. Edward flashed his two-thousand-dollar ticket, which his agent had gifted to him, and slipped through the gate without answering the man's questions.

The gala, complete with champagne, tuxedos, and undersized dresses, was the kind of ego-waving event he loathed. As far as he could tell, most of the people there cared more about being seen around the museum's collection than for the collection itself. They pointed at pieces and spoke of them like so many freshman art majors, with juvenile concepts of artistry and originality.

He overheard two women discussing a display comprised of an iron paperweight atop a stack of crushed cardboard boxes.

"The piece is a delightful contrast of simplicity and monotony," the taller woman cooed. "It's self-gratifying and yet self-loathing. The medium naturally lends itself to critiquing the oppression of the greedy over the poor." She then sipped from a fifty-dollar glass of champagne, and Edward groaned.

A man with an Italian accent whispered into his ear, "I'm not sure if I should give her a dictionary or an art history book. She could use both."

Edward chuckled. He turned to greet whoever made the joke, but his laughter fell to the floor at the sight of him. Luciano was standing beside him, dressed in a flawlessly fitted tuxedo. He held a champagne glass of his own in one hand and a thin, gorgeous woman in the other.

Luciano flashed a bright grin. His joy seemed genuine. "Mr. Humboldt, I had no idea you would be attending. This is the finest surprise of the night."

Edward, far less enthusiastic about their encounter, managed only to be polite. "Have you had a few drinks, Luciano? I didn't expect a warm welcome."

"Why should I be mad?" Luciano raised his glass as a solitary toast. "I'm the artist who finally proved you wrong. I have my own gala. I arrived here in a Lamborghini with

Daria as my personal guest." He nodded toward the woman in his arm. "I have won."

"Congratulations," Edward said, hoping he sounded sufficiently earnest. He gestured toward the stage, where the legs of a solitary easel showed beneath the curtain. "Is that *True Reflection*?"

"It is."

"Will you be showing anything else?" There had been seven other pieces at Luciano's previous MoMA exhibit.

"Why should I? They would only distract from the main attraction."

The admission baffled Edward. Nothing else? The gala was a perfect opportunity to establish a second signature piece, or to make millions in auctions. Luciano was arrogant, but he didn't seem completely incompetent. Why not show more pieces?

Perhaps he had nothing else to show. Edward doubted it was true, but asked nonetheless. "Have you created any other pieces since you made *True Reflection*?"

Luciano shook his head. "My life is too busy."

A sense of pity mixed with Edward's dislike for the man. "So you've exchanged art for fame? You're squandering your talent."

Luciano's demeanor soured. He poked Edward's chest with a finger, spilling champagne on Edward's coat. "Squandered? On the contrary, I've used all of my talent to make my masterpiece even greater. The public loves me for it, and every hope and dream I add to it comes true."

Edward tensed and checked again that the portrait was still covered. The unforgettable discomfort from his first viewing of it awoke. "You talk as if it's a magic lamp. Paint in a wish and the picture manifests it."

"That's exactly what I'm saying," Luciano said without any indication he was joking. "My connection with the piece is such that it speaks to me. I unload my heart and soul into each new rendition, and stars align in my favor."

An overwhelming pang of fear seized Edward like a cold grip around his neck. His knees weakened, and he nearly stumbled into Luciano's silent date. His premonition about the painting's unnatural qualities flared.

If Luciano noticed anything unusual about Edward, he didn't mention it. He swigged the last of his champagne. "For example, I added you to the image as one of my many admirers, and here you are."

Edward's entire body began to ache. His stomach churned at the thought of being on that wretched canvas.

"It's more than just my masterpiece or lucky charm," Luciano said. "I'm painting my own destiny."

A deal with the devil if ever there were one, Edward thought.

His rescue came in the form of the chamber orchestra starting to play. Luciano released Daria and checked his gold Cartier watch. "That's my cue. Time for the show." He headed toward the stage.

Edward, meanwhile, staggered to the drink table at the back of the room. He needed more separation between him and the painting.

The orchestra's melody rose. Luciano strutted to the microphone with open arms and delivered a speech that Edward missed because of his disorienting migraine.

However, he did notice the artist's stage-performer posture and pompous tone.

Was he going insane, or did no one else recognize the suffocating aura in the hall? Edward was rubbing his eyes and considering a swift exit when the crowd cheered. Luciano had undressed the new iteration of *True Reflection*, an ulcerous wound of art that lived up to all of Edward's original, overblown scorn. The eyes were almost as dark as the cavities of a hollow skull. The lips glistened red like a bloody kiss, and the figure's inner glow provided the image's only source of light. The sea of people in the background had not only multiplied but was bowing as well. *True Reflection* had become pride incarnate.

The audience cheered despite the brush strokes having regressed enough that Edward could tell the difference in quality at a distance. The amassed layers of paint looked thick enough to rip the fabric from the canvas' wooden frame. Witnessing the corpulent painting released some of Edward's tension, turning his fear into sorrow for the young artist. Luciano, in his pursuit of pleasure and fame, had turned his work into a hefty mess.

Rather than a celebration of art, the gala was the public suicide of a career. The people's enthusiastic approval was fueling Luciano's self-destruction.

A woman bumped into Edward as she hurried toward the stage. Her casual, gray jacket surprised him. She looked beggarly compared to the other, finely dressed women.

***

Turpentine

The audience vanished from Luciano's sight as a barrage of camera flashes lit up the stage. The cheering and applause shook the elevated floor under his feet. He opened his arms and absorbed the warmth of their praise.

By following the painting's lead, he had not only lived out his dreams, he had surpassed them.

A specter rushed forward from the immaterial crowd and leapt onto the stage. Luciano recognized it was Julia, the object of his past affair, in spite of her frenzied appearance. She reached into the pocket of her gray jacket and withdrew a knife. Her expression read murder.

Luciano tripped and fell in his flurry to get away. Expecting an attack, he shielded himself with his arms. But she ran at the easel instead. Shrieking, she slashed the canvas across the portrait's cheek.

"No!" Luciano screamed.

A pair of security guards tackled Julia. As they dragged her away, her shouts changed to hysterical laugher and then deep, guttural sobs. "You ruined my life," she wailed. "You ruined my family. You don't deserve this, you monster."

Cameras continued to flash, their lights blinking through the portrait's gaping hole. A sickening sense of violation ripped into Luciano. "No. No!" he cried. He needed to hide the damage from the stares of the horrified onlookers. He ripped his masterpiece off the easel. In his haste and panic, he snapped the canvas's upper frame in two.

Luciano ran with his portrait to the prep room behind the stage. Once inside, he slammed and locked the door. He laid *True Reflection* on the wooden table like a medic preparing a critical patient. A frantic search of the supply cabinets turned up only brushes and tubes of paint. He shoved them off the shelves. Where was the tape?

When the reality of what had happened set in, he threw jars of paint and cleaners against the wall. Shattered glass and pools of color covered the floor.

He collapsed on the table beside his ruined creation. Luciano touched the portrait's tear, then he noticed his reflection across the room.

Luciano slid off the table and approached a mirror leaning against the wall. His eyes were red and sunken, his face pale from shock. He gazed at the smooth, flawless skin on his cheek.

He glanced back at the ripped cheek on his portrait, then again at the mirror.

By following the painting's lead, he had not only lived out his dreams, he had surpassed them.

Luciano picked up a shard of broken glass and raised it to his face.

***

Edward pushed through the crowd toward the prep room. The audience was in turmoil, shuffling in every direction and shouting over one another into their cell phones. Reporters and their videographers had dispersed to the hall's perimeter to announce the shocking news.

The madwoman's attack had done more than destroy *True Reflection*. It had released Edward from his nightmarish curse. Whatever its cause, either supernatural or psychosomatic, the affliction was gone. Edward's head felt clear, as if he was finally breathing oxygen after prolonged suffocation.

He feared Luciano's reaction was quite the opposite. In spite of their hostile past, the artist's panic-stricken disappearance worried him.

Several people had gathered around the prep room door, including Luciano's date, Daria, and museum director Franklin Gibbs. He was knocking and trying to coax the artist out. Franklin sent one of the event waitresses to fetch a key from the security staff, but before she could return, the door opened.

A woman screamed, and those closest to the door staggered back. Daria covered her mouth and turned away, heaving.

Edward stood on his toes, trying to peer over another man's shoulder.

Luciano emerged with the ruined portrait under his arm. He walked toward the stage with the heavy, uneven steps of a drunk. His shoes, which were covered with paint, left multi-colored footprints on the wood floor. When Edward caught a glimpse of Luciano's left cheek, he understood what had startled the others. The flesh was flayed open and hemorrhaging blood down his chin and shoulder. The portrait's face, torn and bent around the broken frame, also bled from its wound. Clearly, Luciano had smeared his own blood on the ruined canvas.

The artist climbed onto the stage and held up his new, ghastly version of *True Reflection*. The audience muttered and snapped pictures. Absolutely no one applauded. Luciano, devoid of his usual swagger, searched longingly over the crowd while blood rained from his chin to the floor.

No one moved to help him. Even the museum director stood aside, sickened and dumbstruck.

Edward called from the side of the stage. "Luciano, put the picture down. We need to get you to a doctor."

A hollow vestige of the once-arrogant artist glanced at Edward and shook his head slowly. He looked like a cornered, frightened animal.

"Please, come with me. The museum's restorers can take care of the damage while you get medical help."

The portrait glared at Edward from beneath Luciano's arm. But it no longer intimidated him. If anyone were under its spell now, it was the painting's creator.

Luciano bolted from the stage and back into the prep room. Edward ran after him, but the door was locked by the time he reached it. He knelt and spoke through the keyhole. "Luciano, the painting can be salvaged." He doubted that were true, but he needed to say something encouraging. "There are people out here that can help you."

A heavy, metallic object scraped across the floor inside the room. Edward rattled the doorknob, trying to force it open. If Luciano had already resorted to cutting himself, he was susceptible to doing worse. The guy deserved a lesson in humility, but not self-mutilation.

The museum director was pacing nearby, hands interlocked behind his neck. Edward grabbed him by the shoulder. "Do you have the key?"

"Not yet. I sent Emily—"

"Here it is," the waitress said as she jogged up to them with a ring of keys in hand.

"Open that door," Edward ordered. "He looks scared. He could do anything."

Something crashed inside the prep room.

Director Gibbs tested one key after another in the lock, twice dropping the whole ring in his panic. "This is a nightmare," he repeated several times.

A pungent odor began to waft under the locked door. Edward recognized the rust-like fumes at once. Turpentine. Was Luciano destroying the portrait? Turpentine would wash away the layers of paint.

Edward pounded his fist against the wall. He shouted, "Luciano, you've got an entire lifetime to create another masterpiece. You could even—" He stopped before suggesting the artist make another *True Reflection*. "I want to help you."

No answer, save the sound of more glass shattering.

"Hurry," Edward pleaded with the director. "And have someone call an ambulance."

The director jammed a key into the hole. "I've got it!" He tried to open the door, but it swung only a few inches before banging against something heavy.

"It's barricaded," he said, then fell backwards, fanning his face and coughing.

Edward peeked through the small opening. Luciano had shoved a metal cabinet behind the door, barring their entrance. A concentrated rush of noxious fumes burned Edward's eyes and throat. He covered his face, but too late to keep the tears from gushing.

During his brief glimpse, he saw Luciano, who had the crazed, terrified look of a man plummeting into the depths of Hell. The lower half of his face was entirely red with blood. Luciano was draining a tin can of turpentine onto a table and his chest. He must have emptied gallons of it. The vapors had nearly knocked Edward to the ground.

Between coughs, Edward begged with a strained voice, "Luciano, stop. Will you let me in?" He wiped his eyes and, squinting, peered once more into the room.

Luciano dropped the can. Its clear contents continued to spill over the floor. His head and limbs hung limply like those of an abandoned marionette puppet. Luciano finally spoke, his voice forlorn and disemboweled of all confidence.

"You were right."

Edward pushed against the door, trying to force the cabinet back. His shoes slipped. "Right about what?"

Luciano rubbed his body, spreading turpentine and blood over his tuxedo. "About the painting. I started to hate it, too, but I needed it." He wrung his hands together. "I lost my desire to paint months ago. I don't want to make something else."

"Take a break. With time, you'll fall in love with painting again. It worked for me."

The artist picked up something too small for Edward to see. "It has become such an ugly picture," he said.

"I'm sorry I was so harsh. I admit I'm not a fan of this piece, but I see your skill. You could make an even greater painting."

"Don't apologize," Luciano said. "You were the only one being honest with me. Thank you."

"I want to help you."

"I know, but I don't want it."

Edward heard the quiet but terrible sound of Luciano striking a match.

"No!" Edward dove against the door with all his might, crushing and dislocating his shoulder. His effort and pain managed to move the door only an inch more.

The prep room erupted with yellow fire. Edward jumped back from the flames and intense heat that shot out through the narrow opening. After the initial roar of the ignition, the museum hall echoed with the screams of hundreds of frightened guests and one burning, dying artist.

People shouted "Fire!" and stampeded from the museum. Staff members grabbed paintings off walls and fled as the alarms and sprinklers activated. But Edward shouted for help as he alone continued ramming the door. He kept up his futile rescue attempt long after Luciano's screams ceased. Firefighters eventually pulled him away.

***

Pablo Picasso is the most famous name associated with the Cubism movement, but others share credit for the revolutionary form.

Edward was seated on his front porch, typing the first draft of a textbook on modern art history. He could only use one hand on the keyboard because his right arm was still tied to his body in a sling. The injury from the museum and the subsequent surgery were healing more slowly than he had hoped.

The screen door opened and closed. His wife emerged from their house and headed toward her car.

"I'll be back in a couple hours," she said. "I'll bring lunch."

"Okay," Edward said. "Love you."

"Love you too."

Luciano Mideo had perished in the fire. Thankfully no one else was hurt—besides Edward—and the damage to the museum was minimal. He attended the closed-casket funeral a week later. Job opportunities returned shortly after. Old acquaintances began calling again with offers of work, including the book he was typing.

In the wake of *True Reflection's* destruction, some people awoke to its diminished quality and questioned its status as a phenomenon. Most, however, lamented the loss of what they viewed as one of the greatest masterpieces. A curator in London collected the portrait's ashes and put them on display, creating a new infatuation. Time ran an article of the memorial piece and quoted the curator, who called it, "A savage beauty that conveys the existential consumption of passion."

Edward had no intentions of visiting the display.

His cell phone rang. The caller began the conversation by complimenting Edward's past work but quickly moved on to her real reason for contacting him.

"No," Edward replied to her request for quotes about Luciano. "I'm open to being interviewed on any topic but that. I already told your publisher I won't be discussing Mr. Mideo. It would feel like trampling his grave."

At least a third of Edward's business calls involved Luciano's death. Edward wanted to move on after paying his respects. Dwelling on the tragedy saddened him immensely, in part because he wished he had done more to help. Logically he knew the death was not his fault, but guilt and sorrow were not entirely logical emotions. Time and involvement on other projects would be the best remedies.

"Fine," Edward said to the caller. "This is the only quote you'll get from me. I lament what happened to Luciano Mideo. I may not have adored all his work, but he was still a young man with promise and a full life ahead of him. His death is a greater loss than his painting. I hope the next time someone creates an admired piece, we get to know the real artist as well as the artwork ... You're welcome ... Good day to you, too."

Edward hung up and set the phone next to his laptop. Before typing, he pondered what he would write in the history book about *True Reflection*.

Wrath and Ruin

GHOUL
A GIDEON WELLS STORY

April 21, 1895

Professor,

These letters contain details from our investigation into the Haughtogis Point mystery. I found the beast, and I am trying to stop it before it can kill again.

I know enough at this time to implore the university to send you or one of your peers to this town posthaste.

Sincerely, Gideon Wells

1

We reached our destination by carriage as the sunset bled on the gray Allegheny cliffs. I cannot overstate the trepidation I felt as we rolled up to the pale, weather-gnawed Ragiston house. My concerns were not due to our hosts, for the young owners of the home, siblings Claude and Ida Ragiston, greeted us with relieved smiles.

My uneasiness came instead from the property itself.

Our earlier train ride through western Pennsylvania had crossed dozens of fields with emerald grass and dandelion freckles. By contrast, the brown, stubbly grounds around the mansion made it seem as if winter had only just packed up its snow and departed.

Furthermore, the house begged for restoration. More shutters were broken or crooked than not, and at least one had been nailed over a window to cover broken glass. Dead ivy hung like nets from pitted bricks. One of the house's three round towers had shed the shingles from its roof, and the slate tiles lay heaped at the base of the wall.

The haggard aesthetics were no guarantee the building neared collapse. Indeed, the tour that followed my arrival assured me the aged mansion remained sound, but first impressions forewarned me of the chaos into which we were entering.

The Ragiston siblings proved humble and amiable in spite of their situation. Claude, rather than his servants, opened the carriage door for Rosette and me. Ida bowed as if we were privileged guests. I wondered if their greeting would have differed if they knew about our train ride; Rosette had busied herself by catching flies and feeding them to the spiders under her seat.

Claude extended his open hand toward me, but Rosette took it first and vigorously returned the shake. Her forward manners, or lack thereof, elicited wide eyes and a slight blush from the young gentleman. Rosette similarly greeted his sister and three servants, startling all of them and nearly removing the arm of one servant, an old maid, at the shoulder.

"Oh, my!" Ida Ragiston adjusted her feathered hat after Rosette's violent handshake dislodged it.

I laughed in spite of myself and grabbed one of my bags off the carriage. I tossed another to the old butler, who caught it quite capably for a man of his age.

"Did you have any trouble on your way here?" Claude asked. He pointed at the scratches on Rosette's leather bodice, which for good reason is better armored than normal women's fashion.

"It's from an old incident," I said. "Nothing to worry about."

"I got bit." Rosette beamed. "Would you care to see?" She began to roll up her sleeve to show off the scar on her left elbow.

I took her gently by the wrist. "It has been a long journey. Perhaps it is best if they show us to our rooms."

2

I should explain my companion to you, as you have not had the queer pleasure of meeting her. Rosette, or Rose as I call her, is technically a handsome young woman in the same way an angry, twelve-point buck is technically a majestic deer.

She was fifteen when I discovered her four years ago, fully half my age at the time. While strolling through Scranton, I spied a girl with short black hair and a pauper dress climbing quite nimbly out the fourth-floor window of an orphanage. She scrambled over the exterior walls as ably as I can descend a flight of stairs, and she leapt the gap to the neighboring building without any regard for the thirty-foot drop below.

Curious, I followed the girl, keeping far behind her and acting as naturally as I could. Within the span of an hour, she swam in the river, galloped on a horse through a market, got thrown into the street by the doctor whose horse she had stolen, danced for pennies, bought three apples, gave one of the fruits to a beggar child, and climbed onto the steel truss of a bridge to eat the second apple.

The third she threw at me as I passed by. It would have hit my head had I not caught it.

"I'll blacken your eye if you keep tailing me," she warned.

"When did you notice me?" I asked, then took a bite of the fruit.

"You were in front of the cigar shop when I climbed out of Saint Mary's, behind the woman with the brown hat."

Ghoul

I marveled at her. She had noticed me from the first. Her attentiveness matched her impressive dexterity. "How did you learn to clamber and leap between buildings with such ease?"

"I encourage you to try it first, and if you fall, then I'll teach you." She froze her lips and gaze into an emotionless expression I have since come to know well. I still struggle to interpret it.

"Would you like to work for me?"

"Stay far away from me, you lecher."

Her other, half-eaten apple flew at me. I leapt out of its path. "I assure you my offer is honest and innocent."

"All right, then." Rose rolled off the truss and slid confidently down one of the angled spans. Thus ended our bizarre and abrupt interview. She agreed to hire on as my apprentice, and no explanation of my hazardous work dissuaded her.

The mother superior of the orphanage required far more convincing of my honorable intentions. I was not engaged at the time, nor could I feign the personality of a fatherly figure, thus she considered my request to adopt the girl with due skepticism. In the end, however, she released Rose to my care with multiple prayers of thanks. I gathered the impression the girl's adventures had been a regular vexation.

The children of the orphanage did not share the head nun's enthusiasm. Many cried and held onto Rose with long embraces. The nuns explained she had acted as an older sister to them all.

After four years, I have still not deciphered the enigma that is Rosette Drumlin. She possesses an unrestrained spirit and impressive strength for her slight build. My betrothed,

Emily, has surrendered all hope of training civility into her. She used to fear that Rose would be hurt in my line of work. Now she pleads with Rose not to kick men in their noses or teeth, as blood stains are difficult to wash from boots.

I long for her to stop instigating fights as well, since I inevitably come to her aid, and I already provoke enough fights of my own.

But enough of the past. I will get back to describing the task you hired us for.

3

The Ragistons and their staff led us to our quarters. Claude and Ida had in their employ an elderly couple, Mr. and Mrs. Williams, the latter of whom once served as the siblings' nanny.

The other member of their staff was Mr. Carlson, a tall black man recently hired to be the groundskeeper and caretaker of the home. I did not envy him. He had a tremendous task before him.

They offered us first-floor rooms with freshly papered walls, intact windows, and clean, tucked bedding. Mine featured a wide oil painting of a fox chase. The accommodations surpassed those I usually endure while on the hunt, but the low view of the street would not do.

Mr. Williams knelt shakily before the fireplace and stuffed kindling between the logs. "I will bring your other bags to this room if you desire."

"Pardon me if I sound ungrateful, but do you have another room I might stay in? For Rose as well? I would prefer one with a more strategic view of the property."

Claude and Mr. Williams passed sideways glances to one another.

"Forgive me, Mr. Wells," Claude said. "We have bedrooms on the second and third floors, but they are not yet restored to fitting conditions. I beg you to reconsider this room."

I knocked on the mahogany dresser in the corner. "I will not be offended by a dirty room. Many of my hunts require me to sleep outdoors in the snow or rain. I assure you, unless the spiders are large enough to eat me, the quarters cannot be as bad as the worst I have stayed in."

The two men looked at one another again, this time with bewilderment.

As requested, they escorted Rose and me to the corner rooms on the upper floor. Along the way, Claude Ragiston winced at every cobweb, stain, cold draft, and obscene word scrawled on the walls by trespassers during the home's abandoned years.

Rose's room provided a splendid view of the street and the row houses on the other side. Mine overlooked the garden to the rear of the house. I smashed away any cracked window panes that obscured my sight.

Past the property, fog rose from the river and tangled in the leafless tree branches along the bank. The quarter moon and twilight tinged everything with a shade of purple. I did not expect my first observation of the surroundings to reveal anything, but I spotted a mysterious figure standing on a platform near the water.

"A woman in a bonnet is standing out there in the garden."

Claude and Mr. Williams hurried to the window. The old butler grinned.

"The darkness deceived you, Mr. Wells. That is the statue of Lady Ragiston."

"My grandmother," Claude added.

"Oh." I tossed my bag on the mattress, startling a cloud of dust into the air. "This room will suit me fine. Can we all gather to discuss the matter at hand?"

Most of us walked down the stairs to meet Mr. Carlson in the main hall. My accomplice, however, slid down the curved banister without laughing or screaming, her expression as emotive as a scarecrow. When Rose reached the bottom, she dusted off the front of her leather bodice and sporting skirt. The ensuing whispers between Claude and Ida were likely comprised of questions about our identities and feral upbringings.

Pillars and the second-floor balconies surrounded the main hall on three sides. The entrance of the home, including the gilded door and stained-glass windows, completed the perimeter. More effort had been made in the restoration of that room than most. The marble-and-parquet floor had been polished, the portraits looked pristine, and the grandfather clock melodiously chimed the hour only thirty-seven seconds late.

I paced before the glowing stone fireplace as I traded inquiries with the Ragistons and their staff.

"May I ask how you know Professor Emerick?" Claude asked.

I explained how I came to know you and the other instructors at Cornell through my research at the university. I kept the details to myself, but I let them know you had employed me before to gather and assess evidence from bizarre cases.

"My official title, if it can be called 'official,' is Investigator of Exonatural Phenomenon."

Ida shuddered and shifted in her seat toward the fire. "Exonatural? Is that anything like the supernatural?"

"Similar, but no. 'Supernatural' is a term reserved for ghosts, angels, deities, and other entities that exist, at least in part, outside of our world. In my opinion, such anomalies only reside within the domains of superstition and religion."

As usual, Rose raised her hand to protest my assertion. I continued explaining our line of work before she could reopen our years-long debate about supernatural, mystical beings.

"Exonatural creatures and forces, by contrast, exist only in our realm. I can observe them and dispose of them, should the need arise. They can be explained with biology, zoology, or physics, even if their origins bypass the normal order."

Rose huffed. "*You* exist in our realm, but physics has yet to explain your stubbornness."

"*Regardless,* do not mind the terms. They're the creation of bored researchers who like to debate and complicate life. For your case, you can simply think of me as a hunter. I find and kill things which should not be living in the first place."

Mrs. Williams entered from another room carrying a platter with two glasses of red wine. I gave thanks and, to her surprise, took both.

Claude reached for the second glass of wine when Mrs. Williams passed. Finding it gone, he feigned a stretch. "Mr. Wells, you said you are from Binghamton, no? Are you by chance related to the railroad magnate?"

"You are not the first person to ask me that." I took a sip from one of the glasses. "You do not need to call me Mr. Wells. I'm simply Gideon."

"So you are not related to Aaron Wells, then?"

"Actually, I am." I winked at my hosts and finished the first glass of dense cabernet.

The Ragistons straightened their postures. My connection to Aaron Wells no doubt mattered immensely to them, not only because of his wealth but also because their family's mining business relied upon Wells Rail Industries.

Ida cleared her throat. "Pray tell, how close is your relation?"

"He is my father."

Mrs. Williams, on her way to the kitchen, spun and considered me anew. Claude began to stand, then sat back down. His gazed bubbled up to the higher floors, toward the run-down halls and rooms he had earlier apologized for.

Mr. Williams gave the most delightful response. "Your father? Pardon me, but why in heaven's name do you perform such ghastly work?"

"Entertaining dull, prosperous guests at dinner parties is ghastly work. Reading contracts is ghastly work. My job offers adventure and discovery."

I picked up the iron poker from beside the fireplace and prodded cinders off one of the burning logs. "My elder brothers inherited my father's mind for business. I was born into the same wealth but with less admiration for it. Money is not altogether terrible, and it's quite helpful in my endeavors. I just never acquired a taste for the upper-class lifestyle. Adventure and exploration are preferable investments."

"And what of your assistant?" Ida discreetly eyed Rose, who climbed onto the wide base of one of the pillars.

Rose balanced against a coat stand and pointed at the balcony above her. "The builder was left-handed, like me. I can tell by the hammer marks around the nails."

"Miss Drumlin is something between an adopted daughter and an apprentice," I said, rolling the poker between my fingers. "Her talents make her rather eccentric, I'm afraid. But do not be concerned by her. She is quite harmless."

Either out of unfortunate timing or playful spite, Rose bumped the coat stand off its legs. It toppled and cracked loudly against the floor. Mrs. Williams hurried to Rose and forcefully helped her off the pedestal, warning her about modesty and safety.

Claude began to mouth words, then paused. He probably worried that my familial connections added business ramifications to our conversation. The weighty silence reminded me why I am rarely forthright in mentioning my family. I loathe the awkward moments that follow whenever I admit my father is one of the wealthiest men in America.

I reassured Claude, "Professor Emerick sent me, not my family."

"Yes, of course." He began to bounce his knee. "Our fathers likely knew each other through Dale Carnegie. My family manages many of his mining operations, and yours of course relies on his steel."

"They probably did know each other." I squinted at him. "You used the past tense. Has your father passed away?"

Claude swallowed hard, and Ida spoke up. "Our parents perished in the Pittsburgh theater fire six years ago, or else this home would have been their inheritance instead of ours. Unfortunately, our grandfather, Leonard Ragiston, largely abandoned it to vagabonds during recent years. He only used it when he came to inspect the quarry or to visit Charles Voor, and he kept to just a few essential rooms on the first floor."

I twirled the poker and slid it back into its holder. "Can you tell me about your grandfather's death?"

Claude and Ida lowered their heads. Before they could well up the resolve to answer, Rose balanced on her forearms atop the back of an empty chair. With snarled lips and a slight growl, she said, "I read about it in the papers. The monster tore out his throat."

She snapped her teeth together three times in rapid succession, adding further horror to her impropriety.

Ida got up and moved away from her. She dabbed her eyes with a handkerchief.

"Consarn it, Rose!" I exclaimed. "Show some sympathy for their loss."

Rose stood erect and stared at Ida with her taut, emotionless gaze. "They are innocent of any wrongdoing," she surmised. "Her distress is real."

"I never doubted their innocence. They're the ones who summoned for help."

I moved to a position between Rose and Claude, who was pressing his fist against his lips as he recalled their patriarch's death.

"Forgive her, Mr. Ragiston. May we proceed? Please tell me all you know about this ghoul of yours."

4

The Ragistons shared a number of details about the ghoul, and Mr. Carlson recounted stories he had overheard. I will summarize the ones I feel are most significant here. When I have more time, I will provide you with a longer record, Professor.

Local newspapers reported on the attacks in Haughtogis Point, and while they suggested a number of causes, the writers usually blamed rabid dogs or bloodthirsty wolves. That is because they doubted the eyewitness accounts of the locals, who held a unified claim of a demon or ghoul. At least two dozen people swore they saw it. Given my past experience, that means perhaps eight of them genuinely witnessed the creature prowling around town.

Leonard Ragiston died on the twelfth of January. As Rose so callously reenacted, the beast bit and tore his neck. The cuts on his arms and side indicated he died while fighting off the attack. The first blood fell on the grounds behind Mr. Voor's nearby mansion, and he ultimately perished a hundred feet away on the path that leads to his own property.

I asked Mr. Williams and Mr. Carlson, rather than the still-present siblings, if the corpse exhibited signs of having been eaten. The men flashed sour grimaces. They were surprised and appalled by the question, and I was surprised to learn the body had not been chewed. Mr. Carlson suggested that the quick response from servants at the neighboring Voor house scared off the predator. However, savage dogs are not easily chased from their prey, and ghouls have no recollection of fear.

Ghoul

I suspected, and still do, that Mr. Ragiston was the first of the ghoul's victims. My hosts shared rumors from older, mysterious crimes that have since been attributed to the creature. I remain skeptical of them because of their much-earlier dates.

One involved a man whose corpse the townspeople pulled from the river. His cut and bruised limbs resembled Mr. Ragiston's, but his death sounded like a case of overzealous drinking followed by a nasty tumble down the rocky riverbank.

The second crime involved a middle-aged woman found with deep cuts and bite marks. Her death piqued my interest, but the creature would have needed to lie dormant for a long time after the slaying. The crime happened five years ago.

I similarly doubt the ghoul caused the disappearance of two children who worked in the quarry. That incident occurred three years before these recent events, and no one found evidence of violence against them. It is far more likely they ran away, and if an unfortunate tragedy did befall them, I would wager that a mining accident, drowning, or even kidnapping is to blame.

By contrast, recent events since the twelfth of January share cohesive accounts. Three more people have been attacked, and the survivors and other witnesses describe a monster with a starved man's form that crawls on all fours like a beast. Its forelegs are consistently reported as being slender and exceptionally long. The ears are said to be enormous, as if taken from a human-sized rabbit or bat.

Mr. Carlson confirmed those descriptions and claimed to have observed the creature himself. His sighting occurred while he stared out into the fog from one of the mansion's windows. I thanked him but remained uncertain of his account; poor weather and rumors can make false monsters out of distant animals and bushes.

Other qualities about the ghoul remain less clear, such as the creature's hide. Conflicting accounts describe it as bald, furry, or bristled like a bed of nails. One woman swore it has wings and can fly. The claims that it wears tattered clothes are consistent with other ghouls I have faced; reports that it hides and avoids eating the victims are not. I need more time to sift through the rumors to determine their veracity.

The secondhand accounts are a fine start, but my foremost priority going forward is to visit the sources of the rumors. I plan to examine the evidence from the attacks and to interview the witnesses. However, my assessment thus far is that something unnatural is prowling Haughtogis Point, and the town is justifiably unnerved.

5

I awoke twice during the night. Both times, I spent about half an hour staring out at the tentacled groves of trees in the mist. The ghoul never appeared. After the second watch, I lit a candle and wrote my initial letters to you.

Rose confirmed in the morning that she had seen nothing of interest from her room except roaming cats.

Haughtogis Point is a long, slender village bent by water and stone. Its southern boundary folds around a curve in the Allegheny River, and the north traces the tree-crowned gray cliffs. Brick houses arranged in long rows comprise the majority of the residences. These belong to working-class citizens, many of whom travel by ferry to the Ragiston-owned quarry on the far shore.

Five buildings overshadow all the others. Two are places of worship, and the Presbyterian and Catholic church steeples stand like watchtowers at opposite ends of the village. The other three are mansions belonging to Haughtogis's wealthiest families. Each connects to the others by paths and acres of gardens along the steep riverbank. The Voor house lies at the center, bookended by the Ragiston and Carter residences.

The two fatal ambushes occurred in the Voor gardens, so I decided to begin my search there. After some martial arts practice and breakfast, Rose and I asked Mr. Williams for a tour of the attack scenes. He obliged. I hurried back to my room for my derby, revolver, and bag, and then we set out.

We walked first to a circular, wooden pavilion half-way between Lady Ragiston's statue and a small stable behind the Voor house. Pigs were grumbling in the latter.

Mr. Williams stamped his foot on a spot near the pavilion's entrance. "The sheriff said the blood trail started here."

I tugged on the pavilion doors to have a peek inside, but they were locked. Rose took interest in the cuneiform etchings on the entrance. Meanwhile, I circled around the structure in search of another door or window. Each wall panel had a lion head sculpture but no glass.

"Are these symbols Egyptian or Mesopotamian in origin?" Rose asked.

"I'm not certain," I said. "But Egyptian artifacts are popular with wealthy collectors."

The damp ground sucked on my boots with each step. When I backed up, I spotted a ring of windows between the upper and lower sections of the conical roof. Little good they would do me without a ladder.

A maid, about my age, emerged from the stable with a slop bucket in hand. She stopped when she saw us, and I called her over.

She greeted the butler as she drew near. "Good morning, Mr. Williams."

"Morning to you, Susan."

"Are you in need of something?"

"Yes, your help," I answered for him. "My name is Gideon Wells. I have been hired by Mr. and Miss Ragiston to investigate the ghoul issue."

She wrinkled her brow. "But Mr. Ragiston is dead."

Mr. Williams said, "The young ones, dear. Claude and Ida."

"Oh."

I waved my hand over the ground. "Tell me, is it true the creature attacked the elder Mr. Ragiston here?"

"So said the doctor and sheriff. We found him further down the path, closer to his home. About there." She pointed at a spot where the path bent around a raised bed of flowerless, muddy soil.

"Susan?" A gaunt old man stumped toward us from the direction of the Voor house. He had wiry, white muttonchops, a tweed suit, and the labored gait of a chain gang marcher. "Susan, who are those trespassers?"

Susan closed her eyes as if making a brief, silent prayer.

Mr. Williams whispered, "Oh, curse the devil."

"Who is your friend?" I asked.

"Timothy Barron, my counterpart at the Voor residence."

"Excellent. Just the man I would like to speak to."

Mr. Williams smacked his lips. "You do not want to speak with him under any circumstances."

I chuckled. "I like you, Mr. Williams. We should play cards sometime."

"Thank you, sir, but the missus would not approve."

Susan, a sweet woman, introduced us to the curmudgeon. "Sir, Mr. Williams is here. He is helping Mr. Gideon Wells and…" She gestured toward my accomplice.

"Rosette Drumlin." Rose curtsied.

"They are here to get rid of the ghoul."

"It's not here," Timothy said briskly. "Do you see the monster?"

I could tell he would be a dry well of help. "Before locating the creature, I need to understand its previous attacks. Is Mr. Voor home, perhaps? I wish to speak with him."

"No. He departed on business." Timothy shooed the maid away with shaky hands. "Go on, Susan. Get on with your work."

"Will Mr. Voor be returning soon?" I asked.

"I do not know."

"Where has he gone?"

"He is busy with research in Ontario." Timothy bent in a fit of coughing that shook his body. When he straightened up again and cleared his throat of phlegm, his eyes were red and teary.

"Are you all right?" Mr. Williams asked. He sounded genuinely concerned.

"I will be when I go back in from this cold, damp air. Instead, you have me out here. I will not stand for some inspector trampling the flower beds and causing rumors about the master. It was bad enough after the men died back here."

I stared at Timothy for a long moment. "My, you are a beacon of sunshine."

Rose approached and stood near him, just behind his shoulder. Timothy let out a lesser cough and glared back and forth at the two of us. Addressing Mr. Williams by his first name, he said, "Robert, tell your guests to keep to the paths. I do not want them destroying the gardens or interrupting the staff."

I asked, "Do you have any guesses why the ghoul might have come here or why it attacked the men?"

Ghoul

"I cannot speak for the ghoul, as I have never seen the thing. As for Mr. Ragiston, he was a dear friend of Master Voor. He visited often when in town. He also liked to stroll through the garden and to read books in the pavilion. And Joseph Prentice was our grocer. He delivered food to our back door most mornings."

Joseph Prentice was the other man the ghoul had slain. I had learned about him during my conversation the previous night. The circumstances of his death closely resembled those of Mr. Ragiston's, except he had collapsed on the doorstep of the Voor mansion.

"Is the pavilion always kept locked? How would Mr. Ragiston have gotten in to read?"

Timothy scowled. "It's locked for good reason, to keep thieves away from the valuables in Master Voor's study. Mr. Ragiston had a key, and it has since been returned to us. I showed Sheriff Richt the room. You can bother him about it, or about anything else you want to know. I already gave him my full account."

Timothy strained through the last few words and succumbed to another fit of coughs. He wiped his lips. "I am through. I would appreciate if you keep to the—"

Rose patted a tuft of his sideburn. Timothy swatted her hand away.

"What are you doing, child?"

Rose rubbed her own hair. "They feel lighter than I expected," she said of his sideburns. "How long did it take you to grow them?"

He stormed off, stomping as heavily as his light, frail legs could manage. "Be gone, Robert, and keep them off the grass."

"Grass" was a rather generous description of the brown growth on the lawn.

I patted my apprentice on the shoulder. "Be kind, Rosette."

"He was being a bear."

"Don't you tell me to do unto others as I would have them do unto me?"

"I would let him poke my sideburns, if I had them," she said.

I shook my head. "I apologize for that, Mr. Williams.

The Ragiston butler wore the wryest of grins. "I saw nothing that needs apologizing for."

Honestly, neither did I. Rose was right; Timothy was a bear.

We next sought out Sheriff Richt, a man of little height and even fewer smiles. Based on the loud huff he made when I began my inquiries, I figured he would dismiss us without providing any information. But I have since determined he reacts in kind to all requests for help.

I learned a few new things from the sheriff that are perhaps significant. First, a local doctor found a bullet or a piece of shrapnel in Mr. Ragiston's chest. It was an old wound, and the skin had been stitched over the metal, so it did not cause his death.

I thought little of the detail until I passed it along to Claude and Ida. Neither was aware of their grandfather's injury or of him having served in combat. That leaves a victorious duel as the most likely source of the bullet.

Wealthy men are prone to adventure in their youth.

Second, I asked about the old, unsolved crimes I described in my last letter. He had nothing to add in regards to two of the mysteries, but he did mention that the female victim almost certainly died of a knife wound. The gnawing on her skin came from the rats discovered with the corpse. Upon learning this, I assumed the ghoul incidents were limited to only the previous few months.

Third, the grocer, Joseph Prentice, put up a fight against the creature. He had a swordstaff on his person at the time of death, and the tip of the blade was red with blood. That detail means our fiend can, in fact, bleed, and if it is a ghoul, then it must have emerged recently. The blood of the awakened dead blackens and rots over time, or drains entirely.

Fourth, the fatal wounds on both Mr. Ragiston and Mr. Prentice included deep tears surrounded by wide, shallow cuts. The marks are indicative of a fanged creature. Also, the ghoul left Joseph Prentice's body unmolested beyond the kill, but it plundered the groceries. The evidence unfortunately expands rather than lessens the number of monsters I have to consider.

Finally, I learned that Sheriff Richt coordinated hunting parties for two weeks after Mr. Ragiston's death. Armed men searched the surrounding forests for wolves or bears, but that ceased once sightings of a hellish creature began occurring in the village. The hunters failed to kill the ghoul before it could attack again, which leads me to my next letter.

6

After my garden investigation, I bid Mr. Williams to return to the mansion. Rose and I went with Sheriff Richt to our first interview. Along the way, we crossed a wooden bridge that spanned a creek-sized runoff ditch. After a short walk down a bowed street lined with identical gray homes, we arrived at the desired door. Dozens of garments hung like banners from the laundry ropes that zigzagged between second-story windows. A few women regarded us while they tended to their shops or mended clothes.

Sheriff Richt rapped his knuckles on the door. Several young, muffled voices sounded within, then the cloth covering the nearby window lifted aside. Three children, none more than six or seven years of age, pressed their slender faces against the glass and peered out at us.

Rose, whose list of virtues does not include patience, did not wait for a proper greeting at the door. She raised the window and spoke with the oldest of the children, a boy with disheveled blond hair. "Hello. Is your father home?"

The boy stayed at the sill, but his brother and sister retreated from Rose. "No ma'am. He's gone to quarry. My mama's here."

"We would prefer your father, but she will do." Rose bared her teeth at the boy and gestured at them. "Your teeth are quite yellow for a child your age. Do you own a toothbrush?"

The boy maintained his puzzled stare while calling "Mama?" over his shoulder. A moment later, the door opened. A weary-looking woman with a sleeping infant in one arm greeted us.

She tried to read all of our expressions. "Is something amiss, Sheriff? Is my husband all right?"

"As far as I know, Mrs. Hill." He removed his hat, revealing that his head lacked any hair above the cap's brim. "The Ragistons hired an investigator from a university in New York. May he ask some questions about the attack?"

Her gaping worry changed to squinting suspicion. She blew a strand of hair away from her face and stepped back from the door.

"Welcome to you. Come in."

The house was a simple tenement decorated with an unframed painting, a chipped vase, and an empty wood-and-glass jewelry box. Beyond that, the first floor had an oven, fireplace, table, and four chairs. The daughter and middle boy swept the floor together, spreading dust more than cleaning it, and the eldest boy practiced his writing by copying words from a Bible.

"There's pottage on the oven." Mrs. Hill raised her chin toward an iron pot.

I nudged the ladle sticking out of it. The congealed, brown stew barely moved. At least its smell more closely resembled food than its appearance.

"I hope the neighbor doesn't miss her cat," I said under my breath.

"Pardon?"

"Nothing, ma'am. I'm muttering to myself." I turned and warmed my back against the oven's residual heat. "Mrs. Hill, is your husband healthy?"

Rose, standing prim and proper with her hands clasped, mumbled, "With four young offspring, I would guess quite healthy."

I raised a finger to my lips to hush her, but my snorting laughter undermined the seriousness of my order. "His injuries. Has he healed from them?"

"He returned to work soon as he healed enough for it. He didn't lie none. You can see for yourself his leg is scarred and hobbles."

Mrs. Hill's infant began to squirm. She bounced him on her arm. "You won't fire him, will you? We need the money for food."

"Relax, ma'am. I am honestly here to dispose of the ghoul and nothing more."

"All right," she said, but she was not all right. She remained tense in spite of my calm grin.

I guessed that my association with the Ragiston family, her husband's employer, unnerved her. In order to look less imposing, I moved to a seat and leaned one elbow on the table. When I produced the journal from my bag, I positioned it so she could steal glances at whatever notes I recorded from our conversation. I wanted her to know I had no ulterior motive for being there.

"Sheriff Richt and others have shared plenty of stories about the ghoul, but most of the witnesses are dead or spotted it from afar. Your husband is different. He saw it quite clearly when it attacked him, correct? Can you share what he told you about it?"

She called out, "Boys, take your sister upstairs."

Her two oldest sons led the little girl away.

Ghoul

Once they had gone, she said, "It attacked him in full daylight, it did. It weren't a wolf or some dog. He said it looked like the ghoul's mother were a sickly woman, and its father were every kind of despicable vermin rolled into one. It had the mouth of a coyote, ears of a bat, eyes of an owl, and claws of a rat."

"It sounds like a poem," Rose mumbled.

I finished my notes and asked, "Did the creature have fur or wings?"

"It had long spines on its back, like a porcupine. The rest of the body looked like a gray human corpse. My husband said it was hungry. He could see its ribs through its skin."

"Thank you." I wrote the information down in pencil, then smiled past the woman at her three children. They were doing a poor job of being discreet as they spied on us from the top of the stairs. "Did he mention anything else that might help me find it? Perhaps a noise or smell?"

"Only that it smelled awful, but that's no surprise. It crawled out of the sewer." She chewed her lip as she sifted through her memory. "Oh, and it was wearing cloth."

"Cloth? What do you mean?"

"It had cloth wrapped around its waist, like it was wearing short pants or a skirt that been torn to bits."

I closed my journal and considered all that Mrs. Hill confirmed. My intrigue boiled. Our creature represented a new species, of that I felt certain, but a new species of what? I could not rule out ghouls, but the possibility of it being a lycanthrope increased. Lycanthropes' appendages grow, while ghouls tend to lose ears and other thin flesh as they decay.

Rose voiced my thoughts. "It would be our first ghoul with quills and ears."

"First ghoul?" Sheriff Richt and Mrs. Hill asked in unison. Then the sheriff said, "Have you seen more of these demons before?"

"Yes. I stopped three that kept digging up bones from the Antietam cemetery. They are awakened dead, by the way. Not demons."

"We should investigate all recent mass deaths that might have drawn it here," Rose said.

"I agree."

"It might be a lycanthrope, but have you ever heard of one attacking in daylight?"

The girl's astute mind is an endless wonder. She has caught up to my knowledge of exonatural creatures in a quarter of the time. "No. Ghouls prefer the night, but lycanthropes require it."

"What if they have enough shade?"

"Perhaps." Our conversation left the sheriff and Mrs. Hill in a silent stupor. I asked, "Can you show me where it attacked him?"

"If I must," Mrs. Hill replied.

She headed outside with Sheriff Richt. I followed them until Rose stopped me at the door with a tug of my sleeve.

"May I?" She held up the dollars she stores in her pocket.

"No, Rose. That's too much for you." I opened my billfold and, to her delight, handed over a twenty-dollar bill. "Take it from me instead."

Giggling, she waved to the children at the top of the stairs and left the money on the table.

We returned to the bridge we had crossed earlier. Mrs. Hill pointed to the stone-lined recess beneath it. "My husband was breaking rocks and repairing the ditch. It rushed out from under the bridge and bit him. He kicked it and broke free, and it went back into hiding."

Sheriff Richt added, "We piled rocks under there to keep the devil in the sewer, but it climbed out somewhere else and eventually attacked Miss Murphy."

Harriet Murphy was the other living victim, and I intended to visit her next.

Rose leapt down into the ditch, and her boots sunk halfway into the mud. She leaned to one side and peered under the bridge. "The drain is still blocked."

I kicked a pebble off the lip of the ditch. What kind of monster would ambush and withdraw? Most beasts lack the necessary mental faculties for such tactics.

"Have you searched the sewers?" I asked.

The sheriff paled at the question.

7

We visited the final victim, who was recovering at her cousin's house. Miss Harriet Murphy intrigued me more than any other witness. At the time, she had been working as a maid for Claude and Ida, and the attack occurred in the Ragiston basement.

Her wounds were still grisly despite two weeks of healing. Stitches corrugated the red flesh on her forearm, chin, and cheek. Bandages covered her left eye, the one that had been clawed.

I asked Miss Murphy to share anything she could recall. She prepared tea for all of us and sat down to explain what happened.

She had gone by candlelight into the basement for flour and discovered the pantry door ajar. The room had been raided, and broken jars and torn bags lay spilled onto the floor. She feared a burglar might be lurking in the dark. If one considered the guilty fiend a mere burglar, she was right.

Miss Murphy heard damp, congested breaths like those of a pneumonia patient, and she smelled a stench similar to a corpse or sewer. She cried, "Hello?"

A gray mass wriggled off the top shelf of the pantry. Then the beast looked up at her with a yellow, vicious gaze.

Not surprisingly, she screamed in terror. The creature thrashed about the room and clawed her, then fled into the deeper, darker recesses of the basement. She yelled for help as she ran up the stairs.

Miss Murphy ended her story abruptly. She set her cup of tea down because her hands were shaking enough to spill it. Then she touched the wrinkled skin around her stitches and wept silently.

She was young, pretty, and a maiden. The facial wounds must have disturbed her terribly.

I told her, "The cuts are straight. The scars will be faint if present at all." Hopefully my assurances will one day prove true.

We did not stay after that. I thanked her for her help and promised to kill the so-called ghoul. Guilt gnawed me as I left. I appreciated her insight but lamented that it required her to dive back into the depths of her nightmare.

8

Professor, please forgive my handwriting in this and all ensuing letters, for I now have to write left-handed. You will understand why after you read the incredible new details I have sent you.

Last night, in defiance of Ida Ragiston's pleas, I undid the lock on her basement door. It had been sealed since the incident with Miss Murphy.

"I beg you to reconsider," Ida said. She and the other members of the Ragiston house were standing in the kitchen. "Going down there is not safe for you or Miss Drumlin, and it puts the rest of us at risk."

"Which is why I need you to close the door behind us." I raised my revolver in front of my lips to gesture for them to be silent. I pushed the basement door open far enough to listen for movement in the darkness below. I sensed nothing besides silence and the cool, damp air.

Rose sat on a stool, kicking the front of her skirt. "Do you hear anything?"

I shook my head.

She shrugged and tore pieces from a loaf of bread on the table.

Ida squeezed the folds of her dress. "Oh, dear. Can you not try another plan? I do not want to be at fault for having put the two of you in terrible danger."

"The three of us, ma'am."

"Three? Who is the third?"

"He is." I thumbed at her brother, who was holding up a lantern at my back.

Ghoul

"Me?" He lowered the lantern so swiftly that it bounced off his thigh. His eyes widened with fear. "You said nothing of me going down there when you asked for my help."

"Why in the blazes would I need someone to hold my lantern here in the kitchen while I'm down there?"

Claude turned to his three servants. Mr. Williams's head was bowed in prayer, and his wife looked nearly as flustered as Ida. He called Mr. Carlson by his first name, John. "Carry this lantern for our guest."

"No, he will not," I ordered.

"I beg your pardon?"

I glared at him. "How much do you pay Mr. Carlson?"

Claude stuttered, and then said, "A proper wage, but I do not understand what that has to do with the matter at hand."

"A proper servant's wage is not enough for a man to risk his life."

"I can pay him more for the trouble."

My kind opinion of Claude wavered. "No, Mr. Ragiston. I know too many wealthy inheritors who never earn their respect or way in life. Some of those vermin crawl on the far branches of my own family tree. This is your home, your inheritance, and you are the one who hired me, so hold onto that lantern and kindly follow me into your basement."

His Adam's apple bobbed on a hard swallow. He nodded, at first tentatively, then with vigor. "All right, I'll go."

Perhaps I could hold out hope for him yet.

Mr. Carlson searched me without blinking, no doubt wondering if he should obey me or help his employer. I gestured toward Ida and the Williamses. "Please stay and guard them, Mr. Carlson. Unless one of us calls for you by name, remain here."

"Yes, sir."

"Are you ready?" I asked Rose.

She sprang from the stool. "I'm ready," she mumbled through fat cheeks stuffed with bread.

Rose picked up her handgun and leather medicine bag, which contained tools appropriate for hunting in the dark. I took two weapons for myself. The first was, as I mentioned, my revolver. I fastened a hooked, silver bayonet beneath the barrel before going downstairs.

The second weapon was my light-staff, a special walking stick I commissioned from an Irish fellow in New York. The handle is capped with a metal dragon head, and when I press its spines, light shines out of its mouth. The beam is narrower than a lantern's light and can only be used for brief periods, but you can imagine the usefulness of such a tool.

The hinges squealed an indecipherable warning as I opened the door and shined my staff into the black descent. The beam illuminated a few cobwebs and floating specks of dust. Everything else was shadow.

I tiptoed into the musty stillness. The stairs creaked nonetheless.

"What is the layout ahead of us?" I asked.

Claude followed close enough at my back that I could hear the lantern's flame dancing on the wick. "The basement is rather complex. When we were children, Ida and I used to get lost down here on purpose."

"At least describe the first few rooms." Understanding my surroundings would decrease the odds of me being caught unaware.

Ghoul

"The hall has three doors," Clause whispered. "The wine cellar and ice stores are to the right. The pantry is to the left. The hall splits in two directions after that."

I reached the smooth, stone floor at the bottom of the steps. Bricks formed the corridor's arched ceiling, but stacks of roughly cut stones made up the walls. Just as Claude described, the first door opened into a wine cellar. Racks lined the room, and bottles nested in at least half of the grooves.

I should have risked an expedition to that glorious vault on my first night. Fate rewarded my sweeping inspection of the stock. "Oh, sweet mercy."

"What is it?" Claude shrank behind me, but at least he managed to keep the lantern above my shoulder. "Is it the creature?"

"No. It is far more significant than that." I hung my pistol from the holster by its bayonet and turned off my lightstaff, which had begun to warm. I lifted a bottle of luscious Romanée-Conti wine off a rack as tenderly as one picks up a sleeping babe. "We have come to rescue you, little one."

"You are incorrigible, sir," Rose said from the doorway.

"It's Romanée-Conti, Rose."

Bah, what do the youth know? Professor, if you have ever had the pleasure of tasting that complex, extraordinary nectar, then doubtless you understand my excitement.

I was prepared for my good luck. I took a corkscrew out of my breast pocket and opened the bottle. The aroma cleansed my nose of the dank air.

"Is it expensive?" Claude asked.

"Extreme—I mean, it is extremely difficult to find, but not expensive." I lied in hopes the wine's value would not be deducted from my pay. I raised the bottle to my lips. The drink embraced my tongue.

We next checked the pantry, the site of Harriet Murphy's attack. The door still hung open. My boot struck a toppled basket when I stepped inside. The smells of salt and rotten apples wafted from the dark floor and shelves.

"Move closer," I said to Claude.

He did as asked, and the light recounted the violence that had occurred there.

Glass jar shards covered the floor between two of the shelves. The exposed vegetables and fruits had been chewed, either by our prey or by mice that benefitted from its invasion. Salted pork lay beneath the hook it had been torn from, and I doubted any mouse could be blamed for the chunks ripped out of it. The reddish-brown stains splattered on the floor and wall likely originated from Miss Murphy's unfortunate encounter.

"It attacked her here," Claude whispered.

"I guessed as much." I took another drink from the bottle. That poor girl. Even if she had not been hurt, the sight of a monster emerging from the clutter would have haunted her for ages. I stepped over a spilled bag of potatoes and examined the ragged gouges in the side of pork.

"How did it get in here?"

"We do not know," Claude said.

"Was the door from the kitchen locked at the time?"

"No, but why would the creature come down here when it could steal food from the kitchen?"

He raised a good point. And what were the odds of it going unnoticed inside the mansion? "What entrances are there from the outside?"

"Only one, but the door is locked and has been for years. None of us can open it. We made a poor attempt to find the keys when Ida and I first arrived, but other priorities took precedence."

"The keys are lost?" I asked.

"Yes. The knowledge of their whereabouts died with my grandfather, I'm afraid. He might have lost them years ago."

"But you are certain the door is locked?"

"Yes." He paused. "At least it was when we last checked."

I considered for a moment the possibility that someone did possess the keys, and that they had let the creature in by malice or mistake. Maybe they had stolen into the basement for food and left the door open. It seemed more likely than our ghoul learning to pick locks.

We would need to check the door he referred to. In the meantime, I had information to glean in the pantry. "Rose, come help me survey the food. I wish to know what types attract the beast."

"I cannot," she said, and not in her monotone, playful manner. I noticed a sharp intensity in her voice, and Claude raised the light toward her.

"What is the matter?" I asked.

Her face soured. "I smell a sewer odor."

Tripping over potatoes, I raced back to the long, arched corridor. She was right. A vile stench like concentrated rot oozed out of the deepest darkness of the passage. Miss Murphy had encountered such a smell just before her attack.

I listened for any hint of movement but heard only Claude's rapid breaths and the lantern rattling in his trembling grasp. I pressed the spines on my staff's dragon head and aimed its narrow beam down the hall. There, from around the corner, a pair of yellow, oval eyes stared back at us with predatory rancor.

A chill cut me to the quick.

9

My companion screamed. Not Rose. She pushed forward to my side, readying her gun. The cry came from Claude.

The creature reacted with spastic movements, its yellow eyes shaking wildly and flashing with each blink. It uttered a warbling growl, then it launched down the right-most tunnel branch as swiftly as a fired cannonball.

"Quick!" I cried. After sprinting a few steps, I stopped, seized by my better senses.

Rose asked, "What's wrong?"

I raised the wine for one more hurried sip, then rushed back and set the bottle of ravishingly delicious Romanée-Conti on a pantry shelf. "I dare not waste this," I said as I raised my gun and ran after the creature.

The next branch of the passage narrowed, and we moved in single file. Vertical stains darkened the bleached, dusty walls wherever moisture had trickled down them like blood from a wound. The rusted pipe at the peak of the arched ceiling had taken on the color of an artery.

I rolled my steps from heel to toe, quieting my movements as much as possible. I kept my light-staff aimed ahead and my gun at the ready should the creature surge toward us. The doors to the left and right were all closed, so I assumed the beast had continued on to the chamber at the tunnel's end.

The ceiling in the last room stooped so low that I felt the need to crouch, yet the walls spread out wider than the reach of our lights. I swung my staff back and forth. Its beam became lost in the chaotic mess of bags, casks, and crates stacked into towers. At least three tables occupied the chamber, and the one nearest to us had vials, a scale, and other chemistry tools. Empty sconces reached out like clawed paws from the pillars, begging for lit candles.

Our target was hiding in a bastion of clutter and darkness. The risk of ambush grew tenfold. I crept toward the left. Saws hung from the low ceiling beams ahead of me, and their teeth drew jagged shadows in my light. I had to move with a dancer's grace to avoid stepping on steel rods scattered over the floor.

The farther I advanced, the more the light faded. Claude lingered at the door, too afraid to follow me into the broad chamber.

"Mr. Ragiston, bring the lantern up here," I said.

"But I do not have a weapon."

"For good reason. You are as likely to shoot me as that beast if you had one." A glass vessel tipped over and rolled somewhere in the dark. "Hurry! I have no time for cowardice. I can't fight what I can't see."

He shuffled forward. Halfway to me, he stumbled, and the lantern swung violently as he regained his balance. "Oh, I always hated this room, even before that demon appeared."

"Shh. Keep the light behind my head so you don't blind me." I jerked my light-staff to one side but too late. Whatever I sensed moving hid itself again. "Rose, please release—"

I heard the clasp of her medical bag being undone. She was already setting the plan in motion. Rose removed the lid from one of her jars and released the contents into the air. Glowing, shimmering beads of green took flight and meandered in drunken patterns about the room.

"What are those?" Claude whispered.

"Corpse beetles." I took a step toward the sound of feet slapping on stone.

Rose completed my explanation. "They've been painted with an extract from glowworms, and they're attracted to the rotting stench of the awakened dead."

The beetles should have swarmed in the direction of the beast, but they continued to wander about the various heaps of boxes and bags. I heard a low, gibbering noise but struggled to discern where it came from, so I moved toward the densest cluster of green specks. The insects circled like vultures above a pile of animal hides and skulls.

"What are these?" I asked.

Claude peered from behind one of the tables. "I do not know. My grandfather collected these things while my sister and I lived in Philadelphia."

"Hmm." I mused at the beetles' uncertainty.

"It's not an awakened dead," Rose said, seconding my unspoken epiphany.

"What do you mean?" Claude asked.

"She means it is a living animal and not a ghoul." But an animal of what terrible species?

The hairs on my neck stood upright, not because of the chilling air but because of my tactical blunder. I had led them into terrible danger because my estimation of the beast had been wrong.

Strategies for living monsters differ from those for the awakened dead. With the latter, the straight-forward technique of using oneself as bait is most efficient. But living creatures possess cunning and a desire for self-preservation. Against such a foe, the safest plan is to distract its attention with anything but your flesh.

Oh, how I loathe uncertainty and error. Nothing else is as apt to cause death on a hunt. Did Rose understand our situation? I could only hope, because admitting the danger of my error might have caused our inexperienced lantern-bearer to panic. He was frightened enough already.

I leapt over a large, oddly shaped sack and immediately swept under the next table with my light. My heated staff began to flicker and dim at random. When I stood back up, I shined the dwindling light in the gaps between shoulder-high stacks of rummage. I half-expected to see the creature ambushing me.

"Think of it as a hunting animal, like a lion or dragon. What do animals—"

"Dragons exist?" Claude interrupted.

"Not anywhere near Pittsburgh, but that's not important at this time. Animals desire security and food. Take away either of those and you inspire fight rather than flight. We must force its behavior rather than responding to it."

Rose marched toward me, stepping nimbly over the mess on the floor. In a swift chain of motions, she put her revolver in its holster, stole the lantern from Claude, and plucked two beakers from a crate. She threw them toward the farthest corner. They dashed against the clutter.

Roaring, a slender figure bounded toward me over the tables. It crashed through wood and glass at a frightful pace, and I dove aside to avoid its trajectory. I fired one bullet but knew I missed the streaking beast by a wide margin.

Ghoul

It pounced into a square hole in the wall and scuttled out of sight.

I ran in pursuit and squeezed my head and arms into the hole. When I shined my light up the shaft, I found naught but a swinging length of rope. The creature had escaped.

Emerging from the hole, I asked Claude if his house had a dumb waiter. He stood abruptly. His gaping expression told me he realized our predicament.

We had flushed the deadly monster into the mansion with his sister and servants.

10

I left the lantern with Rose and told her to guard the basement hallway. Then, after taking a wooden box from her bag, I flew up the stairs with Claude on my train. I feared we would arrive at the kitchen to a scene of panic and violence, but Ida and the servants knew nothing of the creature's presence.

Ida sighed with relief upon seeing her brother. Mrs. Williams, however, quickly interpreted my preoccupation with checking the bordering rooms.

"The creature is in here?" she wailed.

Before I could lie, Claude sounded the warning. "It climbed into the house."

Ida screamed and backed into a corner. Mrs. Williams raised her shawl and shielded the mistress. Mr. Williams resumed his prayers but did so while keeping watch. Mr. Carlson took up a knife, so I chose him to come with me. I needed someone courageous and ready to fight.

"What about me?" Claude asked.

I flicked off my light-staff, giving the bulb some much-needed rest. "You did well, Mr. Ragiston. It's your turn to guard the others."

"I will," he said confidently. Our brief hunt had left its mark in him.

With utmost haste, Mr. Carlson lit another lantern and showed me to the dumb waiter doors. The first exhibited no signs of disturbance, but as I reached the second floor and shined my light down the hall, I saw a void in the wall. It was a safe bet the, for lack of a better term, "ghoul" had emerged from that hole and now roamed in our proximity.

"Keep watch behind me," I said.

"Yes, sir," Mr. Carlson replied.

I could hear it, the slap of the ghoul's feet and hands as it skittered over some nearby surface. Yet in spite of the noise's unsettling nearness, the creature eluded me. I began to fear it possessed an ability to camouflage itself. I was, after all, pursuing an unknown entity.

Keeping to the rug to stifle the noise of my steps, I advanced down the hall. Which room had the creature crawled into? I chose the one Mr. Carlson pointed to. He either had keen ears or keen luck because upon entering, I heard a shuffling noise within.

The room had grand, segmented windows on either side of the fireplace, and one of them was boarded up. A cool, moaning draft seeped through gaps in the wood. Moonlight shone through the other window. It cast a luminous blue checkerboard across the leaf-strewn floor and draped over the empty card and billiard tables. A broken pair of antlers hung above the bar to my right.

As Miss Murphy so accurately described, the creature's breathing sounded like a pneumonia patient's. I could hear its forced gasps through bubbling phlegm, but I still could not locate the beast. I raked my staff's light over the floor, then along the wood beams near the ceiling. I found nothing more than a startled rat.

I reached into my coat and took out the wooden box from Rose's bag. "Mr. Carlson, would you kindly avert your eyes toward the floor or shut them?"

He lowered his face. "Why, sir?"

"Because I have only one pair of tinted glasses, and these burning oils are quite unpleasant without them." I opened the velvet-lined box and took out the goggles and ceramic ball. The former I slipped over my head, and their dark lenses devoured what little vision I had. The latter was a sun grenade, a device of my own making. It contains a more violent form of the chemicals we paint onto corpse beetles.

I heaved the grenade against the ceiling, dashing its shell and spraying droplets of liquid sunlight around the room. The incendiary rain stung my scalp and hands, but it also replaced night with radiant day. Not wanting to waste the precious few seconds of light, I sprinted across the room and spotted the creature hiding behind the billiard table.

It looked as hideous and fierce as a ghoul. Its emaciated human body, corpse-like visage, and pallid flesh bore similarities to the awakened dead. However, this being was smaller, about the size of a child of ten, and its features and posture were far more animalistic. It had long jaws like a dog, the hiss of an angry cat, and laid-back ears suited for an immense bat. The sparse quills on its back stood erect and shivered. When it snarled with its scabrous lips, it exposed fangs and a sack of dried fruits in its teeth.

Professor, consider this my confirmation that the creature is no ghoul, but for lack of a better term, I continue to call it as such. I have no previous record of this abomination and thus no official classification for it.

I must confess I faltered in that first moment of beholding the monster. Perhaps I was too eager to study it, or perhaps a detail I have yet to put my finger on caused the distraction. Its golden eyes fascinated me and induced a vague sense of familiarity. Whatever the reason, I was slow to use my weapon, and the elusive creature made an escape.

The ghoul hurled one of the billiard balls at me. I deflected it with my arm, but by the time I aimed my gun at the ghoul, it was bounding on all fours between the card tables. It headed toward the window, dove through one of the broken panes, and vanished outside.

I gave chase and stuck my head through the hole it created. I searched the balcony and lower rooftops, hoping to fire a bullet at the ghoul or at least track its path. When I raised my tinted goggles for a brighter view, the creature lashed out from above and cut the back of my right hand with a shard of glass.

It had used an improvised weapon for a second time, a behavior I have never witnessed from genuine ghouls.

I cried out in pain and surprise. The revolver fell from my grasp, slid down the sloped roof, and plummeted to the ground. It is this same wound which presently forces me to write left-handed. Again, I apologize for the appearance of my recent letters.

With a dexterity that would have made Rose jealous, the ghoul bounded over the balconies and scuttled down a turret to the grass. From there, it scampered through the property's gate and fled into the streets of Haughtogis Point.

11

Bested by the monster, I withdrew into the parlor room. The sun grenade's light, which dimmed to mere star-like speckles, was insufficient for me to examine my wound, so I marched to the kitchen. My hosts fretted over the blood running down my wrist. In spite of the roaming beast, Mr. Carlson braved a ride to the doctor's house. I, meanwhile, wrapped my cut with cloth, then set out to retrieve my gun, my accomplice, and my bottle of wine.

Claude and I found Rose in the cluttered chamber, peacefully arranging vials on the ground. He then showed us the iron basement door that led outside. It was still sealed just like he had said. I undid the lock bar, but a second lock from the other side prevented me from opening it.

How had the creature gotten in?

We returned to the first floor. Ida and the Williamses were lighting every lantern and candle they could find. Mr. Carlson brought Dr. Torani to the house in excellent time. I gathered everyone in the main hall, and while I waited for the doctor and the wine to complete their work, I inquired about our discoveries in the basement.

"That creature has accessed the pantry at least twice. Is there another entrance you might have forgotten?"

"None," Claude asserted, and his sister nodded in concurrence. "The basement has only two entrances, and you saw for yourself we kept both locked."

Mr. Williams added, "The outer door has been locked since the masters were children." He motioned toward Claude and Ida.

Ghoul

"Was the—*ow!*" I flinched from a prick in my hand. "The blazes?"

"Steady now." Dr. Torani pinched my wound shut and pushed the stitching needle through to the other side. I had initially been averse to discussing matters in front of him, but Mrs. Williams assured me the doctor was an old friend and already quite familiar with the goings-on in the house.

Oh, joy for gossip.

I swigged wine and tried to ask my question again. "Was the door kept locked to prevent the children from getting out?"

"No," Mr. Williams said. "It was because the slaves on the Underground Railroad no longer needed the basement for hiding."

Out of all my findings about the Ragiston house, its history on the Underground Railroad was the most unexpected. "I am astonished. Pardons to present company, but I did not take Leonard Ragiston for a man of sufficient character to shelter slaves."

"Not him, but Lady Ragiston did. Bless her, she was a saint. After slavery ended and Mr. Ragiston sent her away, there was little reason to use the hidden door."

He explained the history of the mansion. Haughtogis Point used to be a trading site for the French fur trappers hunting upriver from Fort Duquesne. During the French and Indian War, traders fortified the village, and they stationed a cannon on the very spot where Lady Ragiston's statue now stands. They built underground chambers for storing powder and rations. The cluttered room where we had chased the ghoul was one of those chambers, and it predated the mansion.

Fort Duquesne grew to become Pittsburgh, and the Ragiston and Voor houses replaced the trading camps from old Haughtogis Point. The underground chambers gained new importance when Lady Ragiston began to hide fleeing slaves in them. She concealed the entrance from plain sight and erected the statue as a guide marker for those seeking shelter. A collapsed river dock, which I had seen during my tour of the garden, once served as a landing for the slaves who crossed the water by night.

Mr. Williams confessed, "Your impression of Master Ragiston is not inaccurate. He was not prone to generosity, and he complained the lady's benevolence would bleed them dry. But she kept taking them in, including Mr. Carlson's mother."

Mr. Carlson smiled at the mention of her.

Mr. Williams added, "I do believe her persistent philanthropy led to the divorce. She later managed Mr. Rockefeller's charities until her passing."

The story calmed Ida. She had been on edge since the ghoul incident, but for a moment, she looked almost at peace. She and her brother shared gentle, reserved natures. They in no way resembled the Ragiston patriarch, who was reputed to be a callous boss and ruthless negotiator.

Mrs. Williams said, "In recent years, Master Ragiston occasionally used the chambers for storage, but nothing more. And he always opened the door himself."

"I can confirm that," Dr. Torani said. He tugged and snipped the excess thread from my last stitch. "I ordered medical supplies for Mr. Voor and him, and they opened the door for me when I delivered the boxes."

"Mr. Voor?" Rose asked.

Dr. Torani nodded. "The gentlemen shared the tunnels because they spread under both properties."

I knew then nothing mattered more than finding a way into the tunnels. Given the sightings from the Ragiston basement and the sewer holes beneath the bridge, the odds suggested the ghoul navigated by way of those underground passages. It might have even formed a den in the dark, forsaken chambers beneath the village.

An idea occurred to me, and I absentmindedly tried to snap my fingers until the pain from my stitches stopped me. "If Mr. Voor and Mr. Ragiston both let you into the storage chambers, then it's possible they both had keys."

"I daresay it's more than possible." Dr. Torani dipped his stitching needle in alcohol. "Mr. Voor was the one who took the keys out of his pocket and opened the door. In fact, it was he who placed the order. Mind you, I don't know what help I can be. I didn't go into the tunnels. I just left the boxes with them at the entrance."

"What kinds of medical supplies? We found curious items in the Ragiston basement. Rose, what did you see?"

She answered, "Three beakers, seven flasks, eighteen cylinders, one crucible, two funnels, twelve empty bottles, and jars of chloroform and formaldehyde."

"Thank you. My lovely human abacus found the items in crates that are far less dusty than the other supplies. They have not been there long, and they seem quite out of ordinary for the home of a mining baron."

"I purchased the chloroform and formaldehyde," Dr. Torani said, "as well as scalpels, salves, mandrake, and other things. The vessels probably came from Mr. Voor. He was a chemist, after all."

My instinct bounded and wagged its tail like a hound that had picked up the scent. Evidence and sightings kept rolling toward the Ragiston and Voor properties. The mansions sat atop a hive of vacant chambers with untold substances stored in them. There could be dozens of chemicals and ingredients in the tunnels, any of which might have lured the creature down there.

"What did they use the supplies for?" I asked.

Mrs. Williams said, "Well, whenever we visited Haughtogis Point, Master Ragiston helped Mr. Voor with his experiments."

"What kinds?"

"We don't know. They spent long hours in the Voor house or in the pavilion, and they never discussed the work with us."

"That never struck you as odd?"

"We were curious," Mrs. Williams said, "but we honored Mr. Voor's secrecy. His company depends on research."

I stood and wavered a bit as my balance sloshed in wine. "I understand Mr. Voor's motives, but what about Mr. Ragiston? Had he always been interested in chemistry?"

Mr. Williams sat forward in his chair. "With due respect, Mr. Wells, you of all people should know that rich men can spend their time and money on unusual hobbies. Chemistry seems quite sensible compared to chasing monsters."

I admit he was right.

I asked the young Ragistons for their thoughts. They had stayed as quiet as Mr. Carlson for quite a while.

Claude squeezed one hand with the other. "Forgive me if I am misinterpreting your questions and tone, but it sounds like you suspect my grandfather caused this mess. That would be a terrible charge against my family."

Both of the Ragistons slumped their shoulders like scolded children. I assured them, "I am not blaming anyone. Just intrigued."

"Tell them," Rose insisted. I swear the girl has telepathy.

I sighed. "Fine. Doctor, can I trust you not to share what I say?"

He swore it, so I confessed my suspicions.

"I believe the creature has taken up residence in the tunnels beneath your house, and the experiments might have been the cause. We need to determine if your grandfather created or acquired something that drew it down there."

They said nothing in reply. In the quiet, the fire's pops sounded like bangs in the hearth. The conversation unsettled our hosts. I, on the other hand, was flush with excitement and a belly full of exquisite wine. We had made excellent gains on the creature that day.

I swayed to a song in my head as I finished my drink. "We will inspect the hidden door tomorrow. Unfortunately, we also need to ask dear old Timothy if he has the key. I would rather deal with the ghoul than that man. In the meantime, let's all get some rest."

"*Rest?*" Ida cried. "I don't know if I will ever sleep again after tonight."

"That creature could have climbed into this house at any time, and yet it did not." I recognize in sober retrospect the statement probably failed to comfort her. "It fled once it had the opportunity, so I doubt it considers your house to be hunting grounds."

I ran my thumb over the blood-stained sutures and swollen flesh around my wound. "Thank you for your fine needlework, Doctor. I should heal in no time, though writing is going to hurt."

"What about shooting?" Rose asked as I strutted to the stairs.

Yes, holding a gun hurt as well.

Ghoul

12

Professor, it is Sunday afternoon, and I am watching for the creature from the corner tower of the Ragiston mansion. I can see Rose in the street, still in her Sunday dress and jumping rope with the local children. Earlier today, she befriended a stray dog and sat with it for the span of about thirty minutes.

In moments like these, I remember how young she is. She may be an adult, but she so easily slips into the personality of that child I took in from the orphanage, the one missed by all the boys and girls she cared for.

She amuses me, and my sentimentalism surprises me. One can hardly call me a father regardless of what the adoption records say. Perhaps I am simply further on the journey of life than I realize and thus admire her youth. Aging causes people to long for the increasingly distant shores of childhood.

Whatever the explanation, I appreciated today's hours of normalcy and catching up on writing.

The morning snuck by before we started our work. Rose, as always, attended Mass. Why a girl so bright and logical insists on going to church each week is beyond me. My influences have not dissuaded her from that habit, nor do I try to anymore. I have accompanied her a few times, at her request, and found she genuinely delights in the singing, ceremonies, and teaching.

I spent my Sunday morning on the important tasks of nursing my hangover and writing my latest letters. I intend to post them to you tomorrow.

We further explored the streets of Haughtogis Point in search of sewer holes where we might snare the creature. The village felt altogether different with the men and boys home rather than toiling all day at the quarry. They looked weary, cracked, and sore, like machines on the cusp of breaking down. They shared few smiles and laughs, as joy is expensive to people so impoverished of energy. A lot of them sat on the sides of the street, watching their children play but not joining in.

So while the ghoul may not, in fact, be a ghoul, I nonetheless found awakened dead among these poor workers.

We scoured the gardens and located the door Mr. Williams told us about. It had been built into one of the arched recesses that decorate the pedestal of Lady Ragiston's statue. The hill slope and evergreen shrubs wrapped almost entirely around it. No one would ever find it by chance, except perhaps young lovers in liaison behind the bushes.

The door used to match the marble structure around it. Much of the white paint had peeled, exposing the oak underneath, and the statue pedestal had pulled a blanket of moss up over its base.

After trying the locked door, I contacted Sheriff Richt and asked him to obtain a key from Timothy. I hoped his authority would make the butler a little more cooperative. Unfortunately, Timothy insisted he knew of no such key, and that, since the door resided on Ragiston property, it must be among Leonard Ragiston's effects.

I have made arrangements to enter the underground chambers tomorrow. Claude intends to hire a locksmith from the neighboring village. Meanwhile, Sheriff Richt is conscripting hunters to help us kill the ghoul. I would rather catch it as a live specimen for you, Professor, but it has mauled too many people. I cannot in good conscience risk others by dragging this ordeal out longer than necessary.

I did lay a rope snare near the hidden door and baited it with meat. If we are fortunate, the trap will put an end to this madness tonight while we sleep.

I will be sending these letters to you come morning. Even if we have not captured the monster by the time you receive them, come to Haughtogis Point anyway. I have confirmed the existence of an animal unlike any other, and that should be all the convincing you need to join us.

I await your reply or arrival.

13

The weather awoke drab and dreary. The rains came not so much as a downpour but as a loitering, smoke-like mist. The one benefit of the miserable conditions was that I had an excuse to wear my heavier coat, and its longer sleeves covered my stitches.

I loaded a bag with lanterns and a net, and then I headed with Rose to the hidden door. My snare had captured the same stray dog that Rose befriended the day before. She released the dog, fed it part of her breakfast, and named it Gargoyle. Then she shooed it away for its protection.

Shortly after, Sheriff Richt arrived with his conscripts, a pair of boys with rifles. The older one, named James, looked about Rose's age and was every bit the cocksure hooligan I feared would volunteer. He bragged about almost shooting the ghoul once and swore he would avenge his cousin, Mr. Hill. The imbecile carried his rifle over his shoulder without any regard for keeping it dry from the rain, and he laughed loudly as if we were hunting a treed raccoon.

In a more amusing faux pas, he approached Rose and tried to spur conversation out of her. She responded by saying, "Human flesh would make fine bait for the ghoul. If you touch me, I'll consider your fingers an offering for the task and cut them off."

Oh, if only he had been dumb enough to keep bothering her.

The other hunter, Sheriff Richt's fifteen-year-old nephew, also happened to be named James. He held his gun at the ready and kept a constant, terrified watch. Unfortunately, he provided little help beyond vigilance. Had the ghoul appeared, the younger James would have been shaking too much to shoot it.

"Uncle, do you have any more men who can help us?" he asked. "That monster is dangerous."

I tried to reassure him. "You ought not worry. There are five of us. If the monster did kill one, there is only a twenty-percent chance it would be you. Gamblers would love those odds."

I smiled in amusement. He stared aghast at me.

Time crept at an excruciating pace in that chilling haze. I listened to the river's quiet, relentless procession and to the rocks being shattered at the distant quarry. Every time winds moved through the garden like ghosts of winter, both the naked tree and I shivered.

We jerked at a *galoosh* sound from the river. The older James was throwing rocks into the water. "If I shoot the ghoul, can I keep it?"

"No," I said.

"Why?" He flung a second rock, one that would have skipped on the water had his awkward throw not wobbled and crashed on the shore.

"We need the creature for science," I said.

"But if I hunt it, I should get its head. It almost bit my cousin's leg off."

"Mr. Wells will be taking it with him," Sheriff Richt said. "I want this town to return to normal."

The time reached a quarter past nine and still we had no word from Claude. I paced along the paved footpath. Every time I faced west, the Voor mansion's bizarre form loomed ahead through the mist.

Its conglomerated construction suggested changes in design over time. I doubt the original plans included the elongated layout, squat towers, and gothic arches. If ever I wanted to own a home that discouraged guests, or myself, from visiting, then I would purchase that house. Who would enjoy living in the architectural equivalent of a centipede?

The more traditional Carter residence likewise stood in silhouette, albeit more distant and obscured. Its broad balconies and parapets overlooked the gardens.

I paused mid-step. *The Carter house overlooked the gardens, the site of the ghoul's killings, and I had not interviewed the residents.*

I moved mine and Rose's bags into one of the statue alcoves for shelter, then headed up the path. "Come, Rose. Sheriff, please keep watch until the locksmith arrives."

"Where are you going?" he asked.

"To pay a brief visit to Mr. Carter. I will not be long."

The young, nervous James hurried after me. "What do we do if the monster emerges?"

"You need not worry about that," the other James said as he aimed his rifle at a pinecone.

"Yes, no need to worry." Rose thumbed at the older, dimmer James. "Just stand behind him."

"Shoot the creature," I told him. "That Winchester rifle you brought is a fine gun. If you miss, you can use this." I pulled my knife from its belt sheath and gave it to him.

"Thank you, sir," he said, tracing the seven-inch blade with his finger.

14

The palace-like Carter mansion lay ahead, its silhouette tangled in the rows of wiry brambles separating us from the house. The path meandered through a grove of still-barren trees whose spiraled branches reached up and out like tentacles in the wet air.

I imagine the place feels charming in the summer.

The white-bearded owner of the home must have noticed us walking up the trail. He stood in the back door and greeted us as we climbed the steps to his colonnaded porch.

"Good morning," Mr. Carter said. "Are you Gideon Wells?"

"I am, and this is Rosette Drumlin." I tipped my hat to the man. Water trickled off the brim.

"I heard about you. How fares your search for the monster?"

"Wetter than I care for, but we are getting closer."

I stopped and shook his hand, but Rose continued on. She crouched under Mr. Carter's elbow and passed by him through the doorway.

He stammered, "What ... what ...?"

"May we come in?" I asked. "We have some questions and would prefer not to stand in this dreadful weather."

Rose squeezed water from her dress onto the vestibule's cherry wood floor. Mr. Carter's maid entered the room and, seeing the puddle, gasped. She hurriedly pulled a mop out of the closet.

Mr. Carter squinted at me, half-covering his dark eyes with his bushy brows. "Humph. This is a strange visit indeed." He nodded. "Yes, yes, come in. Would you care for some tea?"

I smiled. "Or wine. Either would be lovely."

Our host showed us to a hexagonal study that would have colored any librarian green with envy. Tiers of books covered the walls except around the fireplace and windows. Rose immediately set to exploring the hundreds of volumes, walking her fingers from spine to spine.

I glanced through the stained-glass windows, which depicted canaries singing on branches. The unstained sections provided a fine view of the gardens.

The maid took our coats and set blankets on chairs so we could sit. She then added wood to the fire and left to prepare drinks.

We began with a trivial conversation regarding my father and a fabricated story about my injury. Mr. Carter laughed at Rose's fascination with his book collection and offered for her to take one. He had no idea he just made a friend for life.

"There are some Jane Austen novels to your right, dear."

"Thank you, sir. I would prefer this one." She jumped and yanked a bestiary of medieval creatures from one of the high shelves. The cover illustration, quite typical of the genre, depicted naked mortals being poured into Hell or snatched from the air by winged beasts. She flipped through the pages. "May I keep it?"

"Yes, but I'm surprised. Such fables are usually of interest to young boys rather than ladies."

"I've killed one of these," she said excitedly and pointed to a picture.

Ghoul

I steered the conversation toward urgent matters. "We should add our ghoul to the book."

As I hoped, Mr. Carter began to talk about the creature. He and the people of his house had been keeping watch at the windows ever since hearing about Miss Murphy's encounter. He pleaded for us to stop the ghoul, lest the strain on his and his wife's hearts kill them both.

I inquired about the two lethal attacks in the garden. To my disappointment, I learned that no one in his house had witnessed the incidents. My visit was not fruitless, however.

The focus of our conversation moved to Leonard Ragiston and Charles Voor. Mr. Carter's response fueled my kindling suspicions about the men. I gathered by the way he grimaced that he harbored little fondness for his wealthy neighbors.

"Have you visited the Ragiston quarry?" he asked. "Have you noticed the hours when the workers ferry back and forth across the river?"

"I have. They're over there for at least twelve hours."

Mr. Carter blew out his moustache with a puff. "The cart horses get more rest than those men. I own the ferry boats they use to cross the river. I cut my rates twice so they can come home with enough earnings to feed their families. Did you know four of them have died in the quarry since last July?"

Rose said, "That means Leonard Ragiston has more blood on his hands than the creature."

"If you ask me, he got what he deserved."

I was struck by a sudden fondness for the man's spirit. "My, the conversations between you and Mr. Ragiston must have been delightful."

He cut off my comment with his hand. "Bah. I stopped speaking directly with him years ago. Charles as well. He's cut from the same greedy cloth. He owns the chemical factory in Penn Hills, and he started hiring competitors for shipping goods after he found out union officials traveled to his factory on my boats. I tell you, those men built their wealth on the broken backs of others and on the graves of their own hearts."

Then Mr. Carter confided something that shifted the ground beneath my investigation.

"I hope you do not think me spiteful, Mr. Wells, but the ways they have abused their people offends me. Plus, I am not comfortable living next door to someone deeply involved with the occult."

"I beg your pardon?" Rose and I threaded glances with one another. I leaned closer to our host. "What do you mean by 'the occult'?"

Mr. Carter lit a cigarette. "I mean what anyone would. Have you not investigated his house?"

I shook my head.

"Charles Voor devotes the largest room to his menagerie. It has the kinds of things one would expect from a man who travels the world to hunt: a lion head, bear paws, and tusks."

The animal hides and bones in the Ragiston basement flashed into my memory.

Mr. Carter continued. "None of those seemed out of place, but the oddities in his collection disturbed me. Grotesque monstrosities. An albino snake with the wings and talons of an eagle sewn onto it. A rat with two heads. Ritual masks covered with human flesh, and the dried corpse of a

212

plague victim. Skeletons, potions, severed tails, and prayer gems he claims contain the souls of the dead. Civilized men ought not have such things."

"You say he brings oddities back with him from his travels?"

"Yes."

Charles Voor, world-travelling collector of the weird. That revelation branded him as a suspect in the mystery. Had he brought the ghoul back from some remote corner of the globe, only to have it escape from his collection? It would explain the creature's presence, not to mention his butler's defensive behavior.

Mr. Carter grimaced. "I see that look, Mr. Wells. I know what you are thinking, but Charles has not traveled overseas for years. I visited his home after his last long excursion. I doubt the demon belonged to his collection."

He might have dismissed the thought, but I could not. Even if Charles Voor did not knowingly bring the ghoul to Haughtogis Point, genuine occult artifacts attracted malicious entities far more than chemistry experiments.

I shrugged and feigned agreement with Mr. Carter, hoping to prevent rumors of my suspicions from spreading.

"You are probably right. If Mr. Voor has not travelled in a long time, and if you have seen his collection, then the creature must have come from somewhere else. His property borders the river. Maybe it swam downstream from a mountain or cave.

"Hmm." He stroked his beard.

"And I would not worry about the menagerie. Those things are rife with harmless forgeries. Nonetheless, if I get the opportunity to inspect it, I will let you know."

"Thank you. It would so put my mind at ease to know there's nothing to fear in that house. You probably think me a coward."

"Not in the least. Forgive me if I never get to verify the collection, though. The butler is not terribly fond of us, and I doubt he will let us in. Do you know when Mr. Voor will return?"

Mr. Carter exhaled smoke from his cigarette as he shook his head. A serpentine cloud drifted away from his lips. "No. He has been gone since before Leonard died. He would have wanted to be at the funeral."

"Would anyone else show the collection to us? His wife maybe?"

"He never married nor had any children. Unfortunately, you have no choice but to go through his butler. I know that man is as sour as Charles is strange."

An urge to return to the statue door grew in the back of my mind. We had stayed away too long. I finished my tea and stood. Rose, still flipping through her new book, walked across the room to join me.

"I knew Leonard Ragiston's reputation as a hard man," I said, "but according to you, I underestimated that quality in him. His grandchildren are amicable enough, and yet they have a strong affection for him."

"They probably fell in love with the idea of a grandfather more than the actual man. When they were children, he kept too busy with work to spend time with anyone. And what children would not have fun playing in the halls of his house?"

"Do you think they will become tyrants like him?"

Ghoul

"I hope not. Their grandmother and parents had soft hearts. But not Leonard. He would have stolen a beggar's only nickel to buy himself lunch."

15

Armed with new insight, I bid Mr. Carter farewell and set out with Rose. During our visit, the clouds had darkened to slate and let loose a pounding rain. Consequently, Rose left her book with Mr. Carter for safekeeping.

I could not ignore the lure of possible evidence in Charles Voor's house. Understanding is the lifeblood of exonatural investigations. Thus, en route to the statue, we detoured to the front door of that bizarre mansion. I held low hope of getting inside, but information can be gleaned from conversations as well, even hostile ones.

Torrents of precipitation, only a robin's breath warmer than ice, ran heavily off our coats and hats. By the time we reached the mansion's entrance, the gargoyle statues on the steps were spewing rainwater that drained from the gutters through copper pipes.

Rose clacked the lion head knocker. Like me, her clothes hung heavily on her body.

The door opened, and gaunt, old Timothy stood in the gap. He had paled to the color of balsa wood since our previous encounter.

"How may I help you?" he asked in a fanged tone.

I grabbed Rose's shoulder, stopping her from forcing her way in. "Hello, friend. Has Mr. Voor returned yet?"

"No." He began to close the door, but I blocked it with my foot.

"That is a shame, but you can still help me. I heard he has an extensive collection of curiosities in his menagerie. I am quite fond of such exhibits. Might we be allowed to see it?"

As expected, he said no. "This is a private home, not a circus. I'll not have vagabonds traipsing in off the street to steal from us."

"Mr. Wells took me to see a circus once," Rose said.

Timothy ignored her.

I peeked over his shoulder but glimpsed nothing more than a wall and mirror. "I wish you would reconsider. Where does his collection come from? Africa? The Amazon?"

He noticed me glancing around him and closed the door against his hip. "He has traveled all over the world. Good day, Mr. We—"

"Is that why he went to Ontario for research? Is he collecting more curiosities?"

Timothy's face hardened, but his eyelids fluttered as if he were fighting sleep. Speaking slowly and deliberately, he said, "I do not know Master Voor's business. He said he was going away for a few weeks to support a university's studies at a mine. Obviously his time away extended. I know nothing more, not even the name of the university. He gave the scarcest of detail before rushing to pack his bags and taking a carriage in the night. He said he needed to catch a train in Pittsburgh very early in the morning."

Rose rocked on her toes and heels. "Twice in that statement you used the term 'he said.' Does that mean you don't believe him, or are you merely conveying what he told you?"

"It means he is away on travel, *girl*." He spat the last word at her. "I have no reason to doubt what he said. Master Voor frequently travels."

Unmoved by Timothy's ire, Rose asked, "Did he lie about being gone for several weeks, or has something delayed him?"

"Listen here, child. I am not amused by your mockery and accusations. My master—"

I stepped closer to Rose. "Forgive her, sir, if my apprentice's questions offended you. She has not yet mastered the delicate aspects of the job. We do earnestly wish to help, and the creature's history of attacks on this property makes us worried it will happen again."

"The attacks occurred in the garden and in the house you are staying in. I would think your time is best spent searching there."

"You do not intend to assist us in any way, do you?"

My question coaxed an ugly smile from him. "Oh, so the detective has finally figured that out."

"I'm sorry. I can be rather slow." I stopped Rose by her shoulder again, this time as she tried to walk away. I worried what she might do out of my sight in response to the old man's rudeness. "Will you at least tell me if anything exotic was delivered to the house within the past year? It might be something that seems ordinary but came from an unusual location."

"Nothing of the sort. Good day, Mr. Wells."

"Thank you. You have been most helpful, but would you be willing to answer one question more?"

"What?" The word popped from his tongue like an ember.

"My question—well, Rose's question—is do you think Mr. Voor lied about being away for several weeks, or has something unexpected kept him away? Did he die at the mines?"

The door slammed in reply. It opened a few seconds later after Timothy caught us peeking through windows, and he shouted at us to leave.

The rain pelted us as we walked down the steps.

"Sorry," Rose said in a rare moment of clear and earnest regret. "I hope my provocations didn't hurt your inquiries."

"Not in the least," I said. "That man is either exceptionally rude or hiding something. We'll come later, with a search warrant if necessary. For now, I need you to go back to the statue and help the sheriff. I hope the locksmith has arrived by now."

"What about you?"

"I want to examine something."

She pleaded, "I want to see the pavilion too."

I laughed. I cannot keep a secret from her. "Run along, Rose. I can break the law on my own."

16

I leaned against the pavilion's wall, not only for shelter beneath the overhanging roof, but to avoid being seen by those at the statue or in the Voor house. Jail is a miserable interruption when on a case.

Rose shoved rain-soaked strands of hair away from her forehead. "Please, sir. If I help, the search will go twice as fast."

"I don't want you in here. It's quite enough I'm setting a bad example. I do not want you participating in the crime as well."

"What if I choose to do so of my own accord?"

I lowered my face close to hers. "If I go to jail, the responsibility of stopping the ghoul belongs to you. Now go help our sheriff friend, or at least distract him. I'll join you shortly."

Rose is gifted at hiding most emotions; disappointment is not one of them. She scrunched her upper lip. "What do I tell them if they ask for you?"

"Make up a story."

"I do not care for lying."

"Rose, just—" I paused to calm myself. Mud splashed out from under my boot each time I tapped my toes. "Just say I am busy with the investigation and will return soon. That is the truth."

"Do you think Mr. Voor summoned the creature?" she asked.

"Not in any sort of mystical way. He might have an artifact in the house or pavilion that enticed the creature to come here. It's even more likely he imported it and put it in a private display. I need to collect evidence, and you need to hurry back to the sheriff. Now go."

Rose finally yielded. She huffed and scurried in the direction of the statue.

The doors remained locked, so I stepped on one of the pavilion's decorative lion heads and climbed onto the lower roof. Two of my stitches snapped as I pulled myself up, and fresh blood reddened the raindrops on my hand. Once I reached the nook beneath the upper roof, I peered through one of the windows.

The floor was made of stone except for a six-foot brass circle with hieroglyph etchings. I spied bookshelves, stoppered jars, and two leather chairs. The darkness obscured all other details. I convinced myself I could no longer wait—that if given time, Timothy would hide all evidence. In truth, I shattered the window because of my ravenous curiosity.

Once I cleared the shards out of the window frame, I slid inside with all the grace of a dropped coal sack. The brass seal on the floor rang like a cymbal under my landing.

As I got up off my backside, I noticed a ring of unlit bulbs hanging from the ceiling. A metal lever with a rubber handle stood erect from the wall, and when I pulled it down into an iron receptacle, it coughed sparks onto my feet. The room illuminated, and a muffled hiss of steam echoed in two pipes near the bookshelves.

Everything was arranged with the meticulous care of a museum exhibit. A taxidermic monstrosity with cat, owl, and bat parts hung from a plaque. I opened the lid of a gold-etched cedar chest and found scientific and medical instruments arranged in parallel rows. The pipettes and sealed powders seemed sensible possessions for a chemist. The same could not be said about the scalpels, syringes, and leather bindings.

A cursory check of the liquor cabinet proved Mr. Voor had questionable taste and an affinity for getting drunk quickly. I found an absinthe kit, and such a drink would have been delightful under other circumstances. The rest of the collection, however, was distilled to abuse tongues and capsize brains.

Atop the cabinet sat nine jars with cork stoppers. Each contained a unique substance such as clear fluids, black sand, or a silvery bead. The one with yellow powder held sulphur. I supposed the last vessel held red wine until I opened it and smelled the blood.

I next inspected the bookshelves. None of the novels and texts on chemistry or history piqued my interest. The other books, however, could have fueled a thousand speculations about Mr. Voor. Medieval science books written in French and Old English. Parchments in Latin and what appeared to be Sanskrit and Chinese. Medical journals with detailed drawings of human and animal anatomy. Spellbooks and ritual records from Celts, Gypsies, and unfamiliar cultures.

Mr. Voor's interest in the occult exceeded fascination and superstition. He owned a library devoted to it.

Tucked among the more exotic and serious tomes was a book without any identifying marks on the cover or binding. To my utter surprise, it contained nothing but childish pencil drawings of houses, trees, and other common objects. I chuckled because of how odd it seemed on a shelf of overly odd books.

Ghoul

The drawings also confused me. According to Mr. Carter, Charles Voor had no children, and by extension no grandchildren, so who drew the images? Furthermore, instead of improving page-over-page, the drawings became more erratic and ill-defined, as if the young artist regressed in ability.

I returned the book and chose another, one which was heavily worn and therefore heavily read. Its blue, leathery cover bore gold lettering and symbols matching those on the brass floor and pavilion door.

As I pulled it out, I knocked a framed picture off the shelf. It cracked against the floor.

Fortunately, the fall was not as damaging as it sounded. I placed the chipped frame back on the shelf and took note of the old, faded photograph. A short, bearded man in a surgical coat was shaking hands with a half-bald Union Army officer. Both men looked about age sixty, making them ninety if still alive today. A note at the bottom of the image read *Charles, thank you for your support. Major General Hitchcock.*"

Charles? Charles Voor? Would a ninety-year-old man have the strength for a winter expedition in Canada? Bravo to him if he did, but it was more likely Mr. Voor shared a name with his father. I made a mental record to later investigate his ancestry for a Charles Voor Sr.

To my frustration, the text in the blue book was written in Latin. I cursed myself for dismissing Rose. She had learned Latin during her years in the Catholic orphanage.

The pavilion door's lock clicked, and I jumped. The door handle turned. Someone was coming in.

Seeing no means of concealment or escape, I tore several pages from the book, stuffed them in my inner vest pocket, and dropped into one of the leather chairs as if I belonged in the study.

The door swung open. Timothy stood at the entrance with an umbrella in one hand and a gun in the other.

I crossed my legs and laid the open book on my lap. Making the most of my predicament, I said, "Thank heavens you are finally here. Have you brought me some tea?"

17

"*Thief*," Timothy snarled. "You have no right to be in here."

I snapped the book closed, laid it on the arm of the chair, and wiped my bloody hand on my pants. "Forgive me, sir. I chased the ghoul to the pavilion and thought it climbed inside. I tired myself out during the pursuit, so I sat here for a quick rest."

He would never believe me. I did not care. I needed a delay and a plan, not his support.

Timothy left the umbrella outside and entered the study. He nudged the glass shards on the floor with his shoe. "You broke a window."

I stood. The moisture from my coat remained on the leather chair. "That window was the ghoul's doing. That's why I thought it came in here."

"A thief and a liar. I'm calling for the sheriff."

"I apologize, but I already summoned him. He is busy with a task I gave him." I brushed my hand over the seat, but of course I could not sweep away the damp spots like crumbs. "I can go find him for you if you like. Or perhaps we could wait someplace comfortable until he arrives. Might I recommend this study? We could pass the time with these books."

Timothy leveled his gun at my chest. "You are coming with me to the sheriff's house."

"Very well." I sighed. "I do hope you plan to share that umbrella."

Timothy moved toward me. He stepped onto the bronze disc, and a faint, metallic ring echoed beneath the floor.

I turned my ear toward the previously unnoticed sound. The ground beneath the seal was hollow. I stomped my heel on it twice and confirmed the echo.

"Quit stalling and go outside," Timothy said.

I began to devise another lie. I looked for any sufficiently unusual object and settled on a blue lily pressed between layers of glass. "It may not be wise to involve the sheriff."

"Why?"

"Because if you do, I will tell him what I found in here. Do you know what that is?" I pointed at the lily. "It's a Jotela flower, an exceedingly rare specimen. Native tribes in Indochina worship it, and removing it from the region is punishable by death over there. I know some officials in Washington who would be intrigued to hear Charles Voor has one."

Timothy frowned at me with equal parts disdain and annoyance. "That's a Siberian squill, you imbecile. It's one of Master Voor's favorites. He brought it back from Russia."

"Well ... 'snails." My bluff failed. "It is a beautiful flower."

I trudged across the pavilion, stomping on the metal floor as I went. I felt angrier at the butler for thwarting my curiosity than for aiming a weapon at me.

"Move along," Timothy ordered, pushing me outside. He stopped to lock the door and pick up his umbrella.

As I waited with arms crossed to conserve my warmth and keep my stolen pages dry, I heard excited cries over the steady hiss of rain. The voices came from the direction of the statue door. All of the people I stationed there had vanished from sight.

Had they been attacked? Dread and urgency tugged at my sleeve.

"We need to head over there at once," I said, not bothering to mask the concern in my voice.

"No. We are going to the sheriff."

"The sheriff is there, you ornery, inbred fossil." I stifled an urge to punch him. "Listen. The ghoul is hiding in the chamber, and I need to stop it before it kills again. If it harms one person because of your interference"—a person like Rose—"their blood will be on your hands, and then your blood will be on mine."

My threat startled him, but he recovered and poked my chest with the barrel of his gun. "Shut your mouth."

I stepped back as if surrendering, then swatted his gun aside while pulling out my revolver.

Timothy froze for a moment as he realized I had turned the tables. He dropped to the ground and shielded himself with his umbrella.

Agitated shouts continued to sound near the river.

"I'm going over there," I said. Without waiting for his reaction, I sprinted toward the statue.

"Halt!" Timothy shouted.

"Shoot me," I replied, unwavering in my run. For a moment, I feared he might.

18

The voices cleared as I drew near. The men shouted, "Keep going," "I can almost fit through," and "Do you need help?"

I crested the steep bank that bends around the statue and slid down the wet grass. The hidden door was open. Claude and an unfamiliar man stood in front of it, peering into the darkness. Sheriff Richt and the two boys called out from inside.

"Where is Rose?" I asked breathlessly.

They pointed toward the river. Rose climbed up the shore near the collapsed dock and waved.

The men explained what had transpired during my absence. The newly arrived gentleman I did not recognize was the locksmith. He succeeded in forcing the door open, but to everyone's disappointment, the inner room proved empty and scarcely large enough for a mule. Someone had apparently walled-off the majority of the room.

My accomplice arrived at that time and assisted the befuddled men. She held a light to the grate on the small room's floor and discovered a trough with two chains. She deduced these were part of a mechanism for opening the passage Dr. Torani told us about. Rose's search led to the old, ruined dock where, beneath the rotted boards, she found a crank and a drain gushing with water.

When she rotated the crank, a portion of the wall in the small room receded, exposing a larger, deeper chamber.

Rose beamed with pride as she strutted to me. "I figured Lady Ragiston built the hidden entrance to protect the slaves. Since they came by boat, the dock seemed a logical place to look for a door knob."

I would have congratulated Rose for her fine work, but her expression tensed. I spun and faced the source of her worry. Timothy approached with his umbrella held high and his gun aimed at me.

Groaning, I removed my coat and handed it to Rose. The rain began to invade the few remaining dry threads of my shirt.

"Left breast pocket," I whispered, then cocked my head toward the room. I needed her to read the Latin text before it could be confiscated.

She donned the oversized coat and escaped toward the door.

"Mr. Wells, stay where you are," Timothy ordered. Despite his umbrella, the rains had soaked his clothes, making him appear weaker and more shriveled than ever. Bruises darkened his fingertips and the flesh around his eyes. His skin looked otherwise pale as washed cotton.

"Sir, a man of your age would do well to avoid being outside in this weather. The cold will be the death of you."

"I am through with your games."

Sheriff Richt and his conscripts emerged from the chamber to investigate the commotion.

"Ah, Sheriff. There you are." Timothy nodded toward me. "Arrest this man."

Sheriff Richt's focus darted to me. I circled my ear with my finger, intimating the butler had gone nuts.

"What is this business about, Gideon?" he asked.

Timothy waved his weapon. "He stole into Master Voor's property. I caught him reading the master's personal documents." A vicious flock of coughs flew out of his lungs, and I hoped he would not accidentally squeeze the trigger.

"Put the gun away, Mr. Barron," Sheriff Richt said to Timothy. "Are you ill?"

"I am fine. I demand you arrest this criminal."

The sheriff puckered his lips as if preparing to spit. "How do you respond to these charges, Gideon?"

I shrugged. "Guilty as charged. I trespassed in the pavilion and flipped through one of Mr. Voor's books. That is all. Sheriff, we've no time for bickering right now. The creature is likely hiding in there, and we could put this nightmare to rest in time to eat a warm lunch."

He shivered. "Curse this rain. Mr. Barron, the Ragistons hired Gideon to rid Haughtogis of the ghoul. We need his help."

"That gives him no right to break the law or for you to ignore your duty."

"Might I suggest we deal with this charge tomorrow?" I said. "You have my confession. Determine the fine, and I will pay it. Our hunt is infinitely more urgent."

Timothy scoffed. "Sheriff, you cannot trust this outsider." A coughing fit bent him at the waist and halted his protest.

Fury burned the last of my patience to ash. The coppery taste of anger tinged my tongue. I snapped, "He is hiding a crime. Charles Voor is responsible for the ghoul. He brought it back from some godforsaken jungle, and he is to blame for it preying on the people of this village."

"No, Gideon. You're wrong." Rose, standing in the doorway, held up the pages I had stolen.

"It's far worse than that."

19

"What do you mean 'worse'?" I asked Rose.

"Where did these come from?"

I cleared my throat. "I found them."

"You stole them," Timothy said, stomping his foot.

Rose shoved the papers back into my coat pocket. "Are these from the pavilion?"

I nodded.

"Then it appears Mr. Voor is dabbling in biological alchemy."

Alchemy. Every clue and suspicion knotted around that despicable word. The vials of sulphur and black sand. The ancient-world symbols. The wretched amalgamations of diverse animals joined into one. Contrary to my earlier impression in Mr. Voor's study, the owl and bat parts may not have been attached to the preserved cat with thread, but by science.

And the critters would have been alive when it happened.

I thought the practice was purely conjecture and myth. The alchemists I knew were charlatans, the shysters of chemistry. They tinkered with the properties of minerals and chemicals, combining and separating their components, then made grandiose claims about what their concoctions could do. Every proponent of alchemy argued for its legitimacy, but none of them ever presented solid proof.

While traversing the fruitless rumors, I had happened upon legends of a darker and more unbelievable variation of the practice. Biological alchemy, the art of altering and combining living flesh. I never found anything more substantial than stories and speculation, but would practitioners of such a vile, nightmarish science ever admit to it publicly?

"I do not understand," Claude said. "I thought alchemists create gold."

"It is more than transmuting gold from baser substances. In theory, alchemists use exonatural energy to expand the limits of natural chemistry. The darkest forms manipulate the biology of living creatures." I exhaled strongly, expelling clouds from my nostrils. "Only a madman would commit such a crime against nature."

"Is it possible?" Rose asked.

"Until this moment, I would have said no."

"I still do not understand," Claude said

I marched toward Timothy in spite of his gun. "It means that if Charles Voor achieved biological alchemy, the real thing, then he did not import the ghoul. He created it in a laboratory from other animals."

"Is this true?" Sheriff Richt asked.

Timothy backed away and lowered the gun to waist height. Based on the quivering of his arms, I doubted he had enough strength to hold it any higher than that.

"They are lying. Master Voor is a chemist, not some witch doctor."

"What will we find in the chamber?" I asked.

"I have no idea. This entrance belongs to the Ragistons."

"Stop slipping away from the questions, you eel! Charles and Leonard studied together in the pavilion, and according to Dr. Torani, they both stored surgical supplies in their basements." I tossed a glance at Claude, who caught it with visible trepidation. He understood that any guilt placed on Charles Voor also tightened like a noose around his family's name.

Timothy lowered both his gun and umbrella. "Utter rubbish." Deep, chesty coughs interrupted him. "Why would he create some monster?"

Rose said, "According to the pages, he also used alchemy to extend lives. Mr. Ragiston, did your grandfather ever require his workers give blood for influenza testing?"

Claude wiped the rain from his brow. "I do not know."

"Yes," the older James said. He grabbed the crook of his elbow. "I heard the stonemasons talking about it, how a doctor from Pittsburgh took blood out of their arms."

"Thank the men for contributing years to Mr. Voor's and Mr. Ragiston's lives," Rose said. "Well, at least until the creature killed Mr. Ragiston. Blood-soaked ruthenium adds thirteen lunar cycles when buried in the chest."

A look of utter horror stretched Timothy's wrinkled face. He backed away from us and then shuffled away toward the Voor house.

"Mr. Barron?" Sheriff Richt called.

"Let him go," I said. "We can question him after we stop the creature."

Rose and I led the others into the chamber. I took two lanterns from my bag and lit them with matches from a tin. For the first ten paces, the sloped passage narrowed enough to be mistaken for a crypt. I stooped to avoid striking my head, and moisture dripped from the ceiling onto the back of my already-soaked neck. The air hung dense and stale as if the room had inhaled and held its breath for years.

"You're bleeding again," Rose said.

Blood and water dripped together off my hand and colored the lantern's glass. The scent from my wound would crowd the passages.

She asked, "Is that safe?"

"None of this is safe."

At the top of the incline, the tunnel opened into a broad room with a half dozen columns and walls of stacked stones. Rat pellets rolled like gravel under my boots, and the light from our lanterns snagged in the curtains of cobwebs. God only knows what the spiders ate in there. Water rushed off a lip of stone that projected from the back wall, flowed down a trough, and vanished into a hole in the floor.

Two more passages branched from the chamber, both of which ended at iron doors. Attempting to orient herself, Rose straddled the water trough in the center of the room and straightened her arms toward the tunnels. "The one to the right leads to the Ragiston house. It's the door we could not open before. Where does the other one lead?"

"To the Voor house," I said. "Or, more likely, to the space under the pavilion."

The others scouted the room cautiously. Claude must have promised a handsome payment to the locksmith because he ventured into the darkness with us. Younger James ducked and clawed a cobweb out of his hair, and older James laughed at him.

"You think the ghoul lives down here?" Sheriff Richt asked.

I raised my voice above the clamor of water. "I do, so keep up your guard."

Ghoul

After checking the left door, I asked the locksmith if he could open it. He dug at the keyhole with his hooks until it clicked, but still the door would not move.

"Something is blocking it," he said.

"All right. Put away your tools. It's barred from the other side, just as the Ragiston door was."

The older James craned his neck to peek around us. His unpleasant breath lingered in the tunnel. "Do you think the ghoul came through here? Can it open doors? That would mean it can break into houses to kill us while we sleep."

"I am not sure how it moves around. I have yet to figure out how it got into the Ragiston house."

"Through here," Rose called from the wide part of the chamber. She motioned toward the spot where the runoff water spilled out of the wall. "It can fit in this hole."

Her teeth chattered as she spoke. Wet clothes and cool air were taking their toll, on her and the rest of us. My skin craved warmth.

I walked back and knelt beside the trough. Rose had placed her lantern in the hole, on a crevice just above the water's level. The air emitting from it smelled dank, rusty, and slightly sulphurous. When I stuck my head inside, my shoulders stopped against the rim like a sideways cork atop a bottle. My eyes reached deep enough for me to peer up the drains, which flowed toward me from two directions. A faint glow illuminated the left duct about fifty feet away.

I pushed back from the hole.

Sheriff Richt asked, "Well?"

"She may be right. It's wide enough, and the creature might be able to reach any sewer drains diverting rainwater to this point. Claude, are there any drains in your basement?"

"Yes. A few."

"I know where next to look to find how the ghoul got in."

"We need to open the door on the Voor side," Rose said.

I paid no mind to her comment until one of the men cleared his throat loudly. Four of them averted their eyes, and older James gaped at Rose. I turned him away when I realized why. She had removed her skirt, exposing her short pants underneath, and she was untying the straps on her leather bodice.

"What in heaven's name are you doing, Rose?" I asked.

"I said we need to open the door."

"So you're stripping to nude and pretending you're a key?"

"No, but perhaps our alchemist friend could help me do that." She slid the loosened bodice down over her slender frame, leaving naught but her chemise and pale camisole covering her torso. "There's a lock bar on the other side. I intend to crawl through and open it."

Apprehension punched my chest. Upon dread realization of her plan, I seized her arm. The fool girl was practically throwing herself into the jaws of the beast.

"Stop this, Rose. We will find another way in. Patience over courage."

Sheriff Richt peeked through his fingers. "You're speaking madness."

Rose pulled free of my grasp, planted her fists on her hips, and scowled. "No one else will fit."

"Rose, no," I said sternly.

Ghoul

She flushed with anger. "What if it attacks someone while we wait? What if it kills a child this time?"

"That child could be you."

"Except I'm not a child. I'm an employee of Gideon Wells Exonatural Investigations, and I have a job to do."

Professor, you have four grown children, correct? And is not one of them an Army officer? I admire your fortitude. Among myriad reasons why I would make a pitiful father is my apparent lack of courage for the responsibility. I have faced dozens of fanged monsters that tried to eat me, and I have trained Rose how to fight back against them. But sending her alone and defenseless into the creature's lair racked me with trepidation.

Her plan was feasible. It was clever. But it was reckless. In the end, I let her go anyway. I knew Rose's stubbornness too well.

In the absence of further objections, she began to climb belly-down into the small, square hole.

"Gideon, she cannot be serious," Claude said.

I held my tongue.

"Wait," the younger James called. He ran to Rose and held out the knife I had given him. "You might need this."

Rose rolled it over so the blade aimed away from her, then bit down on the steel. She grinned at him as best she could with the knife between her teeth.

"Be quick, and stay safe," I told her.

"None of this is safe," she mumbled. Then she slid lithely into the hole. The frigid water surged around her body.

"Mind your thoughts, James," I said.

I meant it for the older boy, but they both replied, "I'm sorry."

I watched and waited from the entrance. The light from the lantern and from the far end of the tunnel outlined her figure. Had Rose been a few inches larger in girth, she never would have fit. Her shoulders and her head, which she had to hold above the water level, dragged against the sides of the duct.

She stopped and plucked the knife from her teeth. "The channel branches."

"Which way?" I asked.

She nodded left and right. "Both ways. The tunnels are the same size, but they are pitch-black."

"Stay on course then. The light is your best bet."

Rose wriggled forward like a squeezed caterpillar. When at last she reached the place where the light illuminated her hair and shoulders, she rolled with noticeable struggle onto her back. Her muffled grunts echoed louder than the churning water.

She slid a hand around her hip and pulled the knife out of her mouth again. "The opening is covered with a grate."

"Can you open it?"

She pushed and pulled at the obstruction. "No. The stench wafting through the grille is revolting. I smell a rotting corpse."

Each second heaped more risk onto the plan. My gut knotted, and my instincts screamed that Rose should abandon her attempt. "Rosette, slide back to me now."

"I will try one of the branches next." Her voice sounded so distant and restricted.

"You will do no such thing. Come back—"

Two-thirds of the way up the tunnel, a pair of oval eyes crept into view. The light reflected off them in a sickly yellow glow. When the ghoul rotated its head like an owl to look at Rose, one of its long ears stuck out across the entire width of the passage.

"Here, here, here!" I cried, trying to attract the beast to me. I balled my wounded hand into a fist and squeezed out blood as impromptu bait, then I drew my revolver. "Rose, do not move. It's here."

The gun slipped in my wet hand, and the remaining stitches strained as I held it. I aimed the weapon down the tunnel, but I never fired because I could not fit my head in at the same time. I risked hitting Rose if I shot blind.

I pulled the revolver out and poked my head in. Rose's and the creature's silhouettes merged into one.

"Don't move," I shouted. "Feign death."

I never would have given that advice while I thought the creature was a genuine ghoul.

Straining to climb in after her accomplished nothing but bruising my collarbones. I heard thrashing in the water and Rose's cries.

Desperate, I sprinted to the barred door and threw my body into it. It threw me back with painful resolve.

"Help me!" I yelled to the men standing off to the side. They hurried over and, as one mass, we slammed against the door like a human battering ram. It shook, and the chamber echoed with the thunder of our effort, but still we could not break through.

Amid my efforts, I remembered there might be another way in. I stopped the others.

"You, try to get the lock bar open," I said to the locksmith. To the younger James, I said, "Stay here and guard him."

"But I—"

"Stay here, James."

I ordered the rest of the men to follow me.

I grabbed my bag and sprinted to the pavilion ahead of Claude, Sheriff Richt, and older James. Someone had already opened the door and turned on the lights. I caught Timothy stuffing alchemy books into a bag.

I aimed my revolver at his head. "Tell me how to open the door."

20

Timothy dropped the books from his arms. "I do not know what you speak of. What door? You are standing in the only one."

"The hidden one in the floor. How do I open it?"

Sheriff Richt hustled into the room, panting. "Holster your weapon, Gideon."

I ignored him. "That seal is covering a hole, and I need to get down there at once. How do I open it?"

"He is mad," Timothy protested.

James whistled his astonishment as he and Claude entered. "So this is Old Voor's shed?"

The sheriff put at least some faith in my claims. He stomped on the bronze disc. The metallic echo rang under the floor. "I'll be darned. There is something down there."

"Do you know how to open the door?" I asked Timothy again.

"No."

My throat clenched with anger. "Tell us now!"

He fell to his knees. "I do not know," he moaned.

And I believed him.

Disheartening visions of Rose crawled into my thoughts. I had no time for interrogations. I instructed the others to search the room for a hidden mechanism that opens the door. Claude tugged at the various decorations. Sheriff Richt and I clawed books off the shelves. James at least stayed out of our way. Meanwhile, Timothy sank into one of the seats, struggling just to breathe.

After we tipped, pulled, and rolled every object in the room, I focused on the decorative bronze floor. I skittered on hands and knees over the images of stars, plants, crystals, and animals. Nothing. Nothing. Nothing.

The bird.

A hole had been bored into the eye socket of the eagle symbol. I pressed my small finger into it and felt a ridge of metal.

"Mr. Barron, did Mr. Voor carry any sort of long, slender key or staff with him whenever he came to the pavilion?"

He looked ready to weep or drink a bottle of cheap whisky from the liquor cabinet. "Not to my knowledge, but it appears there is much I did not know about him."

"What about this?" Claude picked up a three-foot-long steel shaft with a leather grip on one end and a hook on the other.

"Perfect." I shoved the instrument into the hole and, with some maneuvering, tripped a concealed latch or device.

The two pipes near the bookshelves hissed with steam. The room hummed and vibrated. After a few seconds, a ticking reminiscent of a loud, rapid clock sounded, and the round seal divided into sixteen triangular segments. The pieces descended to progressively deeper positions and formed a circular staircase.

I hurried below with my bag and lantern. Three arched doors waited at the bottom of the dark pit. Light and the stench of death seeped around the edges of one of them.

Ghoul

21

Professor Emerick, it is I, Rosette Drumlin.

Mr. Wells asked me to provide a written account of the lair belonging to one Mr. Charles Voor. The world knew him as a chemical magnate who lived in Haughtogis Point. In private, he was a repugnant man involved in the nightmarish science of biological alchemy.

The chore of providing this letter falls on me because of what I alone witnessed in the underground Voor laboratory. Furthermore, Mr. Wells is unable to write because of the tragedy that befell him. I speak of the wound he received from the creature. He currently has to write with his left hand, and his already-poor penmanship has become what can only be described as a tragedy.

This letter is an unpleasant task, one which required much coaxing for me to write it. I did not want to put these words to paper because they forced me to dwell on the things I saw. Consider this my final declaration of the events, and do not ask me questions whereupon we meet. I will not reply. It will take me quite enough time to quell the pain of the memories I now possess.

I am quite serious. Do not ask me in the future about the laboratory. I will strike you.

Here is what transpired from the time Mr. Wells and I became separated.

While I lay under the locked grate, shivering, I heard splashes in the running water. I correctly feared the worst—that the transmuted being was approaching. My situation rendered fighting and fleeing impossible. The tunnel walls pinned my arms against my ribs, and my only path of escape was cut off by an animal that had killed two men.

I stayed motionless and prayed it would ignore me. What other strategy remained?

Not only did I hear the being's raspy breaths, I felt them on my shin. Mr. Wells tried to draw it away by shouting "Here" repeatedly. Meanwhile, using the method I had been taught, I calmed myself by squeezing my fists and focusing on getting past the danger. I breathed through my wide-open mouth to be quieter, even though it meant tasting the rancid, sickening miasma of decay that poured through the grate.

My situation resurrected horrible memories from the orphanage, of times when the older boys stuffed me in a chest and sat on the lid until I nearly passed out from shouting. I felt trapped like one of the victims of Lenorso, the King of Leon who buried chained prisoners in coffins with starved rats.

Small, scaly paws marched up my shins to my knees, then they seized one of my boots. The being dragged me with surprising strength and ferocity into a deeper part of the duct. I struggled to keep my mouth above the water, and Mr. Wells's shouts quieted as my ears flooded.

The being shook my leg, slamming it against the walls. I ripped free from its grip and stomped its paw and cheek. My actions gained me a few moments of reprieve but also retaliation from the angered attacker. The being growled and clawed the skin on my calf.

I yelled, dropping the knife. The dragging resumed. After my body caught on a corner between the duct branches, the boot pulled free.

Ghoul

I could see little of the creature besides the outline of its head. When Mr. Wells crashed into the iron door and the bang reverberated like cannon fire, it snapped its ears back and convulsed. Further percussions caused it to spasm and shriek.

Excessive noise agitated it, and likely to the point of pain.

I used the opportunity to crawl away. I did not get far. The being seized me again and thrashed until it pulled off my other boot. It retreated into the black gullet of the duct with my footwear in its clutches.

This behavior intrigued me so much that once my heart stopped exploding with each rapid pulse, I crawled after it. Along the way, I recovered the dropped knife. I eventually emerged in a room lit only by faint light leaning through a doorway. As I climbed out of the drainage hole, I crawled over the mangled grate that used to cover it.

Like a mothman lured by a mob's torches, I crept toward the light, limping because of my wounds. A sensation like gnawing fire enwrapped my lower legs. I reached a hall where crates stuffed with bones and rolled animal hides were stored. Black mold covered the wall like a mural of indistinct shapes, except for one shape that looked somewhat like a hay wagon.

The air tasted sour, and the reek of death oozed down my throat with each breath.

The chamber at the end of the hall unfurled its horrors as I snuck nearer. The few electric bulbs that continued to burn mottled the shadows with swathes of dim, orange light. Hooks, saws, and knives hung from nails on the ceiling beam. Jars on a blood-stained table contained, according to my best guess, lumps of flesh with a rainbow of grotesque discolorations. The skull of a bear or wolf stared at me from atop a pile of bones. One of three brass vats in the nearest corner had rusted through and bled out a gelatinous, mustardy substance.

A golden plaque hung above the door on the far wall. The finely engraved Latin phrase on it read *De Deo errores, de homine perfectio.*

From God's mistakes, mankind's perfection.

The so-called perfections were on horrifying display in stacked cages. Red, hairless mice with spider eyes and pouches of sagging back skin. Six songbirds connected into one feathered caterpillar with spider legs and a rat skull for a head. An eel with cat jaws and white spikes hanging from a canopy of green slime. An eyeless pig that had swollen until it burst, its dried innards stuck to the surrounding floor and wall.

Those specimens accounted for only a part of the zoo of nightmares. A few of them still moved. If you are curious enough to endure descriptions of the rest, ask Mr. Wells.

I will proceed to the contents of the two large cages. In the open one lay the white-bearded corpse of a man dressed in a butcher's apron. I could tell by his desiccated appearance and the thriving maggot metropolis on his neck that he died quite some time ago. A tipped stool, a misshapen phonograph, and lengths of rope occupied the cage with him.

The other cage remained locked, and it contained the things that pain me the most to describe. An emaciated dog with multiple bald scars raised its head. Its hind legs had been replaced with useless, gangrenous human ones, and it flopped erratically like a beached fish as it tried to get away from me. The mutated dog collided with the recipient of its legs, an object I can only describe as a sack of raw flesh dressed in burlap.

The repulsive mass reached toward the hound with one of its human arms.

The abomination *reached out*, Professor. It is that forsaken image I cannot tear out of my sickened memory.

That thing with flesh like a skinned pig reached out. Mr. Wells has insisted since the incident that the thing was dead. Fully dead, cold, and not awakened like a genuine ghoul. He promised that corpses can twitch involuntarily. I made him swear he was not lying, because once I deduced what the headless mound of flesh used to be, I could not bear the thought of it still being alive.

I spotted a doll in the cage. A child's toy. My sight blurred with tears. I staggered and braced myself against a shelf covered with knives, syringes, and other instruments of torture. Grief, unlike any I have ever known, tore my heart as I tried to comprehend this handiwork of evil that surpassed all rationality.

I heard rustling beneath the table. The creature leapt out from the shadows and landed between the cage and me. It lowered its chin and chest to the floor and hissed with such ferocity that its bared fangs quivered. Its ears pointed back in a sign of clear aggression.

I raised my knife and readied to fight, but after a moment, I lowered it. The being was not hunting me. It was protecting the wretched creations in the cage the way a dog might guard her pups. And I read fear in the being. I terrified it as much as it terrified me.

In spite of the risk, while the creature clawed the ground, I knelt and laid down the knife. The creature lunged, then halted inches away from me and swatted the blade aside. Its hisses changed to an undulating growl. Spittle flew from its teeth onto my vulnerable throat.

I drew in a breath, and slowly reached out one open hand.

The being backed away and sat on its burlap-wrapped hindquarters. We stared silently at one another for perhaps a minute before it reached out and tapped my empty palm with its claws.

"If you won't hurt me, I won't hurt you," I said.

Afraid to make an unwise move, and also because I was awed by the being's behavior, I stayed there on the floor. The being dragged my stolen boots to the cage and slid them onto the swollen monstrosity's canine legs. It dressed the nightmarish mass the way a mother dresses its child—or the way I used to put shoes on the younger orphans. It also tossed bread to the dog and slid cups of water to it through the bars.

The being even spoke to the creations, though with gibbering noises rather than any discernible words. It sat in front of the cage door, held the lock, and spoke with gargles and purrs.

The Haughtogis Point mystery gave up its final secrets. The corpse in the open cage was Charles Voor, the creature's original victim. I guessed he perished when his creation escaped in violent fashion. I struggle to evoke any sympathy for him, for in addition to inflicting countless cruelties, his sins have scarred my dreams.

I tried to deny the reality of my other discovery, but further reading from the pavilion's records has since confirmed the loathsome truth. I know the identity of the creature and the caged abomination because I also know what became of the two children who disappeared from the Ragiston quarry. They are one and the same.

De Deo errores, de homine perfectio.

No, Charles Voor. If the transgressions you created were your idea of perfection, then may we all live as imperfections. The only error was the blackness of your soul, and your creation has dealt with that. You, sir, were the monster of Haughtogis Point.

Professor, you no doubt wonder what became of the transmuted being we called "ghoul." I will let Mr. Wells explain, but understand the threat it posed did not end when I made peace with it. When a gush of steam blew through pipes in the laboratory's ceiling, the being scurried into the shadows. Unseen gears whirred in another room, and a series of dull clangs sounded on the other side of the plaque door.

The noises threw the being into a fit of convulsions and growls, but it recovered by the time the door opened. It ignored or did not understand my pleas to settle down. Instead, it tensed its legs and readied to pounce, and the spines on its back writhed.

Consider this: The last person who entered through that door lay in a decaying heap on the laboratory floor.

22

I, Gideon Wells, stood outside the underground door. I had no idea of the things Rose shared in the previous letter. In order to be ready for an ambush, I pulled the net out of my shoulder bag and offered it to Claude.

"Why are you giving this to me?" he asked.

The answer should have been obvious. "Because the others have guns," I said, referring to the sheriff and James. "I need your help if we fight, and this is better than bare hands."

"You mean to catch it?"

"I mean to stop it by any means necessary." I patted the net. "This counts as any means."

Claude grimaced. "I was never trained to fight like you."

"Mr. Ragiston, I need to save my friend, and you need to redeem your family's name. Do you understand?"

He nodded. His clenched jaw and furrowed brows revealed that at least a seed of resolution had taken root inside of him.

I pulled the door open and entered with my gun at the ready. Incandescent bulbs, half of which had burned out, lit the room with a weak, flickering orange glow. Surgical and butchery tools hung from the ceiling. Iron bars formed about twenty cages of varying sizes along the back and right wall. The sights, though ghastly, were but a trifle compared to the sickening, fetid stench of waste and rotting gore.

I covered my mouth and nose. "The devil's blazes!"

Sheriff Richt heaved and held his hand over his stomach. "What horrible place is this?"

Ghoul

"Evil's birthing room."

My attention galloped from corner to corner, quickly collecting details and interpreting the vile history of the laboratory. I witnessed the same caged atrocities Rose described in the previous letter. Most of the creations had died from starvation or from the strain of their own unnatural existence. Some still lived, swelling and deflating with each growling breath.

I recoiled from something squirming close to my leg, then realized the movement came from maggots devouring a putrefied corpse. The body, which we would later identify as Charles Voor, lay beside a phonograph with a dented, mangled horn. In a neighboring cage, an injured hound wriggled beside the corpulent, lifeless remains of a failed experiment.

The grotesque discoveries spurred my urgency to find Rose. "Follow me," I said and sprinted toward a dark hallway. I traveled no more than a few steps before my accomplice stood up from one of the shadows that streaked the room. Her cheeks glistened with tears.

"Rose! Thank heavens—"

Rose shushed me and whispered, "It's here." She pointed toward her feet.

As quietly as possible, I leaned and aimed my gun around the edge of the table. The creature snarled at me like a rabid fox and uttered a gurgling hiss. I nearly pulled the trigger, but Rose waved for me to stop.

"It's human," she whispered.

How I wished she were wrong. However, the creature's torso, its burlap garment, and most of all its expression confirmed it possessed a vestige of humanity. Its darting eyes, regardless of their bestial form, conveyed desperation, anger, and a calculating mind. Charles Voor had done the unthinkable and transmuted a human.

Truth be told, I still would have shot it if not for my trust in Rose. We faced an enraged monster with a history of killing. I had no proof the creature's human elements could ever quell the savage, animal instincts that had overtaken it. Logic ordered me to end the wretch's life, a life which never should have existed. But Rose held out hope; therefore I did as well.

How then to capture it? The wise approach would have been to calmly lure it into a prepared trap, but we had the older, idiotic James with us.

He shouted "I found it" loudly enough to make even me wince. The creature folded its ears back, rustled it spines, and thrashed the air with tooth and claw.

Professor, permit me some conjecture, and consider the following. The creature killed Joseph Prentice after he found it scavenging through his grocery delivery and wounded it with his swordstaff. It attacked Mr. Hill as he smashed rocks near an entrance to the creature's lair. As for Miss Murphy, she was clawed when she screamed in close proximity to it. Pain and loud noises agitated the ghoul.

It should not then be difficult to imagine the creature's response when James fired his rifle and winged its shoulder.

Rose cried "No!" Sheriff Richt shoved the barrel of James's weapon toward the floor, but the fight was already triggered.

The creature shrieked and scrambled toward the hall while holding its wound. For a moment, I thought we would once again have to chase it, but it stopped mid-sprint and rushed at Rose. She dove out of its path and crashed into a shelf of metal and glass jars. A few fell and shattered.

The creature bounded off a cage, dashed over the table top, and pounced at James. I dove and by sheer luck grabbed one of its hind ankles, saving the boy. Both the creature and I collapsed to the floor, but it recovered more quickly than I. By the time I got to my knees, it flung itself at me and stabbed my shoulder with a swarm of its quills.

I let out a manly cry of pain and tried to shove the fiend away, but it latched onto my forearm with its teeth. A vigorous shake from its head spread the tears in my flesh. Then it released me, jerked its head up, and darted away just in time to avoid a bullet from the sheriff's revolver.

Rose called, "Gideon, are you—"

"Grab a weapon." I clambered backward to a pile of bones and leveled my revolver at the dark, cluttered space beneath the table. The ghoul took refuge in there, hiding in the clutter.

I slid my bag from my injured shoulder and reached in to take the net out. It was empty. I had forgotten I gave the net to Claude.

Sheriff Richt moved into the corner and pressed his back against the cages. His chest heaved with each breath, but at least he kept his revolver ready. The fight had been scared out of James. He fled the room and peeked ever-so-slightly from the doorway.

Claude, to my surprise, stood poised inside the entrance. He held the outstretched net in front of his body.

Rose crouched low into an animal-like posture and picked up a broken glass jar. She also pulled skinned hides out of a crate and tucked them under her arm.

"It responds to loud noises," she said.

"You and I have different definitions of 'respond.'" I raised my bloody shoulder and forearm, both of which felt like I had pried them out of a bear trap straight from the blacksmith's fire. "At least I look good in red."

"Prepare yourselves." Claude shuffled sideways into the open cage, the one with Charles Voor's corpse. Claude righted the phonograph and began to turn the crank. A choking growl emanated from under the table.

"Claude, stop." I got to my feet and crept toward him. "This is a terrible idea."

"Don't shoot it," Rose pleaded.

"It's too dangerous," I said. "I am sorry for what happened to it, but this has to end."

"It's frightened and hurt."

"What about me?" I would have rolled my eyes were I not keeping an unblinking watch for hostile movement. "What am I if not frightened and hurt?"

"We won't shoot you either."

The phonograph clicked to life, and the needle scraped over the record. String and brass instruments blared the opening of Beethoven's Fifth Symphony. The music accentuated the barbarity of the room, and even now I struggle to understand Charles Voor's apparent wisdom and culture coexisting with his depravity.

Claude's action resulted in the desired, but terrifying, effect. The creature flashed into the open, screeching. With only a couple of hops, it flew into the cage and flung the phonograph against the wall, snapping off the horn.

Claude threw the net on the creature but failed to keep his grip on it, which meant he did little more than dress the beast. It pounced on his chest and dug its claws into his sides.

I raced toward the cage. Claude was screaming in pain. In so doing, he raised his chin and exposed his jugular vein.

The creature brought its head back like a coiled rattlesnake, extended its fangs, and snapped at his neck.

I swung my open bag in front of the creature's face and caught it by its jaws, saving Claude.

My momentum wrenched young Mr. Ragiston and the creature to the ground with me. Even though blinded and muzzled by my bag, the creature continued to cut and stab us. Claws flailed and quills thrust in search of flesh.

Sheriff Richt ran toward us, but Rose moved faster. She dove over me and pulled the net taut, pinning the creature to the ground. Then she wrapped the creature's sharp bits with the skinned animal hides, placed a broken bottle of chloroform by its nose, and rubbed the back of its head.

She shushed it. "Stop now. It's over. No more fighting."

Sheriff Richt gathered rope and helped us bind its limbs. After a few minutes, the creature stopped tensing and its eyelids drooped. Eventually it fell asleep to Rose's purring hums.

Claude and I finally let go of the beast and examined our wounds. Our shirts bathed in our blood. His ashen cheeks puffed out as he held his breath and endured the pain.

I nudged his boot with mine. "You get the doctor," I said, "and I'll get the wine."

POSTSCRIPT

Professor, it has been several weeks since you took over the research of Haughtogis Point. I wish to provide some closure with this letter, at least for the time being.

I am mostly healed of my injuries, though that has not stopped Emily, my betrothed, from fretting over every stitch. I cannot so much as ride my horse without her going into fits. I suppose this is partly my doing, what with exaggerating my pain for the sake of some added doting from her.

Based on a message I received yesterday, Claude is mending as well. The festering injury to his family's name will take longer to heal, though.

Claude and Ida's inheritance, both the house and the employees, suffered years of neglect under their grandfather. News about the creature could have incited a riot. Claude thanked me in his telegram for crediting him with capturing the so-called ghoul. My boasts about him greatly improved his reputation, and people who once avoided the young Ragistons now approach and greet them.

But more mending is needed. Before I left, I spoke with them at length about changing the way his managers operated the quarry, and I recommended Mr. Carter or my brothers as counsels. They agreed.

Of course, a heavy hand in business pales in comparison to transmuting human beings into monsters. Leonard Ragiston played his part in the experiments. He coordinated the mining of necessary resources like ruthenium, and he assisted in surgeries on multiple occasions. But the sins belonged chiefly to Charles Voor, who owned the laboratory and the knowledge of alchemy. The man was depravity incarnate.

What more can be said about Charles Voor besides that he was an evil lunatic of the highest order? He performed his "research"—normal people would call it torture—to develop enhancements for mankind and animals. He claimed in his journals he wished to develop cures for diseases, malformations, and other impediments in life. He somehow imagined his endeavors to be noble in spite of the revolting truth drooling and convulsing in front of him.

When I study Charles Voor's writings, I recognize a man who gorged on his own lies until his soul choked on a bone. His musings about bettering humanity were rubbish. He dissected, stretched, and amputated boundaries of decency and morality for one raw, simple reason.

Because he could.

To justify his curiosities, he fitted and stacked questionable ideas until he constructed a worldview that reduced people to mere matter. I wish I could say his ideas died with him, but the writings reference a likeminded group known as the Chimera Society. There are other alchemists in this world. Unfortunately, the only one I can identify is Major General Ethan Hitchcock, who died in 1870.

I will continue to investigate this matter.

You probably heard the butler, Timothy Barron, passed away. Did you also know he, like Charles Voor and Leonard Ragiston, had a bead of silver, or rather ruthenium, buried in his chest? I never determined what measure of guilt he bore. Based on the notes, it seems Charles Voor did pretend to leave for Canada, then slipped away to the laboratory for a few weeks of uninterrupted work.

Timothy may not have known about the laboratory, the kidnapped children, or the experiments on the animals. He knew enough to feel guilty, though. He was the only member of the Voor house staff who moved to Haughtogis Point with Charles twenty years ago. Both men changed their names throughout the decades. And Timothy received the same blood-soaked ruthenium in his chest as the others. Its power had run dry by the time I arrived at his door, hence his illness.

I have not been able to calculate his or Charles Voor's age, but both men lived for more than a century. May the worms find an appetite for those shriveled, old prunes.

I know you requested to read Mr. Voor's writings for yourself. I am still undecided about whether to disclose them, to you or anyone. I trust you, Professor, but I worry that you or other researchers may be tempted to tinker with biological alchemy. The tug of curiosity would be fierce. Whoever started down that path would eventually cross their personal ethical boundaries with a few acrobatic leaps of logic.

For now, I am also keeping the creature in a quiet, secured place. Rose has grown quite protective of him. She demands I refer to him as "him," not "it." She will not allow him to be studied and dissected. She visits him and hums songs, and I confess, he seems to enjoy her company. Sadly, I doubt she can domesticate the creature enough for him to be released from his enclosure.

Charles Voor's writings confirmed the creature and the thing locked up with the dog were the boy and girl who disappeared from the quarry three years ago. I wrestled with that knowledge for days before looking for the parents, all the while wondering if revealing the painful truth would be a mistake.

People remembered the children, but none could identify a single relative. That led me to believe Mr. Ragiston specifically chose orphans for the alchemical experiments. Fate poured too much cruelty into their young lives.

I conclude with a report on Rose. Her legs have healed splendidly, but she aches inside. She struggled for days after the case because the cruelty shown to the children and animals pierced uniquely tender parts of her heart. The pain drove her to oversee the creature's recovery and to care for the dog we rescued from the Voor laboratory.

We of course had to amputate the human legs attached to the hound. Rose built a cart for it, and now it follows her around like a furry, two-legged wheelbarrow.

As for the other creations, I personally made sure all were completely dead, then buried them. Our little ghoul had managed to keep some alive with food and water, but none had much fight left in them.

Rose has been more willing to talk about the case of late. Recently while we sat feeding ducks by the river, I asked her what should be done about the creature.

"Keep him alive, and take good care of him," she said.

"But he labors just to breathe, and his unnatural body aches."

"As long as his humanity is in question, we must err on the side of caution. If we ignore the things that make him human just so our decision is easier, we become a small reflection of Mr. Voor."

"Are you still getting nightmares?" I asked.

"On some nights." She threw a handful of breadcrumbs into the crowd of ducks. They beat their wings and raced for the largest pieces. "I'll sleep better when I can forgive him."

"Forgive who?"

"Mr. Voor."

"You don't need to forgive him. He's dead, nor does he deserve it."

"Mother superior used to say forgiveness is soap for the soul. I want the memory scrubbed away."

I tousled her hair. "You will be fine. Time heals."

"So does wine, correct?"

I bit my lip and sighed. "Not as well as you think. It disappoints me to know you want to forgive him. I hoped you would stay angry enough to help me hunt down his friends in the Chimera Society."

Rose stared at me with her unique, emotionless expression. "Why should forgiveness stop me from helping? I want to catch every one of those villains, Mr. Wells. I want alchemy to become myth again."

"That's good to hear. Without you, I would need to hire on James as my apprentice."

She smiled. "You are too hard on the boy. Stop blaming him just because you were too slow to avoid getting bitten."

"You're right." She so often is.

I will soon be healed enough for new work. My next hunt will not be for monsters but for the society that creates them.

So tell me, Professor, do you have leads on any other cases that might involve alchemy?

Wrong Number

Jordan tipped back his water bottle and guzzled every drop. His legs burned as he trudged up his apartment building's steps. A training run shouldn't have exhausted him this close to a race, but was the setback all that surprising? Idling away a month's free time was a terrible way to prepare for a half-marathon. Unless his stamina rebounded over the next two weeks, he had no hope of winning.

The wood-paneled hallway at the top of the stairs seemed twice as long as before his run. He plodded to his door, wrestled with the doorknob to get his key to turn, and entered his sparsely furnished apartment.

On the way to his bedroom, he found his Aussie roommate, Pete Miller, seated at the table in the kitchen. He was slumped over his smartphone. The device's glow highlighted the bags under his eyes and three days of stubble growth on his chin.

They'd been friends since Pete moved to the States with his family in tenth grade. They attended college together, pledged to the same fraternity, and fought side-by-side in two separate fistfights, both of which Pete had provoked. In all those years, Jordan had never seen him look as distraught as he did that morning.

Through heaving, post-run breaths, Jordan said, "I should've started training sooner."

Pete didn't answer. He dragged his finger over the phone's screen, panning through a list of text messages.

"Jeesh, you look more tired than me. Did you go out last night?"

It wouldn't have surprised him. It had been Friday night after all, and over the last few weeks, Pete had begun frequenting bars again. Finally. He seemed to be coming out of the funk that settled over him after his girlfriend, Courtney, left him.

Jordan waited a moment for Pete to respond. His roommate closed the text messages and opened his pictures. *What's up with him?*

Louder, he said, "Hey, Pete? I'm back from my run."

Pete blinked repeatedly at Jordan before showing any recognition. "How was it?"

"Terrible. Thirty-eight seconds slower than Thursday. What's up with you this morning?"

"Nothing. Just … some bad news is all."

"What happened?" Jordan's already racing heart added a nervous beat. "Did someone pass away?"

"It's a family thing. Nobody you know."

"Are you gonna be all right?" Jordan asked.

"I'm fine," Pete insisted to no one in particular.

"Yeah? Well, EMTs also tell trauma patients they're 'fine' while they bleed out."

Pete stood and walked away. He held the phone close to his body and out of Jordan's sight as he scanned through it.

"Don't take up the bathroom. I need to wash."

Jordan huddled for a long time under the shower's weak stream. He paused repeatedly while scrubbing, unable to move on from the look he had seen on Pete's face. His eyes had been so intense. What could have put his friend into such a state of—what kind of state was he in? Depression? Shock?

And what's with being secretive all of a sudden?

The situation was unclear, but his response was not. Pete clearly needed help, regardless of what he said. Plus, Jordan needed to redeem himself. He hadn't exactly been supportive when Pete's relationship with Courtney broke down.

After dressing in shorts and a casual button-down shirt, Jordan sought out his roommate. He was sitting at the end of his bed, staring at his phone as if waiting for it to cure whatever ailed him.

Jordan knocked on the open bedroom door. "Hey, you wanna head out to get some fresh air and lunch? It's my first Saturday not on call in a long time."

Pete looked up and licked his lips. "I guess I could." His muttered tone strengthened his accent.

"Just tell me, man. Did something happen to a distant relative, like a grandparent or cousin? Do you need to fly back home?"

"No. Nobody died." Pete checked the phone once more, then pocketed it.

"Courtney giving you a hard time?" Jordan's lips puckered toward the end of the failed, stupid joke, but there was no taking it back. He tried to salvage it with an awkward grin.

Pete sucked in half a breath and said a drawn-out "No." He blinked rapidly. "It's not Courtney."

Did he just lie? Jordan couldn't tell. Regardless, he swallowed a pang of guilt.

"I'm going to shower, too. Can you give me a few minutes?"

"Sure." He watched to see if Pete would leave his phone on the charger or someplace else where Jordan could peek at it. Unfortunately, Pete kept it in his pocket when he stepped into the bathroom and shut the door.

He emerged from his room ten minutes later, dressed and wearing sunglasses. His blond hair was still damp. He looked refreshed, both mentally and physically.

"You ready to go, mate?"

"I was waiting on you." Jordan slid off the counter he was sitting on. "Want to go to She-Brew's?" It was a bit early for drinking, and She-Brew's Tavern wouldn't open for another fifteen minutes, but they both could use a bigger distraction than coffee.

"No, let's go out and get some sun. But can we swing by my parents' place first to pick something up?"

"They're all the way out in Westfield. We'd have to take my car."

Pete shrugged. "Do you mind?"

Jordan sighed and picked up his keys. *I owe it to him.* "Fine."

The half-hour drive was a quiet one, not including the country music. Pete usually changed the radio to a different station—any other station—but not that day. Instead, he maintained a silent watch over his phone, opening the frequent text messages as they appeared.

Jordan tried to kindle conversation. He brought up topics like Australian Rules Football and Pete's job at the bank, but every response was briefer than the incessant phone vibrations. His concern grew. Lacking an explanation for their bizarre morning, he imagined them on his own. Drug problem? Gambling debt?

"Who's texting you so often?" Jordan asked.

Pete angled the screen away from him. "It's nobody you know."

"Okay, but how do *you* know them? Is it family or someone from work?" Jordan elbowed Pete's bicep. "A new girlfriend, maybe?" *That would certainly help him move on.*

"It's hard to explain, and it's a bit of a personal matter." Pete's phone illuminated with another new message. He flicked his hand over the glass.

Jordan couldn't steal a glance at the text, but he could see behind Pete's shades. His roommate's eyes repeatedly widened and narrowed.

He parked in front of the Millers' home, a white split-level surrounded by three broad oak trees. One or both of Pete's parents were likely away, given that their blue Mazda was missing from the driveway.

Pete climbed out. "I'll be right back."

"Do you want me to wait here?"

"Yeah." He shoved the car door shut and jogged across the groomed yard.

He'd left his phone in the cup holder.

Jordan glanced up three times at Pete, making sure he wasn't turning back to get it. As soon as Pete unlocked the front door and entered the house, Jordan turned the phone toward himself.

The phone shivered like a startled animal, and he recoiled. It had vibrated with another new message. The wallpaper image, a selfie of Pete, Courtney, and Jordan at Myrtle Beach, glowed on the screen.

Should I check it? He tensed at the thought of snooping, but it felt like he was being dragged into something serious. Pete was a great guy but not immune to bad decisions. He could be a reactive hothead. Maybe he ticked off the wrong kind of people when he went out to a bar or club. Maybe he slept with someone's girlfriend.

Courtney. The hidden text conversation might involve her, in spite of him insisting otherwise. His earlier reactions to her name suggested that was a possibility. But that ship had sailed, and she was not the kind of spiteful person to dig into someone else's wounds, unless—

No, she wouldn't have mentioned what Jordan did, would she? It might explain why Pete was being so elusive, but what gain would there be in that?

A door slammed. Jordan looked up with a gasp. The sound came from two houses down the street. A woman in heels was hurrying to her car.

Jordan's heart was racing.

He checked the Millers' house again. The door remained closed, and Pete was nowhere in sight.

The phone awoke when he picked it up. The message alert hovered near the top, taunting him from above the nine dots on the unlock screen. He would need to draw the correct pattern to access the messages. Jordan thought back on the times he'd seen Pete connecting dots with his thumb—a vertical line with a hook to the left.

He swiped through the center dots and veered to the upper-left corner. Nothing. The attempt had failed.

After another quick glance at the house, Jordan tried a similar pattern, then a third. None of them worked. *How many times can I try before it locks me out?*

Finally, he swiped up the right side and back to the center. A dozen app icons appeared.

He was in.

He went immediately to the messages. The latest one had come from someone not saved on Pete's contact list. 686-3223. The number looked familiar, and it had a local area code, but the name was missing. The anonymity of the sender amplified the creepiness of the text. He felt a sudden chill, as if an arctic wind had blown through the car.

"Are you afraid of what I'll do?????????"

Jordan shivered at what he read. Was it a warning? A taunt? Scrolling up, he found equally disturbing messages without any replies from Pete.

"What's worse? Telling everyone my secret or telling no one?"

"Are you sure you know where I am? Someone else does."

"Isn't it?"

"It's killing you not knowing, isn't it?"

This is some seriously messed-up psycho business.

Something moved in the corner of Jordan's eye. He spotted Pete sprinting toward him in the rearview mirror. His roommate had come around the side of the house.

Jordan hurriedly shut off the phone and dropped it in the cup holder, hoping he hadn't been caught.

Pete banged on the trunk of the car.

Shoot! He did see me.

"Can you open the boot?" Pete called.

Jordan tightened his chest, trying to slow his breath. "Sure." He pulled the lever, and the trunk popped open.

Pete tossed a plastic bag inside, and its contents landed with a thud and clanked together. He slammed the trunk shut and hurried to the passenger seat, then immediately checked his phone.

Jordan froze with his hand on the ignition key, waiting to be accused of messing with the phone. But if Pete knew, he didn't show it.

"Where to next?" Jordan asked. *Stop acting nervous.*

"How about the park?"

"Which one?" Jordan forced a smile to mask the worry pounding the back of his mind.

"Reuben Creek Park," Pete answered flatly.

Reuben Creek? Why would he choose there? He has to know more than he's letting on.

Jordan rolled his shoulder, wiping away the bead of sweat rolling down his neck. "Why not Chester Park? They have the farmers' market on Saturday."

"Reuben Creek is along the way."

Feigning indifference, and probably failing terribly at it, Jordan said, "I wish I'd known. We're not dressed for hiking."

"We don't need to hike. I just want to visit a favorite spot. Clear my head, y'know?"

"Okay." Jordan started the car and pulled away from the Millers' home. He turned off the radio, eliminating the distraction. Instead, he focused on the phone number he'd seen, committing it to memory.

He drove down the parkway, past miles of business signs from various decades. Every stop at a red light was both a relief and a jolt of tension; he wanted to know what was going on but simultaneously dreaded finding out. He headed to the main entrance of the park, the one likely to have lots of people around.

"Can we go to the North Gate, please?" Pete asked. He had been silently staring ahead for most of the drive.

A resurgence of worry pulsed through Jordan's body. *He must know what I did, or at least suspect it. I should just apologize and get it over with.*

"Brake!" Pete shouted.

They were rushing toward a line of stopped cars. Jordan jammed the brakes. The tires squealed, and they lurched forward against their seat belts. The car came to a jarring halt only a foot from the rear bumper of a white sedan.

Pete let loose a string of "bloody" curses as he tugged his seatbelt, loosening the shoulder strap.

"Sorry. I'm sorry." Jordan released the steering wheel and flexed his pale, stiff fingers.

"What are you trying to do?"

"I said I'm sorry. I got distracted. Look, we're almost at the South Gate. Can't we just go in there?"

"The North Gate is closer to where I'm headed, and I want to avoid a long walk. I promise this won't be long."

He wants to see how I react. "Fine, but you're buying me a drink later." *Two can play at this game.* "Has Courtney called you lately?"

Pete didn't say "no." He laid his phone on his lap and looked out the side window.

That confirms it. It involves her.

The North Gate was more secluded. It featured a small, gravel parking area and access to a dirt jogging path that followed short, plump evergreen trees into the heart of the woods. Only two other vehicles were parked there, and their passengers had wandered out of sight.

Pete fumbled through an excuse about needing a few minutes alone, then collected his bag from the trunk and headed down the trail. His pace wavered between a fast walk and a slow jog.

The North Gate was one of Jordan's favorite spots, not Pete's. The undulating, scenic terrain was perfect for serious runners trying to improve their conditioning—people like him. Pete preferred the gym and weight benches when he exercised. Had he ever visited this part of Reuben Creek without Jordan in tow?

That didn't matter right now. He finally had a chance to contact the person who had been sending the texts. Using his own phone, he typed, "This is Pete. My phone died. Please contact me on this one instead." Then he entered the stranger's number, and it automatically updated to someone saved on his contact list.

Courtney.

Jordan hit send.

Courtney and Pete's breakup had not been bitter enough to warrant how they were acting. Why had Pete refused to admit she was sending the messages? And what "secret" was she taunting him with?

You know well what secret. It's the one that's been killing you. If he brought you here, then he knows about you and Courtney.

Jordan was a flurry of tics as he waited for his phone to respond. His knee shook, his teeth chewed his lips, and his fingers drummed on the door. It looked like his friendship with Pete was all but over. He wouldn't be forgiven for cheating with Courtney, especially since it happened right before she left.

A message from Courtney appeared on his screen.

"MEET ME IN THE PLACE WHERE WE LAST GOT TOGETHER."

"No, no, no," he said in gunfire-like repetition. Jordan bolted from the car and sprinted down the trail. The rush of adrenaline purged his muscles of all fatigue from his morning run.

Her message was identical to the one she'd sent before their last rendezvous at Reuben Creek. Did Courtney know she was actually contacting him, or did she buy the lie that Pete was using his phone? Either way, she was waiting in the park, and Pete was heading toward her.

Jordan hurried over the first forested rise, then veered from the main trail down a narrow, rarely used path to the creek. His legs slapped through the ferns that leaned over the deer trail, and the sun blinked like a strobe light through the passing canopy. The air was warm and heavy, devoid of any breeze, and he began to sweat heavily through his shirt.

Coming around an outcropping of boulders and birch trees, he spotted the back of Pete's blue shirt at the bottom of the slope. His roommate was kneeling behind a lip of earth and brush, where the forest ended abruptly and dropped several feet into the creek bed. Because the water had receded to its summer low, it flowed only near the tall, cliff-like opposite shore. The rest of the bed had dried into a wide swath of stone and mud.

Pete must have heard Jordan's footsteps because he popped up and scrambled onto the trail. He stood less than ten yards from the last place Jordan met up with Courtney.

"You didn't need to come." He brushed soil off his empty hands and glanced over his shoulder. "I'm almost done. Just a few more minutes of quiet and meditation, and I'll be ready to get some lunch."

Jordan slowed to a stop. He balled his hands into loose fists and pressed them against his thighs. *Here goes nothing.*

"Pete, I know why you're down here. I know Courtney's been texting you."

Pete's eyebrows shot up from behind his sunglasses. He glanced back at the creek again. His mouth hung open for several seconds. "This has nothing to do with her."

"It's her number. She's the one contacting you and making you freak out this morning, and probably for a few days now. You've seemed off lately."

Pete stepped back awkwardly. He stumbled and nearly fell. When he looked toward the creek for the third time, Jordan tried to follow his suspicious gaze.

"It's not her, mate. It's someone else using her phone, and it set me off. It reminded me how much I miss her."

Jordan blew out a long breath through pursed lips. His pulse beat loudly behind his eardrums. "I'm sorry, man. Maybe that's true, but you've figured out at least part of the story if you're down here. Courtney and I started running here a few months ago. We'd meet up and train together, but then … we eventually did more than just run. I slept with her a couple times."

Pete's expression tightened as if someone were pulling the skin on the back of his head. His face reddened. "You? It was *you?*"

Jordan moved his hands up and down, patting the air between them. "I'm sorry. It wasn't like that for a long time, and it only happened after she admitted she was thinking about breaking up with you. It still sucks, I know, and the regret has been eating me up for weeks."

His confession was not only true but an understatement. Wrestling with coming clean had wrecked many nights' sleep. After Courtney broke up with Pete, Jordan lost his ambition to run and stopped talking to her. Maybe the relationship had been doomed, but he still felt guilty for getting involved near the end.

Jordan felt fifty pounds lighter without the shameful secret riding on his shoulders, but he couldn't relax while bracing for the response. Pete could be explosively animated and temperamental when angry. Jordan expected a verbal tirade. In fact, he deserved one. But he hoped their decade-long friendship had earned enough grace to prevent punches from being thrown.

After a long, brooding pause, Pete mouthed soundless words. He turned his head back and forth, as if trying to figure out where he was and how he'd gotten there. His breaths became loud and staggered.

"I'm sorry, man," Jordan said.

Pete's eyes flared like flames agitated by wind.

"I never meant to betray you like this, and neither did Courtney. It just sort of—"

Pete grabbed Jordan by his shirt, spun, and threw him toward the creek.

He tore through wiry brush and tumbled down the four-foot embankment. Fireworks of pain exploded through his body. A boom shot through his head when he crashed into the rocks, and deep cuts fired hot, crackling aches down his back and limbs.

Groaning, Jordan rolled to his side. "Pete, I'm sorry! Stop!"

Pete stomped toward him down a gravel ramp. His buttoned shirt strained against his tensed muscles and heaving breaths. He brandished his phone and screamed, "*I knew she was cheating on me!* She sent a message to me by mistake, telling me to meet in this park. I caught her standing out here, but she wouldn't tell me who the stupid bastard was. And it was *you* the whole time! It's *your* fault."

Jordan needed to retreat, to give Pete space to cool off. He managed to push himself into a seated position, but as soon as he tried to stand, his faltering balance pulled him back down. His vision swayed, then half of it vanished as he closed one eye, shutting out the blood flowing from his wounded eyebrow.

Yet in spite of his pain, dizziness, and fear, Jordan's focus snared on a nearby bit of familiar yellow cloth on the ground.

Spit flew from Pete's lips as he yelled, "Who is texting me from Courtney's phone? Is it you? How? I broke it and threw it in a lake, and somebody's *still* sending me messages from it."

A disorienting chill washed over Jordan. The implications of Pete's questions collided with the sickening recognition of what he had discovered. Garden spades from the Millers' house lay next to the plastic bag Pete had used to carry them. He'd used the tools to dig into the sloped soil on the bank, exposing a gray, decaying hand. A white purse and a strip of yellow cloth also protruded from the dirt.

Courtney used to wear a yellow dress of the same color, and she always paired it with a white purse.

"Oh, Pete, what did you do?"

Pete picked up a rock the size of a softball and held it menacingly by his ear. He shouted, "Tell me who has the phone."

"I don't know what you're talking about."

"Tell me *now*." Pete moved within striking distance.

Jordan scrambled away over the rough ground. "Pete, don't do this."

A blue glow reflected off Pete's sunglasses, and he looked up. For a moment, he backed up in slow motion, his mouth gaping. Then he turned and rushed toward the bank, screaming in a horrifying, high-pitched voice. He didn't get far.

The source of the blue light glided over Jordan. It was an azure vapor shaped like a human dressed in strips of flowing cloth. It wrapped ethereal tendrils around Pete, tore the rock out his hand, and smashed it into the side of his head. Pete's screams stopped, replaced by the sound of blood splattering on stone. He collapsed onto the raised ground where he'd buried Courtney's corpse.

The specter descended onto Pete's body, wrapping its form around his legs and hips. Jordan caught a glimpse of the specter's face and recognized her. *Courtney*. Her cheeks were gaunt, and her frozen eyes were filled with the same icy blue diffused throughout her body, but without a doubt, it was her. The specter's head bore a concave wound similar to the one she'd given Pete.

Courtney's ghost acted unaware or disinterested in his presence while it went about its task of dragging Pete's body into the ground. Both she and her dead murderer slid into the earth as if it were no more than a curtain to the underworld. The earth devoured them inch-by-inch, and in a matter of seconds, they were gone. Vanished.

He was alone.

Jordan snapped out of his trance of confusion and disbelief. His pain hadn't eased, but his dizziness had. He approached Courtney's body slowly, testing the ground before each step to make sure he wouldn't be devoured by it as well. He tugged her exposed white purse out of the dirt, and as he did so, his fingers brushed against the cold, spongy flesh of the corpse's hand. The sensation, as well as the stench, turned his stomach.

Jordan opened the purse, looking for evidence to prove the identity of the body. The wallet was missing, but he did find Courtney's phone. It had been crushed, its back cover and battery had been removed, and water dripped from its circuit boards, but it was there.

Wrong Number

***

Jordan couldn't tell if the cramped, yellow interrogation room was warm or frigid. He shivered, and his hairs stood erect from the goose bumps on his arms, but he was also sweating. The air reeked of the dirt caked on his clothes and hands. Or maybe the smell was in his mind, a lingering residue from the nightmarish experience of digging Courtney's decaying body out of the ground.

At some point—he couldn't remember when—he'd apparently called the police. They arrived at the crime scene en masse, spotted Courtney's remains, and ushered him out of the creek in handcuffs. A lengthy interrogation ensued, and even though he was completely honest, the police seemed skeptical of his story.

He didn't know how his situation would progress. Would they think him a liar and arrest him for murder? Would he have to go through psychological testing? One of the officers had suggested the specter was a hallucination from his head wound. Better for him to be considered a concussion victim than a murderer, but neither affirmed the truth of what happened to Courtney.

Two doors opened, and he looked first at the one in the mirror, then at the real door. The tall, gray-haired policeman with a moustache walked in. Just as he had during the interrogation, he maintained a firm, solemn expression. He had Jordan's phone in his hand.

"The chief says we're going to let you go home for now, but you are not to leave the area, do you understand?"

Jordan nodded. He should have been relieved at the news, but he felt numb.

"It's best for you if you remain cooperative. We'll be stopping by your apartment and calling you while we finish our investigation. If we can't find you, you'll have half the officers in this state chasing you down. Understand?"

Jordan nodded again.

"Here's your phone." He set it on the table. "You can make any calls that you need to while I get your paperwork ready."

The officer closed the door, leaving Jordan isolated once more. His eyes warmed, and he almost succumbed to another bout of tears. Grief morphed into confusion as he recalled the blue figure and Pete's death. The cops were not the only ones having difficulty believing what he'd seen.

Questions about the mysterious text messages drummed steadily as a heartbeat. Who had contacted Pete? How had they come from Courtney's destroyed phone? Why torment him rather than just contact the police?

Jordan dialed Courtney's number and raised the phone to his ear. The call connected to her voicemail, so he hung up. He couldn't bear listening to her recorded voice. It triggered anguish over her death and terror at the thought of her blue spirit.

Guilt that had taken weeks to ease weighed heavily on his chest again. If only he could apologize one more time, to both Courtney and Pete. If he hadn't screwed up and betrayed his friendship, they might both be alive.

Jordan brought up Pete's info on his phone. He smiled at a picture of the two of them in their graduation caps and gowns. Then he typed "I'm sorry" and sent it to Pete's number. He'd never see it, but it was the best Jordan could do.

Wrong Number

After a few seconds, a text response appeared on the screen, one that caused him to throw the phone against the wall. He fell out of his chair, yelling and shielding his body.

The message read, "THIS WAS YOUR FAULT."

The Parable on Thorne Ave *was my second story published in an anthology. I included it in this collection as a "Bonus Story" because it's not a speculative fiction (fantasy/sci-fi) tale like the others.*

It still bears resemblances to the other stories, such as its use of allegory and the inclusion of an "Easter egg." (A few stories in the collection possess what I consider Easter eggs — have fun searching, all who are so inclined.)

Bonus Story
THE PARABLE ON THORNE AVE

Luke Shepherd rolled over in bed toward his grumbling cell phone. He made a half-conscious attempt to grab it but struck the corner of the nightstand instead.

"Ow!" He rubbed the back of his throbbing hand. Awakened by the pain, he picked up the phone on his second try.

"Is it work?" his wife, Leah, mumbled from the other side of the bed.

The brief phone vibration meant he had received a text message. If it was his manager, he would have gotten a call instead.

He realized who was contacting him while his sight was still focusing enough to read. His pulse quickened. He squinted against the screen's garish light, and the blurry letters sharpened into view.

"No. It's Dina."

Their oldest daughter.

His wife threw off the covers and raced out of their bedroom toward Dina's room.

She won't be there.

He reread the text: plz come pick me up. Luke dialed his sixteen-year-old daughter, and while the phone rang, he glanced at the clock. 1:54.

His wife returned to the bedroom and flipped on the lights, causing them both to wince at the sudden brightness. Her face was stitched with worry.

"She's gone again. Where did she go?"

Luke hung up and redialed. "I'm finding out," he said with forced calmness, trying to reassure his bride of twenty years. "It went to voicemail."

Dina's screaming ringback tone blared through the speaker until another text alert interrupted it. The new message read: plz dad.

Luke sighed. As usual, she was communicating only through text messages and refusing to speak over the phone. He typed: Where are you?

They waited through seconds that felt like minutes. Leah paced at the foot of the bed, her hands clasped against her chin, fear and anger swirling in her searching gaze. Luke remained in bed, clenching his phone, but he felt the same as she did.

The reply text appeared on his screen. "She's at Thorne Park playground," he said.

Leah hurried toward her dresser, but Luke gestured for her to stop. "No, no, I'll go. She contacted me."

His wife turned sharply toward him. "Luke, I need to help her."

"What you need to do is let me handle this." He rolled out of bed and hugged her. "Please, stay here with the other kids while I get her. In the meantime, try to stay calm and pray she's safe."

She puffed up and started to say something, then sighed. He was asking a lot of her. Of course she wanted to rush out to Dina's aid, but he handled these situations better than she did. There was no telling how their daughter would react if Leah intervened.

Leah mouthed "Okay," then bit her lip. Tears bled from her reddening eyes.

"Are you going to be ok?" Luke asked.

She stepped away from him and threw her arms up. "I don't know, Luke. What have I done wrong?" Her voice wavered. "I mean, I've tried to bring her up right. I warned her about what a mess I made of my life at her age, you know, so she wouldn't have to go through all the same mistakes. I thought she was smarter than this."

"She is smarter than this, but smarts are not her problem."

Leah's expression hardened. "Go get her. And she is going to be in such big—"

He cut her off with his hand. "I said I'll handle this, and yelling when she comes through the door won't help."

Luke put on a pair of jeans and fleece sweater, then made his way through the dark house. He checked on their son as he passed by the boy's room. He was sleeping soundly by the glow of his nightlight. Luke likewise checked on their middle daughter, who was only a year away from joining Dina in high school. She too was fast asleep.

He navigated the barely lit stairs without issue, but en route through the living room, he crushed his toe against the leg of the sofa. The bones in his foot chattered against one another. Sucking air through his teeth, Luke withheld a cry of pain and limped to the garage.

The garage's metal door rolled up with a hum. Cool night air rushed in and sapped what little warmth remained from the previous day. Luke put on his shoes, an act which heightened the throbbing in his foot, then slid into their SUV. As he started the vehicle, he noticed Dina's rusted blue scooter just beyond the front bumper.

She used to ride that scooter for hours. It had since been handed down to her sister and then her brother, but they never smiled as widely on it as she once did. Now Dina stuck to her bike, which was missing from the garage. Again. He knew where she had ridden to. Her boyfriend, Liam, lived with his mother only a block from Thorne Park.

Luke backed out of the driveway and sped down the vacant suburban street. The night was submerged in a sea of churning fog, and the streetlights projected seemingly tangible cones of light in the mist. The only other glow came from his headlamps. The whole neighborhood was asleep save for the Shepherd family.

Please let her be all right. That thought, his dual-purpose hope and prayerful plea, played on repeat in his mind.

He sped down several residential streets and then, after rolling through another stop sign, turned onto Thorne Ave. A half mile later, he came to a hasty stop at the park. The beams from the vehicle's headlamps reached only a short distance into the consuming fog, but it was far enough to illuminate the two-story playground. In the drifting mist, it looked liked a ship on the move.

A small figure was seated on the lowest platform, thighs clutched to her chest, chin resting on her bent knees.

The Parable on Thorne Ave

Luke stepped out of the SUV, wincing when he put weight on his tender foot. He walked toward the playground. The night was silent, save the hum of a dim, faulty streetlight above the parking lot. Luke was halfway to the fog-shrouded figure before she coalesced enough for him to identify her.

"Dina?"

Still curled up, Dina raised her head and looked at him. She had been crying. Her tears had stolen from her dark, painted eyes and stained her cheeks.

"Dina, I'm here to take you home."

She released her legs and swiped a forearm across her nose, sniffing hard. Without saying anything, she picked up her phone, slid off the platform, and righted her bike. She began to push it past him.

Dina's unzipped, oversized sweatshirt exposed her outfit underneath. She was wearing a small pair of jean shorts and a black tank top with scrawled, misshapen hearts on it. The headlights and fog exaggerated the contrast between Dina's pale face, darkened eyes, and tri-colored hair.

"Dina, talk to me. What happened?" Anger kindled within him. He already knew the answer; he only needed confirmation.

She stopped with the bike between them.

"I don't want to talk about it." That had practically become her catchphrase in recent years. "Can you just take me home?"

"Dina, tell me."

Stronger, "Nothing happened."

A teenager who sneaks out at night doesn't ask for a ride over "nothing."

Luke clenched his fists, then slowly opened his hands and released his caught breath. He drew out his plea. "Dina, just be honest for once. Did Liam hurt you?"

"No," she snapped. "Liam has nothing to do with this. I just want to go home and go to bed, all right? I have a test in bio tomorrow morning."

"That's not important right now." He tried to touch her shoulder, but she recoiled. "Did he hit you?"

Dina buried her gaze into her hip pocket. She mumbled, "No, he didn't do anything like that."

"Dina, please, just tell me. I know something's wrong."

"But you'll freak."

"No." Anger flared up within him in anticipation of the imminent truth, but he kept it in check. "I need you to talk to me."

She looked in every direction except toward his face. "He"—she briefly bit her lip—"asked, and I told him yes, but—"

Dina choked on the tears dammed up inside of her. "Then I just wanted it to stop, but it was too late. I made a mistake, okay?"

His anger surged into tenuously restrained fury. Luke's lips twisted into a scowl, and his muscles tensed beneath his shirt. "Did he force himself on you?"

Dina's head fell forward, and she began to wail. She shook her head with a hollow 'no.'

"I need to have a little chat with him," he growled. Thoughts of pummeling the punk into the floor played in the back of his mind. Luke started toward Liam's house, but he heard Dina's bike crash to the ground, and a hand grabbed his arm.

Dina pleaded through sobs. "No, it's not his fault. I told him yes. I told him yes." She gasped for air. "He doesn't know I didn't really want to go that far. I mean, I thought I did, but after ..."

Her lips kept moving, but the words melted into incomprehensible moans.

All at once, Luke's attention returned to Dina. Healing compassion overpowered his vengeful anger. Liam could wait. He wrapped his arms around his beloved daughter, her cold skin soaking up his warmth. She sobbed into his shoulder.

Dina kept her arms between his chest and hers. When she had regained her composure, she pushed out of his embrace and shuffled into the back seat of the SUV.

Luke collected her bike and secured it to the roof rack, wondering the whole time what to say or do. He considered confronting Liam in spite of Dina's protest, but he settled on taking her home. Luke slipped into the driver's seat and glanced back at her. Dina was resting her head against the side window and staring down the street. The only thing visible in that direction was an illuminated CLOSED sign. The fog blushed with its diffused red glow.

The sign belonged to a diner. "Are you hungry?" he asked. Dina didn't reply, so he took the SUV out of park and pulled out onto the street. He drove slower now that the urgency had passed.

She said nothing. He could feel her retreating into the same pit of silence she had been hiding in for months. He glanced at her in his rearview mirror.

"Are you feeling any better?" he asked, inviting her to conversation.

Dina merely rolled her eyes, then texted someone with her phone. The screen's blue glow illuminated her face and reflected off her nose and lip rings. He and Leah hadn't been pleased when she came home with the piercings without asking first. She had insisted on keeping them so she could be unique, just like all of her friends.

Luke squeezed the steering wheel until his knuckles paled. His mind swung wildly between the past could-haves and future should-dos. What other options were there for getting her life on track? They had already tried grounding, rewarding, family retreats, long talks, short talks, restrictions, pleading, reprimanding, and apologies. All that remained was to release her to the hard schooling of repercussions.

They had warned her about Liam, and they told her she was being irrational. Each conversation had been met by the same expression now on Dina's face: looking at nothing in particular, head listing to the side, lips in a taut, slight frown.

"Dina, if you ever just want to talk, your mother and I are willing to listen."

Her eyes darted away in the rearview mirror.

"We'd understand more than you'd expect."

The uncomfortable silence persisted.

Luke drove up their street. They would soon be home, together yet separated. He rummaged in his mind for a way to utilize their final moments, to make some connection before Dina could return to hiding between her earbuds. *What should I say?*

He reached back to reassuringly pat her on the knee, but she twitched away from him. With a voice as low, strong, and calm as he could muster, Luke said, "I love you, Dina. We love you. We're here for you, and we want to protect you. We only ask that you open up to us, and stop resisting everything we do and say."

Dina curled her legs toward her chest again. She flicked the window lever absentmindedly. "I don't have anything to say."

The light on their front porch emerged from the fog like a lighthouse beacon. A few seconds later, the rest of their house materialized. Luke pulled into their drive slowly, even coming to a brief stop before turning off the road, in order to give Dina more time to speak.

All he received was, "Don't hit the bike on the garage."

His daughter unbuckled her seatbelt and hopped out a moment before they came to a complete stop. Luke hastily turned off the ignition and joined her on her walk to the front door. He wanted to put his arm around her shoulder, and she needed an arm around her shoulder, but he did not. He could not. No good would come of it until she was ready for his embrace.

As they climbed the stairs together, she muttered, "umm," then spoke. Her voice was soft and sweet, but her request struck him hard.

"Please don't tell mom."

Somehow, that was the most painful thing she'd said all night. *Stop hiding, Dina.*

He opened the door. "No promises, but I had kind of hoped you'd tell her yourself."

The screen door crashed shut behind them, and Luke's wife stepped into the entryway from the kitchen. She was as visibly distraught as when he left.

The moments that followed were an all-too-familiar pattern of strife. Leah greeted their daughter with love and relief mixed with disappointment and condemnation. She hugged Dina, who tolerated it for a few moments before shrugging her off. Leah offered tea as invitingly as she could, but the offer went ignored.

Dina marched past Leah and her deluge of questions. She headed up the stairs, toward her room and toward isolation. In response, Leah ordered her back to the first floor, then chased after her. Their lopsided conversation, which started out warm but salty, devolved into shouting through a slammed-shut bedroom door.

"You're not the least bit sorry for what you've put your father through! Do you have any idea how much you're hurting him? He drove out in the middle of the night to get you!"

"I wouldn't have to sneak out if you let me have some fun once in a while!"

"We can't trust you to go out when you're secretly going to your boyfriend's like some whore!"

"Shut up, mom!"

Back at the open front door, Luke Shepherd fell to his knees while the cold drifted in at his back. His shoulders rose and fell as he wept into his hands. Warm tears flowed between his fingers, and his deep, muffled sobs echoed in his palms.

There would be no peace or sleep that night, only sorrow. He wept for his beloved daughter, for the pain she continued to put herself through. He wept because he was helpless until she was willing to accept help. He wept because after the pain of that night had numbed and scarred, she would sneak out again, forgoing his love and wisdom for a world she couldn't overcome, a feral world that cared nothing for her. He wept for all of the senseless tears and regrets she would needlessly endure.

Wrath and Ruin

Acknowledgments

This book would not have been possible without the support of my Kickstarter backers, who raised over $1,000 toward editing and printing costs. I am extremely thankful for all of them.

The following backers gave above and beyond the cost of the book.

Bonus Backers

Stacey Morshedi	Shawn & Patty Birchard
Paul Smith	Lindsay Franklin

Extra-Bonus Backers

Bradley Streeter	Scott Sasina
Danielle Heidrich	Chad Bowden

Extra-Extra-Bonus Backers

Nikki Wasielewski	Judith Morningstar
Kimberly Kinsley	Robert Rhoades

About the Author

C.W. Briar is the pen name of Charles Wasielewski. Briar grew up in woodland country near Barton, a miniscule town in Upstate New York. He currently resides near Binghamton, NY, the birthplace of Rod Serling and spiedie sandwiches.

Briar has an Industrial & Systems Engineering degree from Binghamton University. He has worked as an engineer on various helicopters, airplanes, and trains. His interest in theology and philosophy led him to earn his certification in apologetics through Biola University.

Escape from Wrath and Ruin, which is included in this anthology, became Briar's first published story in 2012. His writing focuses on fantasy and sci-fi stories threaded with quiet, traditional horror. He has always had a fascination with toothy, dangerous creatures, both real and imaginary. That fascination is reflected in the monsters that inhabit this anthology.

Briar is married to his college sweetheart. They have three wonderful children, two adorable corgis, and a pair of fluffy chinchillas. The children are adept at making messes, the corgis shed everywhere, and the chinchillas raise ruckuses while the family is trying to sleep.

C.W. Briar

Made in the USA
Middletown, DE
24 July 2016